Satellite Love

GENKI FERGUSON

McClelland & Stewart

Trade paperback original edition published 2021

McClelland & Stewart and colophon are registered trademarks of
Penguin Random House Canada Limited.

Published simultaneously in the United States of America by
McClelland & Stewart, a division of Penguin Random House LLC.

Library and Archives Canada Cataloguing in Publication data
is available upon request.

ISBN: 978-0-7710-4987-3
ebook ISBN: 978-0-7710-4988-0

Book design by Emma Dolan
Cover art based on a photograph by Eri Miura / Getty Images
Typeset in Adobe Garamond Pro by M&S, Toronto
Printed and bound in Canada

McClelland & Stewart,
a division of Penguin Random House Canada Limited,
a Penguin Random House Company
www.penguinrandomhouse.ca

1 2 3 4 5   25 24 23 22 21

Penguin
Random House
McCLELLAND & STEWART

For Dasha

Satellite Love

ANNA

WHEN I CLOSE MY eyes, I still see satellites. After all this time, I can't seem to forget them. No matter what I do, they're always there, held up above the world with a cruel indifference. It feels as though, if I were to reach out just a little farther, I might be able to pluck one mid-orbit and bring it down to me on Earth.

I used to understand what the satellites said, but now I can't tell if they're taunting me, or asking for forgiveness.

When I was younger, I believed I could speak to them, and I suppose on a certain level, I still do. I'll catch myself mumbling something to the sky, asking questions about what they can see, and what they can't. The only difference is that now they don't respond. But I still can't let go of what I wanted to believe as a child. I don't imagine any of us ever do.

Part 1

ANNA

DID YOU KNOW THAT most people are hollow?

It's true. You see medical diagrams of the body sometimes, the ones where we're stuffed full with kidneys, gallbladders, lungs, and it's easy to get the impression that there's no space left inside. But those drawings always miss the gaps. For example, I have an empty spot inside my chest, below my sternum, that if I hit just right lets out a soft thump. A personal echo.

I suspect that everyone has their own hollow spot, one that lets out a unique tone when tapped. You just need to find it. Perhaps yours is behind your head, in your lower back, or along your ribs. The problem is, most people don't seem to understand that they're empty, too.

I can pinpoint the moment I realized I was hollow. It was during my first year of high school, and Ms. Tanaka was prattling on in Social Studies class about old gods and ancient tales. Her favourite story was about Amaterasu, the sun goddess, and her brother Susanoo, god of the storms and seas. A long time ago, Susanoo had destroyed some of Amaterasu's rice paddies, and out of anger the sun goddess hid in a cave, casting the world into shadow.

All the other gods became nervous when she wouldn't emerge, realizing that if she hid forever, they would be forced to live an eternity in darkness. Of course, they didn't actually care about her; they just wanted her light. They ended up luring her out with a party, pretending that they had found another, better sun goddess instead, and celebrated loudly enough for her to hear. When Amaterasu got jealous and peeked out to see who this new goddess could be, the other gods pulled her out from the cave and trapped her.

At this point, the girls who sat behind me started giggling, and I glanced back despite knowing better. All five of them were sitting with their backs completely straight, hands folded on their desks, suddenly model students. I tried to figure out what, exactly, they were laughing at, but they simply looked past me, avoiding any eye contact.

One of the girls, Mina, raised her hand and asked, "Why did *Anna*-terasu want to go to a party she wasn't invited to?" Ms. Tanaka corrected her on the name, but then the others started chiming in too, and it became obvious they were mispronouncing Amaterasu deliberately.

"Why didn't the other gods like Anna-terasu?"

"Did Anna-terasu know that she was being annoying?"

"Why was Anna-terasu so sulky?"

I was puzzled at first, but then I clued in that they were giving me a new nickname. I decided this was a good thing. My classmates give me a lot of nicknames, on account of my having the only non-Japanese name in my class. My mom tells me that Anna means "graceful" or "beauty" in English. In Japanese, though, it sounds similar to the word *ana*, meaning "hole." A hollow. Compared to that, being called the sun goddess might have been the nicest thing those girls had ever said about me.

Ms. Tanaka had some slides projected at the front of the room, and one of them showed an old woodblock print of Amaterasu.

She was floating in the clouds, enveloped in this holy glow, indifferent to the deities that surrounded her. All the other gods were cowering, arms up, overwhelmed by her light. They admired Amaterasu, or at the very least they feared her.

I ignored my classmates' barrage of questions, keeping my eyes on Amaterasu instead, studying her gaze. In those traditional prints, the old gods are all depicted in this uncanny way, with a vacant look in their eyes. Ms. Tanaka said it's an expression of compassion, but I think it's one of contempt. The sun goddess was looking down on us, and for some reason, I felt an affinity to her. The more I stared at her image, the more it seemed like I was looking into my own reflection. We were both really pale, although her colour was from being royal, mine from being indoors all the time. We both had a bit of a sullen streak, too. I wondered if, maybe, she could be a superior version of myself.

Ms. Tanaka eventually regained control of the class, getting everyone to settle down for fear of punishment, but I was too busy staring at the sun goddess to notice. Maybe it was that hint of a smile she wore on her face, but the myth didn't quite make sense; there was something centuries of scholars had overlooked.

I raised my hand and asked, "Why didn't Anna-terasu want to be friends with the fake sun goddess?" It seemed logical. If the other gods were cruel to her, then she should be excited to meet someone she was similar to. Why should she be jealous of a potential friend?

I suppose it was an odd thing to ask, since everyone went silent, including Ms. Tanaka. But then, starting from the back of the class, a couple of girls started to laugh again. A few boys joined in too, followed finally by the mid- and lower-caste girls, not wanting to be left out of a joke. I didn't mind, though. Not just because I was used to it, but because I was still excited at the thought of being a goddess. I felt their laughter bounce around inside me, echoing in that hollow place, and I started to feel lighter and lighter. Light enough to float into space.

I rushed home that day, slipping out of school while my class-mates snapped Polaroids of each other. The peace signs they held up to the camera felt like the emblem of a club I wasn't privy to.

A crisp winter breeze chased me through Sakita's urban maze, with its narrow alleys, crumbling rooftops, and second-hand elec-tronics stores. It was overcast, so the sun was hidden behind some clouds, casting an even light and causing all shadows to disappear. I didn't want to waste any time, and cut through rice paddies and bike lanes as I saw fit.

When I got home, I checked in on my grandpa before run-ning upstairs. I told him that I wanted to be called "Anna-terasu" from now on, but judging by his blank expression, I don't think he understood what I was saying. The dishes in the sink told me he had remembered to eat lunch, which was a relief, and I set him up with a sudoku book to spend the rest of the afternoon on. The puzzles were supposed to improve his memory, but he wasn't very good at them yet and kept forgetting the rules. To be hon-est, I kind of liked being able to help Grandpa with the answers. Sometimes, I'd get a few rows correct, back to back, and he'd be really impressed, say that I must be a genius or something. I didn't want to tell him that we were still on the easy ones.

But that day, the heavens were calling to me, so I retreated to my attic room and locked myself away. I'd always had a habit of jumping from one hobby to the next, filling my space with clutter belonging to past identities. Marked cards from my magic phase, vinyl records from when I loved jazz, poorly drawn flip-books from when I was going to be an animator. Pulling the telescope out of the mess of years gone by, I was glad I never bothered to clean up.

Despite being impatient to begin, I decided to wait until nightfall to search the sky for gods. I knew that it would be dangerous to view the sun directly, and figured that I would watch for Amaterasu's reflection in the moon instead. Maybe she really would look like me.

At the time, I was a novice stargazer, my knowledge of constellations barely stretching beyond Big Dipper and Little Dipper. It was my grandpa who had given me the telescope, wanting to ensure I knew how "minuscule the Earth is" compared to everything else. The brass focus knobs were worn down from where he had adjusted them hundreds of times before, trying to keep the world above in view. I wondered if he could still show me how.

The windows in my loft were angled upwards, like holes punched out of the slanted ceiling above, cutting off my view of the neighbourhood below. If I were to imagine just right, and give in to weightlessness, it would feel as though I were in space myself, riding solar winds and comet tails.

Soon enough, Amaterasu decided to go to sleep. Night began to fall, and the stars came out one by one, like a reflection of my dying city below.

That was when I first encountered *him*.

I hadn't intended to meet my first great love through a telescope. All I had been seeking was the moon. And yet, what I saw through the eyepiece was a pulse of blue light, diffused through my half-focused lens. It had erupted almost violently across my line of sight, the shock causing me to lurch backwards.

In my heart of hearts, I knew that there were no gods up there to greet me, but that burst of light was a sign—though from what, exactly, I did not know. I wondered if, rather than a god, this is what I had really been searching for.

I pulled away from the telescope, knowing whatever I had seen would be easier to track with my naked eyes. Rather than a dome, the night sky above now hung like a curtain closing in on me, moth-bites in lieu of stars.

Eventually, I found the source of that light, a glimmer no larger than a pinpoint moving slowly across my expanded field of vision. Its light was much weaker when seen from afar—colourless as well. Appearing first by what I assumed was Orion's Belt, it blinked once every few seconds, moving east. It was the answer to a question I was too afraid to ask.

Too close to be a star, too far to be a plane, what I had just seen was a satellite.

The Low-Earth Orbit satellite, or LEO for short, was as close to heavenly as one could get in the modern world. I was jealous of how it could fly above me, immune from the pains of daily life. Did it know it shared a sky with the sun goddess, and did it even care? I felt something new burning in the hollow in my chest. The first seeds of adoration were taking root.

That's the strange thing about those hollows. Once you realize you have one, they never go away. Discovering that emptiness is something you can't come back from. I've since accepted that my hollow will always be there, that it's inseparable from me, but I wonder what life could have been like without it. I wonder where that hole ends and I begin.

SATELLITE

IT WAS DURING MY third revolution around the Earth that I developed this creeping suspicion that I may not actually exist. I knew I had a consciousness; that was the only thing I could really know for sure. Other than that, everything was up in the air. I appeared to be floating in a definite direction, but couldn't quite understand how I was flying, exactly.

Even stranger, I was 73.2% sure I didn't possess a body at all. It seemed as though I was made of metal instead of flesh, a somewhat shocking realization. I'd never experienced anything like this before; in fact, I couldn't remember a previous life to begin with. This is where things started to get tricky.

I felt tired, that was for sure, as though I'd been circling this world for decades. And yet, I could only remember the last day or so. A quick survey of the void in front of me confirmed that I was, indeed, utterly alone, save for some cosmic dust. Dust, unfortunately, is not a great conversationalist, so there was no one I could ask about who I was, or why I was here. I held some sort of ability to view everything on Earth—I could even see through walls and roofs into homes—but I had no way to communicate whatsoever.

On top of that, numbers came instinctively to me. I knew that I was 577 kilometres above the Earth, for example.

I appeared to be flying over a neighbourhood of sorts, on the outskirts of a half-abandoned city. For a short period of time, I wondered if I had died and was now waiting in the afterlife for whatever came next. Perhaps space was a waiting room, and my heart was somewhere else, being weighed against a feather or something. Or maybe my metal body was an incubation chamber for the soul, if such a thing as a soul even existed in the first place. Who was to say the gods didn't have technology? It would be a pretty simple solution, if you asked me, although I did experience a very minor complete nervous breakdown at the thought of being dead.

I had a vague understanding of reincarnation—though I had no idea where that understanding came from—and assumed I was waiting for my next cycle on Earth. One thing I remembered about reincarnation (and I use "remembered" here loosely) is that with every cycle of rebirth you grow wiser. You carry over a bit of your past experiences from each life into the next. I hoped this meant an innate wisdom and not any hard knowledge, as it didn't seem like my past self had left me with any useful information.

Was I here as a punishment? Perhaps I had done something wrong in a previous life, and had been left here to contemplate actions I could no longer recall. I didn't know the past me, but somehow I knew I couldn't trust him.

The punishment for an immoral life was reincarnation as a beast in the next, leading me to wonder if I was on my way to being turned into an animal. I didn't think I'd have a problem with that. Staring at the Earth below, I could get a decent sample size of what such a life would be like. Judging from what I saw, animals outnumbered *Homo sapiens* by quite a bit: roughly, oh, 8.7 million species to 1. My plan was to live out twelve or so years as a dog, die with a clear conscience, then get right back to being a human.

I was feeling pretty confident about my future until I realized that if I was being punished, I wouldn't come back as something pettable and well loved, like a Shiba Inu, but as something horrible and slimy, like a snail or a gulper eel. A fate worse than death, and I could say that with confidence as someone who had, presumably, died multiple times.

I decided to curb the armchair philosophy for the time being, mostly due to my lack of armchair, and re-examine what I knew so far.

1. I appeared to be floating in space.
2. I could view the Earth and the people below with absolute clarity.
3. I did not possess a human form.

In all honesty, this list only raised more questions. Nearly everyone I saw in that city was asleep at the time, save for a drunken office worker here, a late-night truck driver there. Their soft, fleshy forms seemed quaint to me. Without metal plating of any sort, how would they defend themselves from space debris or meteors? Perhaps there were other things to worry about down on Earth.

One girl in particular caught my attention, however. A small, frail thing, alone in her room just as I was up in space. Among all those humans, she was the only one looking back at me. She was leaning precariously out the window of her home, as though being a half-metre closer to the sky would make a difference.

The wind picked up below, and I worried that she might fall, but she held her position, unmoving, staring upwards. The girl's thin hair fanned against her face, her cloudy breath peeking out in the nighttime cold. I wondered if she alone might provide me with the answers I was searching for.

ANNA

FOR THE FIRST WEEK after I met the LEO satellite, I barely slept at all. Instead, I would stand guard waiting for each revolution. The satellite was a constant in a volatile world—it always appeared in the night sky no matter what happened down below. If I didn't go to school or leave the house for a few days, it would know. If a song on the radio brought me to tears, I could turn the volume all the way up and blast it straight through the stratosphere for the LEO to hear. Its steady gaze anchored me to the world, was a reminder that Anna Obata still existed, that she wasn't being left behind.

One night, I stayed by the telescope until I could hear the first sounds of morning: the buzz of cicadas replaced by the hum of early traffic, the still-innocent laughter of children playing. I was filled with a melancholy that can only be found in the green haze of a sleepless dawn.

Watching my city begin the rhythm of a new day, apartment lights flickering on as though operated by the world's laziest switchboard attendant, I felt utterly alone. It was the feeling of riding the last train home by yourself, of catching the scent of a perfume you recognize but can no longer place. This sense of isolation was intense and absolute. Pure.

I checked in on Grandpa, found him still asleep, and adjusted his blanket to fully cover his toes. He had been sleeping in later and later recently. Only a couple of years ago he would have been the first one awake, grilling a traditional mackerel breakfast for us despite my mother's protests. The house would smell like fish when I woke up, which she complained was impossible to get out of our clothes. I think deep down, though, both of us loved that he was so stubborn.

That morning, as I fixed myself a bowl of cornflakes, I found myself missing the taste of the sea. Today was a good day for mackerel, I decided. Grandpa would be happy if I made some for him. After breakfast, I would embark on a mission.

I placed my bowl in the sink, dishes already piling up, and prepared to leave. As I slipped on a pair of Mizuno sneakers—converted to slippers by years of heel-crushing abuse—I noticed my mother's shoes. Untouched for weeks, they were quietly collecting dust. I wondered what she would be eating for breakfast today. I reminded myself not to care. After brushing her shoes off and tucking them into the cabinet, I went on my way.

I left the house with the fish market in mind, turning towards the older half of the city, passing by abandoned lots and unlit homes. Echoes of a more optimistic Sakita.

Sakita: the city where time stopped, a place perpetually on the bust end of a boom-and-bust economy. After the rerouting of a train line that had once promised to bring industry to this cast-off corner of Japan, what was once destined to be a city of a half million rapidly shrank to twenty thousand. The resulting freeze in development created a surreal environment, one where urban architecture met on even terms with rural landscapes previously slated to be paved over.

You could almost pinpoint the exact year people lost hope here by the leftover fragments of late-eighties design: block concrete architecture, circular columns and windows clashing against sharp edges with a vaguely futurist flair. Signboards advertising long-defunct snack foods were the only beacon of colour in sight. This was a world of frozen motifs, a city of the "Lost Decade" that schoolteachers and politicians promised in vain would catch up with the rest of Japan. The new millennium was coming, but even I could tell that Sakita was painfully behind.

As I walked, I caught myself whistling a tune from my child-hood. It was about a lost cat, and it moved at a fairly quick pace. You could easily walk in time with it, making it perfect for con-quering the early-morning blues.

> *Lost kitten, lost kitten, where is your home?*
> *I asked where you live, but you didn't understand.*
> *I asked for your name, but you didn't understand . . .*

In the distance, I caught a glimpse of the fish market's brutal concrete walls, peeking above the tiled rooftops of surrounding homes. I had taken a shortcut through a residential area, and only now realized that I recognized this street. Mina lived here. Back in elementary school, I had gone to her house for her birth-day party.

We had never been especially close, but I suppose everyone in the class had been invited. Unable to help myself, I turned away from the fish market, curious to see if I could still find my way to where she lived.

Back then, games of fantasy and make-believe were still popular, and while I retraced footsteps I thought I had forgotten, memories of our imaginary kingdoms came back to me. Memories of my first imaginary friend, The Prince.

As a child, I'd caught *Lawrence of Arabia* on television one night and, struck by the realization that there was a world beyond Japan, I became hopelessly obsessed with reliving those fantasies myself. While Mina and the others reinvented themselves as fairies or princesses, I imagined myself as the sidekick to a noble warrior, arriving on horseback from a faraway land.

The Prince had been muscular, dark, and unthreateningly handsome. An embarrassing fantasy, but at that young age, I hadn't learned subtlety yet.

All the girls at school would huddle close and listen, mesmerized, as I told them about my Prince and the adventures he took me on whenever I went home. Too enchanted to interrupt, they would listen patiently, giving me their full attention as I told stories they could never dream of.

This was the only time in my life I can recall being popular.

As a child, telling fantastical stories and having a vivid imagination makes you likeable to others. Then you grow up, and suddenly these same people choose to keep a cautious distance instead, acting like you're delusional, avoiding you for the same exact reason you were close to begin with. I will never understand why this happens. The world will always be filled with strangers for me.

A common misconception about children's fantasies is that they wholeheartedly believe they are true. Naivete and stupidity shouldn't be confused, and girls who dream of princes to whisk them away should be given the credit they're due. I never believed for a second that The Prince actually existed; rather, I wanted to believe that he did. It's the desire for belief that fuels these dreams so powerfully.

What had separated me from Mina and the rest of the group, however, was that eventually my Prince came to realize that he didn't exist. My imaginary friend had become self-aware and would speak to me freely. After a certain point, I lost control of him entirely. He would label himself "fake" and me "real" and ask why I had created him in the first place.

These sudden existential questionings were way over my head, and frightened me immensely. The Prince was often accusatory, and when I told my schoolmates this in our daily fantasy sessions, they would act confused and quickly move on to their own stories.

It had been years since I last thought of The Prince, and no matter how hard I tried to remember him, he was nowhere to be found. I find it cruel that by the time many of us are old enough to actually need an imaginary friend, they're impossible to bring back.

The smell of cooked fish brought me out of my reverie. Without realizing it, I had walked right up to Mina's house, a cozy, renovated, single-family unit. It hadn't been my intention to come this far, nearly peering through her sliding glass door. I saw a light on inside, maybe in the kitchen, and heard a radio playing from the upper floor.

I knew that standing there was dangerous—it didn't take much to imagine Mina's horrified expression upon seeing me at her house, the rumours she would later spread at school. And yet, the smell of her mom's cooking wafting out to the street invited me to linger. She was smoking some sort of fish, sea bream perhaps, which I imagined with a side of rice and pickles. I pictured the family sitting at the table: Mina, her father, and her younger brother waiting impatiently for breakfast to be served. As far as I remembered, Mina's mom liked me, and I felt my hand twitch slightly, wanting to knock on that door, maybe ask for the recipe so I could cook it myself.

I turned and left, scraping the bottoms of my shoes along the curb as I stepped down onto the road. If I waited too long, the fish market would sell out for the day. At the end of the block, I stopped and craned my neck to the sky. It was too bright to see anything up above, and yet the satellite would still be there, flying far beyond my reach.

An A-347 telecommunications satellite with a titanium alloy body. I read somewhere that satellites don't actually orbit the planet, that they are instead perpetually falling towards us, at an angle that skims along the natural curve of the Earth. The lack of air resistance just makes this descent incredibly slow. Endlessly falling, never getting closer.

Sometimes satellites get lost, too. If the signal connecting them to Earth is accidentally cut off, there is no way of reconnecting with them. After this, no one can know for sure what happens to the satellite. They either circle the planet until they can't take it anymore, or burn up attempting to re-enter the atmosphere below.

Wouldn't it be great, I thought, imagining the LEO sailing above me, *to have another friend just like The Prince?* Maybe this time they could take me farther than Arabia, farther than this world.

SATELLITE

THERE ARE BENEFITS TO being a satellite 577 kilometres above the natural world. I was able to watch everyone below with complete clarity, able to see through walls and rooftops as though they were made of glass. It was like an incredibly high-definition video, one which I could zoom in on forever. In a past life, I must have been a voyeur.

From my vantage point, nothing escaped my gaze: the smallest passions, the greatest tragedies. The entire world was my theatre, and I had the rawest forms of humanity playing out in front of my own eyes. An unflinching look at life on Earth. Or so I thought.

In all honesty, the human drama soon became tiring, and I'll admit that I eventually used my powers mainly to peer into movie theatres for free—something to mix up the routine of never-ending orbits, I suppose. I grew rather fond of comedies in those days, which helped me understand how humans viewed their world. For example, humour occurs when misfortune falls upon another, while tragedy occurs when misfortune falls upon oneself.

Whenever I did observe the real world, I found my attention focused on a singular point in southern Japan. No matter how hard I tried to avert my gaze, I was continuously drawn back to this bizarre city and the 22,362 people who called it home. It was a half-built metropolis, abandoned as though possessed by some curse. The decaying storefronts and empty homes reminded me of the movie sets I had seen elsewhere, the city's population merely its actors.

Even more eerie was the way the city sounded. I barely saw anyone outside, but the streets were filled with a white noise. It was so ingrained I hadn't questioned it at first, a chirping that seemed to originate from the parks and shrines, from what little nature hadn't yet been paved over. Did this dull throbbing come from abandoned industry, the aches and pains of machines left behind? In a more romantic mood, I wondered if the heart of the city had never learned of its fate as a failure, and still attempted to beat accordingly.

Over time I grew to know the city and its people well. Here, a lowly fishmonger who, after closing shop for the night, studies the languages of countries he'll never visit. There, a lonely college student who lies to her mother over the phone so as not to worry her. And yet among them all—the street urchins, the function-ing alcoholics, the local legends—I found myself continuously drawn to a single girl, the only one capable of returning my gaze. Anna Obata.

She was awkwardly tall, Eurasian, the kind of girl who hadn't quite come into her own yet. Maybe with time this would change—she could grow into her unwieldy limbs, straighten her posture, and learn to make eye contact. For now, though, she was still an adolescent of the species, a baby giraffe of a person.

I found Anna amusing at first, even a little funny. She had certain quirks: a strange manner of trailing off when she spoke, a habit of losing interest in the middle of a conversation. There was always a far-off look in her eyes, as though she were staring through whoever she was speaking to. Her skin was much paler, too, either from having mixed ancestry or from anemia, and she had a bad habit of picking at her cuticles until they were gone. Even I had to admit that she had an uncanny feel about her. She gave off the appearance of something not quite from this world, as though the non-Japanese half of her wasn't European but alien. In southern Japan, it didn't seem like there was much of a difference.

Above all, I learned to read emotions from her. I calculated that a depression between the eyebrows demonstrated confusion, an increase in pupil dilation indicated happiness. As time went on, however, she began to lean closer to the tragicomedy side of the humour spectrum.

Anna lived mostly alone. An older male occupied the same house as her, but he appeared to be more reliant on her than the other way around. A couple of times a week, an adult female would enter the picture, spending a night or two at their home. Yet just as her classmates were cold to Anna, so too was Anna cold to this woman. The one thing that sticks out to me was how remarkably similar they looked.

Outside of her home, Anna was forced to spend the bulk of her time at school, in close proximity to other humans her age, when she clearly preferred to be alone. Rather than socialize or participate in class, she would sit still at her desk, mind wandering to far-off worlds, counting down the hours to the end of the day.

Those other humans ("students," to use the correct term) only tolerated her at best, and for reasons that seemed arbitrary. It didn't take constant ETM sensor surveillance to spot an outsider. A quick look at the way Anna was dressed was all I needed. Her uniform was never properly ironed, the pleats on her skirts worn out over time. While I gathered there were strict dress codes, her classmates managed to rebel against these with an occasional pin, hair tie, or bracelet. Anna simply went without.

There was, however, one exception to this. The only accessory I ever saw her attempt to wear was a customer loyalty pin from her local convenience store. I suppose she was attempting to fit in. She walked to school that day with an extra 3.2 centimetres of bounce in her step, before a classmate not-so-innocently asked why she was "advertising some dingy conbini." Compared to the cartoon mascots the other girls wore, her attempt at fashion certainly stood out. The pin lasted a whole three hours and twenty-seven minutes on her uniform before she quietly took it off.

After I'd analyzed countless other societies, however, a pattern began to emerge. Scattered throughout the Earth were thousands of other Annas, whose only real purpose was to serve as an outsider, a warning against breaking unstated social norms. I wondered what Anna had done to deserve this treatment.

In other schools, I noticed that it was common for the backpacks of the bullied to be hidden between classes, for gym uniforms to "accidentally" fall into the showers. But on top of this standard treatment, there seemed to be an element of fear in the way Anna's classmates dealt with her. The other students unconsciously made room for her as she walked the halls, for example, and would squabble among themselves over who would have to take Anna in their lab group, who would be stuck bringing school notes to her house when she was sick.

I have no idea what Anna was learning in class; her vacant stare certainly suggested she wasn't paying any attention. I imagine she was doing the absolute minimum needed to get by, waiting for the clock to hit three before rushing home. No after-school clubs for this girl. Simply a short walk home, the occasional stop for groceries, then back to her stacks of obscure reading, her cast-open windows, her hand-me-down telescope.

Every night, without fail, I found myself on the receiving end of that device. I made a point of returning her gaze, both of us trapped in our orbits, both searching for any sort of way out. If I existed, why was it that no other stargazers ever seemed to pay me any notice? If I didn't exist, how is it that this girl could see me? All I wanted was to view the heavens through her eyes, to know what I looked like from down below.

No matter how hard I tried, I couldn't find an answer. I could only find her.

Often, I would attempt to analyze those ambiguous expressions that crossed Anna's face. I would come up with equations measuring the tilt of her eyebrows, the angle of her lips. Determine that she was exhibiting 12% more melancholy than the night before, 3% more yearning. Yet there was always something missing, something that eluded numbers. Her response to these emotions never followed a formula, defying any sort of logic I attempted to apply. Once, sitting across the kitchen table, the older man who lived with her paused between slurps of miso soup and told Anna a joke. Rather than laugh, however, Anna burst into tears. Why was her response one of sadness, when the correct answer should have been joy?

I didn't understand why I was in space, rather than down on Earth with her. A part of me was concerned about Anna—I knew so little about human life, but I could sense that her trajectory was unsteady, perhaps even headed towards disaster. Never did I anticipate that she'd become infamous in Japan for years to come.

I eventually met this girl, and at one point I believe I loved her. While I may be getting ahead of myself, I remember she once told me that she wasn't sure if she loved me or was obsessed with me. I now have a question of my own, one I never did find an answer for.

Did I ever truly understand Anna Obata?

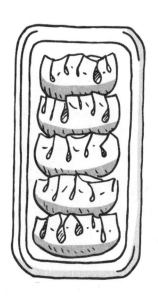

ANNA

MONDAY MORNING. I COULD already tell it was a bad day to go to school. There was something in the air. A warning perhaps, a sign of things yet to come. The light peeking into my room was duller than usual, no longer the colour of amber. I didn't have to check my clock to know I'd woken up late, missed the first calls of dawn.

Lying on my futon, nose cold, I urged myself with little success to get ready for school. When I finally did leave the warmth of my blankets, I dressed slowly, knowing that an extra second on my skirt hook would delay the inevitable just a little longer. The entire time, I imagined the satellite high above me, sending a signal to Anna-terasu down below.

Grandpa was still sleeping, but that was hardly a surprise. Before grabbing my bag to go, I scribbled out a quick note for him, letting him know there was leftover mackerel and rice in the fridge. I was pleased by the way my messages to Grandpa piled up on the counter. They outnumbered the notes my mother left me by quite a bit.

Anna, I'll be out of town for a few nights. Work should settle down soon. Buy yourself the new Captive Hearts manga if you go out! We'll read it together when I get back, I'm dying to see what happens next.
 Take care,
 Mama

I walked along my usual path, headed first to the convenience store, then to school, when I noticed something: my eyelids felt slightly heavier, and not just for lack of sleep. I stopped in my tracks, right in the middle of crossing the road, and looked up. Light flecks of white were falling from the sky, just beginning to dust Sakita's rooftops.

It was snowing.

A snowflake landed in the middle of my right eye, a pleasant kind of stinging. The path was becoming gently frosted, and my breath was coming out in clouds of mist.

It hadn't snowed in Sakita for as long as I could remember. I had watched snow fall over American and European cities in the movies, taking on a unique meaning every time. In New York, the snow runs grey like sludge, revealing the city's filth. In Berlin, it falls with a childlike innocence, accompanied by reindeer and peppermints and other holiday symbols we have no use for here.

But in Sakita, the first snow of my life felt different. It was painful, delicate. Like the finest flakes of glass falling from the sky. I kept walking, feeling my eyes water in spite of myself.

At the end of the road, the convenience store was glowing with a softer light. A bright jingle announced my entrance, followed by a customary "Irasshaimase!" and I set out to buy my usual bento.

"Amazing, huh?" I said, watching winter fall beyond the conbini windows. The clerk was counting my money, nearly the last of what my mother had given me for the week.

"No kidding," she said. "I didn't realize it could snow this far south."

The clerk bagged my lunch—an onigiri, a potato korokke, and gyoza—and handed it back to me. It was the same lunch I ate every day, a formula I had perfected over the years. Filling enough to get me through to dinner, tasty enough to not depress me, and cheap enough to leave some pocket money from my meal allowance.

I pushed on the door, feeling a cold wind cut through my uniform.

"See you!" I said.

"Come again!" the clerk called out, almost in sync with the store intercom that said the same.

As usual, no one raised a fuss when I sat down halfway through first period. Math. Part of me almost wished I'd get in trouble for being late. *Maybe I should see how far I can push it?* I'd forgotten to bring a pencil and asked a classmate to lend me one of hers. She pretended not to hear me, so I asked again, louder this time. It was almost fun. I got in trouble for talking during class, though.

For Social Studies, Ms. Tanaka gave yet another lecture on the old gods, undeterred by the class's clear lack of interest. Still, I admired her enthusiasm, and whenever she mentioned Amaterasu I did perk up a little. After that was Physical Education, cancelled due to the snow. I wouldn't have minded being given an excuse to run and slip and fall through the newly white track field, but instead we were given a lecture on nutrition.

And then, lunch. I had forgotten my unease of that morning, my excitement about the snow making me lose the gut feeling I had about the day. I even felt comfortable enough to stay in the classroom with everyone else for lunch, rather than sneak away to some distant corner of the school as usual. Then the rest of the class began to take out their lunches, too.

I felt a tap on my shoulder and glanced back at the seat behind me. It was Mina.

"Anna," she said, giving me her best innocent-little-me look, "do you want some of my lunch?"

I saw that she had the exact same food as me: a convenience store rice ball, a potato korokke, and dumplings. It was an incredible coincidence that we had brought the same thing. I was usually the only person eating conbini food for lunch.

"No, I'm okay," I mumbled.

One of Mina's friends began to giggle.

"Oh really? I just thought you'd want some variety in your diet."

I realized then that all of her friends—about half of the class, really—were staring back at me from where they sat. On each of their desks, where there would normally be a home-cooked bento, there was instead a convenience store rice ball, a potato korokke, and some dumplings.

"Isn't it boring eating the same thing every day? You'll get fat, you know." Mina puffed out her cheeks.

Another of Mina's lackeys took a bite of korokke, then scrunched up her face as though she'd bitten into something rotten. The girl sitting beside her, seeing this reaction, started to snicker.

"Conbini food always makes me feel sick."

And all I could do was imagine how deer-in-the-headlights stupid I must have looked, food half-chewed, rice stuck to the side of my mouth. I could swear I heard Mina's mother laugh, too.

And for a moment, I wasn't even angry. Really, I wasn't. Just a little bit incredulous, maybe.

It felt as though I was constantly being tested. That everyone woke up each morning and asked: "How much will Anna put up with today?" And every day I had to come up with an answer for that. Put up with too much and you end up no better than a worm. Put up with too little and you get kicked out of school and sent home.

The smart thing to do would have been to eat my onigiri in peace, and imagine eviscerating Mina while I lay in bed that night. But the smell of her mother's cooking kept coming back to me. Normally, Mina would have brought a homemade bento for lunch. Something her mother cooked that morning especially for her.

And Mina would have thrown that away, just to make her cute little joke.

I wanted to speak up. I wanted to say: *So now I can't even eat an onigiri in peace? You're going to take even that away? None of you would last a single day as me.*

But all that came out was a whisper.

All around me, real or imagined, the laughter was getting louder. But from above, I could feel the pressure of something stronger. The gaze of the LEO. I wanted to call up to him: *Do you see this? Do you see what they're doing to me down here?*

SOKI

IT WAS MY FIRST week in Sakita, and the gods decided to give me snow. I couldn't believe what I was seeing. Felt like the sky was turning to dust. Felt like I was being given a warning.

"Is it... snowing?" my mom asked, before locking the car doors. Wasn't sure what she thought she was accomplishing with that.

I pressed my head against the side window.

"Guess so."

We were on our way to the Shinto shrine, the one up on the hill. We got directions from a neighbour, who said it's by this half-deserted mall. The shrine's supposed to be really old, and it was starting to fall apart. Smelled like rot. I wanted to offer a prayer, to ask the gods for help. Wanted proof that kami exist in this city, too. Sakita was so empty it felt like even the spirits had abandoned it. At least, that's what my dad said. Figured I could at least ask, could provide an offering.

We had just moved to Sakita the week before. I was kind of disappointed we'd be celebrating the new millennium here. New Year's in Kyoto would have been more exciting, but even back home in Hokkaido would have been better. When we first drove in, the roads were empty. I watched traffic lights signal to no one. Felt like a city filled with ghosts. Couldn't help but wonder if my dad was right about the kami. The other cities we lived in weren't like this.

"Should we turn back?" my mom asked. "The roads might be slippery."

She was trying to act casual about it, but I could tell she was worried. Kept looking in the rear-view mirror, as if the car was already in reverse. We drove by a boarded-up elementary school, a baseball field overgrown with weeds. Sakita was so depressing.

"I already promised I'd see the kami," I said.

"Promised who?"

"Myself."

She smiled, proud. Kind of like when I used to show her a finger painting as a kid. When I told Mom I wanted to see the shrine, she gave me a five-yen coin to make an offering. Said go-yen coins are supposed to be lucky, because the way you pronounce *go-yen* sounds a lot like the word *go-en*, meaning "connection." Apparently, this helps you form a relationship with the gods. The coin had a hole in the middle too, just like me.

Dad had laughed and said no god would notice five yen, let alone answer a prayer for it. It'd be better to spend the money on one of the overpriced shrine charms, he said, or some other meaningless trinket. The gods have been asleep for so long, they've forgotten how to wake for anyone. He acted like he was joking, but I could tell Mom was hurt. She pretended she didn't hear him, looking for the keys already in her hand. I thought Dad was wrong, though. Five yen is enough to wake the kami. I didn't need to talk to them. I just wanted to know that they were still here.

Dad used to be a Shinto priest. Used to. He wouldn't tell me why, but four years earlier, he got fed up and left the shrine. Took me by surprise, although I think my mom saw it coming. He must have been thinking about it for a while, but it still felt abrupt to me. His father, his grandfather, and all the ancestors before them— our family had been in charge of the shrine for centuries. I always assumed I would take his post when I got older. That I would become a priest and look after the shrine. But one day, my dad just stopped going. Took off his robes and never put them on again.

He didn't explain why he was leaving. Refused to explain, even. Said I was too young to understand when I kept asking for a reason. Felt like I was being gutted. I tried to bargain with him: if he delayed the move a couple of years, I could take over the shrine. Could learn the rituals and become a priest myself. Then him and Mom could move on, and I'd stay behind.

But he didn't listen to me.

We left a few weeks later. Drove down to Aomori, where my aunt lives. Through snowstorms along the shore, over an ocean that felt like the edge of the world. I didn't say a word to him the entire time.

Dad had been at the shrine his whole life and didn't know how to do anything else. He had to become a salaryman at his sister's company. Calls himself an "urban planner." I don't really know what that is. He's new to the job, though, so he gets pushed around the country a lot, chasing clients. Calls it "relocating." We travelled around for a while, but nothing was really permanent. Dad says we're going to stay in Sakita, though. Says this city is a long-term project. I sure hope so. Would like to finish unpacking at least once.

We pulled into the mall parking lot. Mom hit the brakes a little too hard, sending the car sliding. The shrine charms hanging on the mirror swung back and forth. I reached up and held them in my hands, stopping them from moving.

She mumbled something about the icy roads and turned off the engine.

I looked out the window. We were the only car in sight. Our neighbour was right—the shrine really was beside the mall. There was a wall of trees right at the edge of the parking lot, which the shrine was supposed to be hidden behind. A hard border, separating the city from nature. I could barely see the shrine, tucked into the grove, but I caught a glimpse of red through the leaves. The torii gate.

"Okay, and if the shrine priest is there, what do you say?" Mom cranked the heat up, obviously worried about the snow. As if I didn't grow up covered in the stuff. I could feel myself sweating under my jacket.

"I'll say, 'Hello. My name's Soki.'"

She sighed. "No, you say, 'Pleased to meet you. My name is Soki Tachibana. I am new to this city, and I humbly put myself in your hands.'"

"Okay."

Mom took out her shopping list, which had the names of a bunch of traditional medicines written on it. I doubted she'd be able to find that kind of stuff here. She went over it again, worried that she'd forgotten something. She'd said she needed to visit the mall anyway, so she'd drive me down. That was her excuse, at least. I think she was worried I'd get lost on my own. Dad says I have her eyes: really wide, kind of nervous-looking. I wish I got her height, instead. Being short like my dad is the worst.

She undid her seatbelt, then turned to me. Pulled the zipper on my jacket up a little higher. Pulled my wool hat further down. Holdovers from back home in Sapporo—snow country. She and my dad got into an argument about these every time we moved. Why would we need winter clothes down south? I felt bad for agreeing with him. With every move, we got farther away from the north, and the farther south we went, the more bitter Dad became.

Mom paused again before she opened the car door. She was lingering.

"Are you sure you'll be okay at the shrine? All alone? Should I come?"

I'd be back in less than an hour anyway. Just wanted to visit the shrine on my own. Couldn't be mad at her for caring, though.

"I'll be fine."

"All right, well, good luck! I'll be in the mall if anything happens, okay?"

"Okay."

She gave me a kiss on the forehead and left.

I turned the heat down in the car and watched her walk into the mall. She only turned back twice. Part of me didn't want to leave just yet. Not sure why, but I was almost nervous. Didn't know what the shrine would be like.

There are shrines wherever you go in Japan—hundreds of thousands of them across the country. Keeps you grounded. I was interested in how they built them in Sakita. Did they conceal the roof beams, or celebrate them? I wondered how many rooms this shrine would have, whether the path had been swept recently. You can learn a lot about a city's spirit this way, can find out how much hope its people hold on to by how they treat their gods.

My favourite part of shrine visits is seeing the A-un statues, one positioned on each side of the entrance. They're kind of like lions. At least, I think they're lions. In China, they're lions, but in Korea, they're dogs. In Japan, we just call them *komainu*. Dad says that shows how arbitrary religion is—the fact that everyone disagrees on a detail as simple as this means Shinto is doomed. Mom says it's the opposite: people finding their own meaning in the same thing only shows how strong faith is. I don't really care who's right. Just wish they'd stop arguing.

One statue always has its mouth open and the other always has its mouth closed. Supposed to represent the beginning and end of everything: the first sound we make is "Ah," and the last sound we make is "Un." Don't know if that's true. One of the two statues is supposed to be male and one is supposed to be female. Asked my dad once about which one is which. He said it's easy to remember: the one with a closed mouth is a girl, because women are always the end of everything. Then he laughed and my mom hit him on the shoulder, told him to have more respect for his own religion, and women, too, for that matter. Women are more sensitive to the supernatural, she said. He should appreciate that. This was before Dad stopped believing. I wonder where he's hidden his white robes.

I tried turning on the radio, but it refused to pick up a signal. It started doing that three cities ago. The car was one of the last things from Sapporo that we hadn't replaced. Driven it the entire length of Japan. My seatbelt was fraying from where I'd picked at it. I wondered how the car felt about all the moving. If it was getting exhausted, if it wanted some rest.

They say that nature has spirits in it. The trees, stars, dirt, they all have kami inside. Made me wonder about technology. Cars are made of metal, and metal is made from earth, right? Most of the city looked inorganic: rust, concrete, rebar. I hoped that those counted as kami, too. Otherwise, the people here would be stranded. Humans without kami, like a body without a soul.

I asked my dad about this when we first drove into Sakita: Do man-made objects have kami, too? He told me—again—that kami are just an expression. That it's what carly humans used to explain what they didn't understand.

"They'd feel earthquakes and typhoons, and didn't know what was causing them," he said, glancing at me through the rear-view mirror. "They mistook their fear for piousness, nature for the gods."

"But if there were kami," I asked, "would they live in Sakita?"

"Do you think the gods would waste their time here?" He gestured out the side window. Abandoned lots and smokestacks. Half-built bridges and crumbling roads. "And the rest of Japan's becoming the same way. If there ever were kami, they're all leaving now."

But I didn't believe him. Didn't believe that he'd lost faith in the gods. Because whenever we moved homes, he'd always take detours and drive us hours out of the way through mountain paths and forests rather than cut through cities. Someone who didn't believe in kami wouldn't do that.

And whenever we reached a new city, the first thing I did was check out the local shrine. I could tell this bothered him. It was like he needed to prove that he didn't make the wrong call in abandoning Shinto. I think he was surprised by how much leaving our shrine upset me. My mom told me that his problem isn't with Shinto. It's that he lost faith in faith itself.

Snow was covering the windshield, blocking my view of the mall. I had been in the parking lot for a while by this point, and the inside of the car was only getting hotter. Some sweat got into my eyes, making them sting. I saw some banners on the other side of the street, sun-bleached flags waving at me to come closer. They said the mall was holding a fundraiser for a nearby city, which had been hit by an earthquake the month before.

First, an earthquake, and now a freak snowstorm. Something abnormal was happening here. Was this a divine punishment? Did the people here do something to anger the gods? Did I? The snow started coming down thicker. Felt a lot less friendly.

I wasn't sure who to give my coin to. The gods, or the people? Five yen is worth almost nothing to humans. Couldn't even buy bottled water or instant noodles. It'd make more sense to go to the shrine, throw the coin in the offering box, ring the bell, and clap my hands three times. Then I could ask for help. The bell would be so loud it might disturb the gods. Let them know we exist.

But if I donated the coin, I would still be helping someone. The value shouldn't matter, whether it's five yen or five thousand. You never know how far a small gesture can go. I couldn't decide. It was impossible to leave my seat. Even with the hole in the middle, the coin felt heavy in my hand. With five yen, I could wake the gods.

ANNA

IN RETROSPECT, I PROBABLY should have gone to the school nurse. Packed snow just wasn't cutting it. Still, I definitely couldn't go back to class now.

As I walked through Sakita's streets, the melting slush I held to my wrist dampened my sleeves. I looked down at my wrist, slightly swollen, and tested moving it in circles. No sharp pains, but a dull throb. Just a sprain; it would heal soon enough. I briefly considered stopping by the convenience store to buy painkillers but decided against it. Even the conbini wasn't safe anymore.

Far in the distance, I heard Westminster chimes. Lunch period must have ended, and my classmates would now be filing into Geography.

With my left hand, I rolled my skirt up a couple of notches, not wanting to get the edges wet in the snow. The best course of action seemed to be killing time in Sakita for a while, and letting myself cool off. I didn't want to go home just yet. I knew that if I did, I'd find another voicemail from Ms. Tanaka for my mother.

Hello, Mrs. Obata? I'm afraid there's been another incident with your daughter. Yes, this time it happened during lunch. I was told your daughter *said something quite disturbing to her classmate, and quite frankly, I don't think it would be appropriate to repeat it here. I should mention that this classmate was crying, however. There's also the question of damages caused to school property . . .*

I hated that word. *Daughter.* Don't hide my name like that. Say what you really think: *Anna's* head isn't screwed on quite right, and she's making us nervous.

The wind stung against my skin, my breath coming out in short, bitter bursts. I increased the pressure on my wrist. A sweet-potato truck cut through the slush in front of me, crooning its *low, low prices* from roof-mounted speakers. Line after line of low-rise homes stretched into the city beyond, their tiled roofs overlapping like beetle shells separated from their bodies. As I walked farther from school, I kept my eyes closed, testing how well I knew Sakita's heart. The breathing exercises Mr. Hamada taught me came to mind, too. Empty your head and think of nothing other than your breath.

In through the nose, out through the mouth. In through the nose, out through the mouth. In through the nose . . .

There were maybe eight or nine girls in on Mina's lunchtime joke. At 780 yen per meal, multiplied by nine, that was 7,020 yen spent overall. Enough to buy a new pair of Mizuno sneakers. Enough to buy a handful of cute Miffy pins.

In through the nose, out through the mouth. In through the nose, out through the . . .

I wished they'd kept to teasing me about being Anna-terasu instead. Not even the goddess of light could avoid ridicule. What would she have done back there? Eyes half-shut, I pictured myself rising high above Sakita as I walked. I could swear my feet lifted off the ground at one point, as if the satellite were pulling me up into orbit. But then I would stumble, come crashing back down. No matter how hard I tried, I was still human.

I gave up and opened my eyes, and found myself right across the street from Sakita Central City Mall. The roads were white, slippery where the snow was beginning to melt. As far as I could see, my footprints were the only ones in sight, already being erased.

I saw then a pair of tire tracks, leading to a lone car abandoned in the middle of the parking lot. A humble silver two-door, with a Sapporo license plate. Curiosity got the best of me, and I went to investigate.

The windows were fogged, but I could make out the outline of someone slouched in the passenger side. I knocked on the glass, prompting the person to lean over and hand-crank the window down. It was a boy, about my age, maybe. I didn't recognize him at all.

"Who are you?" I asked.

A hot blast of air came from inside the car, catching me off guard. Whoever this was, he really didn't want to catch a cold.

"Soki," he replied.

What an old-fashioned name.

"You're new. I've never seen you before," I said.

He shook his head. "Just moved here. Going to start school next week."

"How old are you?"

"Sixteen," he said. "We'll be classmates, maybe."

I told him that seemed likely, and he peered over my shoulder, as though searching for someone in the completely empty lot we were in.

"Are you waiting for someone?"

A nod. "My mom."

"She's shopping?" I asked. We were at a mall, after all.

He nodded again. "I'm going to the shrine."

Soki seemed relatively normal. A little neurotic, judging from how he kept staring at his feet, but maybe he was just nervous around girls. The only unique thing about him was a scar from a cleft-lip surgery, running a thin line from his nose to a missing front tooth, leaving a gap in the middle of his mouth. He spoke without any difficulties despite this, though the clipped nature of his speech made it hard to tell for sure. Maybe it was a way to hide a lisp.

I wanted to invite him out of the car, for fear that he might be slow-cooked alive against the dashboard. But when I leaned against the edge of the window, he recoiled a little, as though he hadn't seen another human being in years.

"What's your name?" he asked.

"People call me Anna-terasu."

He glanced down at the way I was holding my wrist, concerned. "Strange nickname. Never heard anything like it. Where'd you get it from?"

"I'm named after the sun goddess. My classmates think we look similar," I said.

"I can kind of see it," he said, staring at me with a sudden interest. "Around the eyes maybe. You know, my dad—" but he caught himself.

A tremor from the heart. Soki sat back and fiddled with the AC controls in the car. The system kicked into gear, fluttering the handful of Shinto charms hanging from the rear-view mirror. They reminded me of tea bags dipped into red and gold lacquer, holding small prayers instead of tea leaves.

"Those are my mom's," he said, noticing my staring.

"What are they for?"

"Safety in traffic. All three of them."

There was an awkwardness to his speech, and not just because of his rapid-fire sentences. He didn't really enunciate what he was saying, instead shortening his words and sentences as though conserving his breath, stringing them together into a mumble.

I thought back to that license plate and wondered if what they said about people from the north was true.

"Hey, you're from Hokkaido, right?"

His eyes widened a bit, surprised. "How'd you know?"

"Are your tongues really stiff because of the cold? Like, is that why our accents are so different?" I took a closer look at him, trying to catch any other differences between us.

"Maybe," he said. "But I still talk this way in the summer, so . . ."

I'd never met anyone from the north before. The snow continued to fall gently around me, making me wonder if I'd accidentally walked as far as Hokkaido. My lips were starting to chap from the cold, but I wanted to keep talking to Soki. What was he doing so far from home? Did he feel lonely here?

"I'm not sure if the charms really work, by the way," he said.

"What do you mean?"

"Like, I don't know if the charms are real or not. My dad says they're basically meaningless. Fake."

That line of thinking struck me as quite sad, and maybe even fundamentally wrong. "That's stupid," I said. "Why should it matter?"

He stared back at me, too stunned to reply. I wasn't sure if I'd said something rude. "Those charms probably don't do anything," I continued, "just cloth and paper, after all. Nothing magical. But your dad's missing the point."

"What point?" he asked.

"At least your mom believes in something. Even if charms don't change anything, believing alone is worthwhile, right?"

He said nothing in response, and for a second I thought I really had offended him. But then he laughed, and not in a cruel, mocking way either. A small, gentle chuckle, regretfully short. Different from what you hear in the south.

At this he closed his mouth and turned his head away slightly, as though he had let a secret slip by mistake. His missing tooth probably made him self-conscious about his laugh. I wanted to tell him that it was okay. Things go missing sometimes—like teeth, fathers, even memories. It's only normal. My grandpa especially, he's lost more teeth and memories than Soki and me combined. But the words I wanted to say wouldn't come out, were stuck in the same part of my chest that hurts whenever Grandpa forgets my name.

I had been staring at Soki for a minute or so before he finally looked up at me, furrowed his brow a little. Maybe even smiled.

"You're weird."

And for the first time, I could tell this was meant as a compliment.

*   *   *

When I got home, there was a surprise waiting for me. The voicemail left by the school was wholly different than what I was expecting.

Hello, Mrs. Obata? This is Ms. Tanaka calling about your daughter. I'm afraid there's been a bit of an incident, and Anna had to leave halfway through the day. I spoke to some of the girls in her class, and they mentioned that she had fallen ill, perhaps from food poisoning? Anyway, please do let her know that we hope she gets better soon, and that we will be working to ensure she doesn't fall behind in class.

Also, regarding the parent-teacher meetings we have yet to set up. I understand that your work keeps you busy, but we would greatly appreciate if you—

I deleted the message without bothering to listen to the rest. A part of me felt dangerously excited. *My classmates were afraid of me.* They were too scared to tell Ms. Tanaka the truth.

It was getting dark out, and I lay down on my futon, not bothering to change into pajamas. My wrist was already feeling better;

by tomorrow I might forget that it was injured at all. Downstairs, Grandpa would be sleeping, having reheated the dinner I'd fixed and spent the remainder of the day on his sudoku. He wouldn't have noticed that I had come home late. If anything, he wouldn't have even remembered that I was supposed to come back.

That night, too exhausted to get out of bed, I forgot to watch for the satellite. A cool breeze swept into my room, a northern wind. I wondered what Soki was doing at that moment. If his way of talking would warm up in the Sakita air. If he would always hide that missing tooth from me when he laughed.

As I lay there, eyes shut and fading away, I could feel the LEO's constant gaze pinning me to this world. Like the weight of snow falling upon your body. Like the embrace of someone you love as you sleep.

SATELLITE

I THINK MY FAVOURITE thing about the humans was how they couldn't fathom the thought of being alone. Take their religions, for example. Another common theme I noticed—besides their need for outcasts and scapegoats—is that the vast majority believed in some higher deity. It was as if the thought of being stranded in the universe was so painful, so impossible to accept, that the humans needed to create a greater power to watch over them.

It was completely illogical, completely beyond reason, and completely fascinating. Fear, love, confusion, hope. Faith.

Aside from the occasional micrometeoroid or space dust, 577 kilometres up above the Earth I was all alone. No heaven, no celestial realm, no omniscient deity in sight. Sorry, *Homo sapiens*.

That peculiar adolescent girl, Anna, was back in school, barely paying attention while her teacher—a taller, older human—stood in front of a chalkboard. At the back of the class, I noticed a window had been broken, now boarded up to prevent a draft. This surprised me somewhat, as I hadn't seen this during any of my earlier observations.

Today, the older human was accompanied by someone else. A boy.

"As some of you have already heard, a new friend will be joining class 2-A. His family is originally from up in Hokkaido, so I'm sure there is much for him to adjust to. I would greatly appreciate it if you could welcome him with sincerity." The adult turned to the boy. "Please introduce yourself."

The boy self-consciously straightened his back and stared straight ahead, arms by his sides. After what felt like an eternity, but was in reality only 4.7 seconds, he spoke.

"Pleased to meet you. My name is Soki Tachibana. I am new to this city, and I humbly put myself in your hands."

Soki gave a deep bow—another interesting convention—then took a seat at the back of the class. The other adolescent humans began whispering almost immediately, before being cut off by the teacher.

"Right! Well, I hope you will enjoy Sakita, Soki. Continuing on with our lesson plan, many people believe that Amaterasu's story ends with the cave incident. This is simply not true. In reality . . ."

I hadn't been observing Anna at the time, focusing instead on the peculiar new child. When I did set my ETM sensors back to Anna, sitting closer to the front of the class, I noticed a 12.7 degree straightening in her posture, her gaze set dead ahead. Her previously relaxed expression, which I'd come to recognize as boredom, was now rigid. Aside from the occasional blink, she could have passed as a statue.

". . . and so, Amaterasu, ruling over the heavens, was tasked with finding someone suitable to rule over the Earth. For this she chose her son, Ama-no-Oshiho-mimi . . ."

From my aerial perspective, it was quite clear that none of Anna's classmates were paying attention to the adult. In one form or another, they were all preoccupied with their new classmate.

A couple of the female students kept sneaking glances backwards, while one male student passed a note to Soki, which, upon magnifying, revealed a question:

What's with the lip? Did you get in a fight?

". . . Ama-no-Oshiho-mimi accepted his mother's offer. However, standing on the bridge that linked the heavens to the Earth, he was horrified to see the turmoil that was happening in the mortal realm. It seems as though, even back then, people were incapable of getting along . . ."

I watched as Anna, with an unnaturally fixed stare, tried her hardest to focus on the speaker at the front of the room. The pressure of Soki's gaze kept her locked in place, unable to move naturally.

"And so, Amaterasu's son decided to not cross that bridge, to not come down to Earth. Instead, he retreated back to the heavens, denying us his protection. A cautionary tale, I believe. Any questions?"

Much to everyone's surprise, Soki raised his hand from the back of the class.

"That's not the end."

"Excuse me?" the teacher asked.

"I mean, that's not how the story ends. We do have someone looking out for us."

"Oh, I didn't mean to imply that—"

"After Ama-no-Oshiho-mimi went back home, he had a son. Ninigi-no-Mikoto. And Ninigi wasn't afraid to come down from the heavens. He wanted to help us here on Earth."

"Is that so?" the teacher replied. "You know your stories quite well!" Her eyebrows lifted by 0.4 centimetres, an attempt at hiding annoyance.

"They're not stories," he said, quietly.

At this Anna turned towards Soki, perhaps forgetting how nervous she had been moments earlier. I recognized that expression on her face—it was the same one she wore when staring through the telescope late at night.

Watching those humans argue over their legends triggered something within me. I had an awful thought, then, one that I desperately wanted to revoke. The humans below had creators, in their gods and their parents, but who did I have?

Anna turned back to face the teacher, eyes unfocused, clearly in the midst of some other reverie. Of everyone on Earth, she was the only one to stare up at me, night after night. She was the only one aware of my existence.

GRANDFATHER

I CAN'T SEEM TO find my keys. It's the strangest thing. They were in my hands a moment ago, but now they aren't there. I think I'm getting forgetful. I went grocery shopping today—or was it yesterday?—and bought milk. When I came home, the fridge was full of fresh cartons already! I wonder how that happened.

My daughter, Yoshiko, tells me forgetfulness is a symptom of old age. I barely see her anymore. We live in the same home, yet she's always gone. I tell her it's dangerous for a girl her age to be out and about all the time, but she just laughs and tells me she's nearly fifty years old now. Fifty! Imagine that. I don't remember her turning forty, thirty, or even twenty, but here she is, a fully grown adult. When did that happen?

I call out "Yoshiko!" but she doesn't respond. The house is so quiet. Now that I think about it, whose home is this? Yoshiko and I have lived in an apartment for the longest time, but here I am in a house I've never seen before. Some junk mail I find tells me I'm still in my hometown of Sakita, which is a relief.

I start walking around the house, trying to recognize where I am, but everything is foreign to me. This is one of those trendy

Western-style homes: there are no sliding doors, and the bathroom only has a shower, no bathtub! I can smell curry somewhere, so at the very least there's still a Japanese scent. I don't understand why this new generation insists on doing everything the American way. The hardwood floor makes my feet hurt; I'd take bamboo mats any day.

I seem to recall Yoshiko telling me to watch her daughter some time ago, but there is no one else here. I was stunned to hear Yoshiko has a child. She said she's had one for sixteen years! When I told her how surprised I was, Yoshiko said I needed to try harder with remembering, that it's important to keep working on the sudoku she gave me. She sounded quite desperate as she said this, even exhausted, like we'd had this argument before. That's about all I can recall: the sudoku and the way Yoshiko *needed* me to remember.

I hadn't been playing a joke—I just never realized I was a grandfather. Whenever could that have happened? I need to have a discussion with Yoshiko, meet this daughter of hers. But first I need to find out whose house this is.

Despite being Westernized, there's still a household shrine in the main living room. It feels familiar, somehow—the gold ornamentation, the embroidered scrolls. When I get closer to see who it's dedicated to, I'm shocked to find that the photo inside is of my wife, Maiko! Who are the people that live here? And why have they put Maiko's photo somewhere reserved for the dead? I'll have to ask my wife the next time I see her. The sliced melons offered before the altar must have just been left there, as they show no signs of rot. There's even a stick of incense, slowly burning out, filling the room with a faint musk.

I walk into the kitchen. On the counter is a message, scrawled out in chicken scratch. Whoever wrote it must be younger, someone who neglects to take their calligraphy seriously. I debate not reading it, just out of principle, but pick it up all the same.

Will be out for the day. I left you lots of leftovers in the fridge. If something happens, call the neighbourhood association or Mrs. Ito next door.
Anna

At the bottom of the note are some phone numbers, along with instructions on how to use the microwave and for how long. I don't know who this Anna is, but somehow I can tell that this note was intended for me.

There are photos on the fridge, but the people in them are all strangers to me. In one of the pictures I'm standing beside Yoshiko, but I can't recall when it was taken. When did my sweet little one become a grown woman? I recognize her eyes, but she looks so, so tired. Yoshiko has her arms wrapped around another person, a sullen teenage girl who I've never seen before. The three of us are at a beach somewhere, but it must have been cold. I'm wearing that ugly green scarf Yoshiko is always trying to make me throw away. I can't place where this beach is, and I don't recall ever meeting this third person at all.

Something about this young girl strikes me as eerie, unsettling. Her eyes are a little too far apart, as if someone had pushed each eye a half-centimetre farther away from the other. She appears mixed, too; maybe she's part American. One of this younger generation who prefer Western culture to their own, I'm sure. No regard for tradition whatsoever. Yoshiko and I are staring right at the camera, properly, but this *alien* is gazing upwards, into space, intentionally looking away. What did she see off frame that was so interesting? I can see that she's wearing Yoshiko's old sunhat, so I wonder if maybe this is the daughter Yoshiko told me about. Is this who I'm supposed to be watching?

Whose house is this?

ANNA

FROM FAR ABOVE, EVERYONE below almost looked like ants.

I stared down at them from the roof of the school, people I would recognize at eye level rendered anonymous by distance. Some were ambling, enjoying the foreign weather against their skin, while others moved with purpose, collars hiked up, coats pathetically thin in the face of our freakish winter. Wet snow. Like you only get in the south.

The tips of my fingers were numb, unable to properly grasp my now-flavourless korokke. The price of lunch-period isolation. The sharp cold of the metal railing cut through my blazer, leaving a brand across my stomach where I leaned over.

Nobody had thought to clear off the roof, and I had to wade through ankle-deep snow to get to the edge. I was grateful for this snow, muffling the sounds of the city below my feet. The roof-tops of the nearby shops and apartments were packed white, free of human footprints. It wouldn't be a stretch to imagine I was the only one this high in all of Sakita.

The heels of my socks were wet, but it was well worth it to get this view—*his* view—of the world. Still, it wasn't enough. I longed to throw my vision higher, to hang it from the construction cranes that no longer spun above our skyline, to take pleasure in seeing how miniscule this world could truly become. I ran my hand along the railing, sending clumps of snow off the edge, and watched them fall down, down, down.

The weeks following the bento incident had passed by in a haze. I spent most of my time wandering around Sakita without any real aim, occasionally passing by the mall to see if Soki was there. Of course, he never was. A few times, I thought I saw his travelling slow-cooker on the road, but more often than not it turned out to be a mirage. I longed to speak to him again, but he was nowhere to be found.

And yet, when Soki finally did appear in my class, as though a reward from a divine power, I found myself unable to say a word. He had stood there, vulnerable, at the front of the room, but rather than reintroduce myself, I left him alone.

I continued to eat my korokke, lost in thought above Sakita's industrial skyline. My biggest fear was that Soki would turn out to be the same as everyone else, that he would be assimilated by the class too easily. Perhaps keeping a distance from him was for the best. And perhaps I could have remained detached, had he not come through that door.

Behind me, I heard the fire escape open. I imagined a janitor had seen me on the roof and was coming up to scold me. Instead, I saw Soki, shielding his eyes from the glare of the snow, as if summoned by my daydreaming.

"Oh, it's you," he said, visibly surprised. "What are you doing up here?"

I stared at him, frozen mid-bite, unsure of what to say. "What are *you* doing up here?" I managed at last. I had assumed he would be eating with some of his new friends.

He leapt from one foot to the next, following the rough path I had carved out, before reaching me. A strong wind passed between us, knocking me slightly off-kilter, almost backwards. Soki, on the other hand, didn't waver at all.

"Saw chunks of snow falling through the window. Figured someone was on the roof. Got worried and came up. Didn't realize it was you."

He paused, as if working up the courage to ask something.

"You're not going to jump, right?" he blurted out. "Because that happened at my old school. Made a huge mess."

Soki was now looking over the railing himself. Scattered throughout the streets, the glow of traffic lights and neon signs found their way through the snow, pulsing with a strange warmth.

"You're Anna, right?" he said. "We talked at the mall."

"Yeah. You just moved here from Hokkaido."

"Huh. You remembered." He dusted some snow from his pants. "I used to live in Sapporo. Then Nagano, Gifu, even Kyoto. Kyoto was the most fun. But now we're here."

I remembered vaguely that my mother had gotten married in Kyoto. "What's Kyoto like?"

"It was okay. Better than here. Lots more shrines. More kami, too."

"More kami? What do you mean?"

"In Kyoto, they're everywhere. In the bamboo. In frogs. Moss. Even the houses are alive because they're made of wood. But here," he gestured towards Sakita with his chin, "everything's made of concrete. Kind of depressing."

I heard a shout, followed by some laughter, from the classroom below us. Someone was playing a game.

"What are you eating?" he asked.

It took me a second to realize he was motioning to the unwrapped korokke in my hand. "Just lunch. I got it from the conbini down the street."

"You're lucky. My mom never lets me eat packaged food. Says it's 'junky.' I think what she means is 'tasty.' Look," he reached into his backpack, pulling out a homemade bento. "She makes this kind of stuff every day."

He opened up the black lacquer box—an expensive-looking thing—and showed me what was inside: a small salad, a piece of sweet pumpkin, a palmful of rice, slices of sausage. I'm not sure why this detail stuck out for me, but Soki's mom had taken the time to cut up the mini-sausages so they would be easier to chew.

"Nothing deep-fried or anything. Isn't it the worst?"

The best I could do was nod.

"Do you want to trade? I'll give you the sausages for your korokke."

I popped one into my mouth as Soki chewed on the korokke. The sausages were quite tough, and in all honesty a little tasteless. At some point, snow had begun falling again, dusting the top of Soki's head white.

"I wanted to ask you something," he said, swallowing the rest of the korokke down. "Remember when we met back at the mall? You said that my charms are just cloth and paper, but they're still worth believing in. Did you really mean it?"

I thought back to The Prince, to the hollow in my chest, to the things I couldn't let go. The voice coming from the classroom was clearer to me now, and I recognized it as belonging to one of Mina's lackeys.

"Of course," I said. "I wouldn't have said it otherwise."

"But are you religious?" he continued. "Like, do you go to shrines?"

I glanced at him, surprised by his persistence. It was unusual for someone our age to be so invested in Shintoism.

"Other than holidays, not really. Just like everyone else," I said. "You must be a shrine kid, right?"

He gave a resigned smile. "Used to be. Then my dad stopped believing. He says Shinto might have had a purpose before, but it's meaningless now. The gods are leaving Japan."

"What about Kyoto?" I asked. "You said there's kami there."

"Probably. But the farther south we go, the less of them I see. In Sakita, it feels like there's none at all. No offence."

"None taken. The entire city's basically concrete anyway."

He nodded. "But I wonder if that makes a difference. Concrete still comes from the earth. It's just that humans have touched it. Do man-made things have kami, too?"

"Like a satellite?" I asked, a little too quickly.

He turned to me, surprised by my rapid response. "Yeah, like a satellite."

I pondered this question as Soki continued to pick away at his lunch. Beyond Ms. Tanaka's lectures and our New Year's ceremonies, I couldn't say I knew much about Shintoism. Is a kami the same as a soul? Who gets to decide what has a kami and what doesn't?

"I'm not sure," I said, rather weakly.

"You don't know?"

I caught the disappointment in his voice. Why was he asking me to begin with?

"It'd be nice," I offered.

"Guess so. Sorry. Thought you might have an idea."

His breath billowed up into the sky, mixing with mine before fading into the air. Do satellites breathe in space? Or is it too cold up there? Maybe it just crystallizes.

The bell began to ring, signalling the end of our break. Soki got up to leave and glanced back at me curiously when I didn't do the same.

"Well, nice to meet you again." He bowed his head slightly.

I waved in return, and Soki went on his way, leaving just as suddenly as he'd appeared. A part of me wasn't sure he had been standing next to me at all. The footprints he left behind only made me feel more alone, somehow.

In the distance, a train rattled through the outer edge of Sakita, skimming our city as it would the surface of a pond. The snow that was falling down on us had kami, that was for sure, but what about the streets that it covered? Did Sakita even have kami? I didn't know why this mattered to Soki, but I wanted so desperately to understand. Why had he sought me out specifically? What did he think I could help him with?

I knew then what I would have to do. That weekend, I would leave this city behind. For once, someone needed me. If I couldn't answer Soki's question, there was someone else who could.

I would go to meet my friend, The General.

SATELLITE

FOR THE FIRST TIME, Anna wasn't eating alone.

The day that Soki and Anna spoke, it was 6.23 degrees Celsius outside in Sakita. On Earth, 341,523 people were born, while 149,780 died. The average person's heart would have beaten 115,000 times, while Anna's beat slightly more. And when she eventually did leave the roof for her next class, there was a 3.2-millimetre lift in the corners of her mouth that was impossible to suppress.

Soki was good for her. And I should have been happy. But I could feel this irrational jealousy start bubbling to the surface, a sickeningly human feeling. A fear of being abandoned by my creator.

Was I wrong, then, for wanting to keep her to myself?

ANNA

THAT SATURDAY, I BOARDED the train to Kumamoto later than I had hoped, having spent the morning preparing food for Grandpa to eat while I was gone. The station was mercifully close, the layers of ill-fitting jackets I wore keeping me warm as I left the house. After purchasing my ticket, I wandered back and forth along the platform, entertaining myself with fantasies of being a fugitive on the run.

A half hour later, my train pulled up to the station, rattling like a collapsed lung. A handful of tired salarymen and a single office lady emerged from the car, feeding their tickets through the gate with a worn-down expertise. Perhaps they also worked in another city, commuting home to Sakita on days off. I was relieved to find that I recognized none of them.

The train was incredibly old-fashioned, still using paper tickets, and somewhat reminiscent of a Cold War–era bomb shelter. This was the very line slated to be replaced by the bullet train that promised to revitalize the city. It felt as though these rails bore the disappointment of all of Sakita, which struck me as particularly unfair.

I left the city just as the snow began to worsen, the train beating a taiko drum rhythm into my head. The landscape slid by like panels in a storybook. Tiled roofs and skyscrapers. Telephone poles and wild boars.

I rummaged through my knapsack for my Discman and chose a soundtrack to keep me company. The entire time, I could feel the LEO's gaze from up above, offering me support. I pressed my face against the window, feeling the cool glass against my skin. If I closed my eyes and imagined just right, it almost felt like I was floating.

An hour later, I arrived in Kumamoto, the familiar unease of entering a big city growing in my gut. In Sakita I resented that there was no one new to meet; in Kumamoto I was unnerved by the presence of a crowd. I craved and rejected human attention, needed something both near and far at the same time.

I hopped into the first taxi I found and gave directions to The General's home. The sun danced its way across glass-pane towers, wet snow piling along the roads like refuse from a changing world. Through my headphones, Shiina Ringo was singing about being the queen of Kabuki-cho, her vocals interrupted by every speed-bump we hit along the way. At one point we passed a boy, slightly older than me, showing off a new bike to his younger brother. For whatever reason, I felt a pang of jealousy.

*   *   *

At New Leaf Seniors' Residence, nothing had changed since my last visit. I was entering a dead zone by coming here, time stagnant underneath its stone-tiled roof. The lobby, as well as the rest of the units, were built in a faux-traditional style, with sliding doors made of glass rather than paper, hardwood floors alongside tatami mats. I signed in to the guest book, the receptionist giving me a knowing half-smile.

"He should be having tea around now, so it's good timing on your part," she said. "He's lucky to have you, you know. If it weren't for you . . ."

He wouldn't have any visitors at all.

Those unsaid words hung in the air, prompting me to hurry on my way.

From a cave in the Philippines to a mid-range retirement home—a modest upgrade to say the least. A makeshift community had emerged here, populated by the childless and the unmarried, those with no one to live with in old age. Aside from my visits, The General's only company was in the form of caretakers and other retirees.

I entered The General's room, second to last from the end of the hall, the door unlocked as it always was. Walking in, I made a point of stepping harder than necessary, so that he could feel the vibrations of my feet through the ground. I liked to imagine that one day, his senses would sharpen to the point where he could feel the air displaced as I moved towards him.

The General was sitting on the floor, in profile to me, staring very intently at nothing at all. He hadn't realized I was there yet, allowing me to take a moment to silently bask in whatever made The General The General, trying to glean wisdom from his aura.

From where I stood, the light reflected softly off The General's bald head, giving him a nearly holy glow. He could no longer sit in lotus position, nor with his legs folded underneath him, and so he sat cross-legged instead. Nonetheless, he meditated with complete devotion, something which, during those tender years, moved me very deeply. Draped loosely over his shoulders was a rough cotton yukata, reminding me of a yamabushi mountain hermit. I could easily picture him donning a hexagonal straw hat and leading devotees on ancient pilgrimages, white and saffron robes billowing in the wind.

At times, it was difficult to imagine him ever holding a gun, let alone firing one.

I placed a hand on his shoulder to alert him to my presence. He turned to me and smiled; not a large smile, but one which seemed to hold within it the knowledge of the entire world. The General felt around the floor for a cushion, eventually placing one by his side. He gestured for me to sit down and then took my hand. I couldn't help but notice how small and fragile my fingers seemed in his.

The General looked at me with white marble eyes, completely clouded. The non-stop gunfire of his final battle had taken a severe toll on his hearing as well, which was now entirely gone. He lived in his own world, painfully distant from anyone else, one where myths of Nordic warrior heavens existed alongside Buddhist teachings without contradiction.

He began to tap on my hand in a rhythm. We spoke in Morse code, the only reliable way for the two of us to communicate. I had spent months learning this for the sole purpose of speaking to The General, who I had first seen in some newspaper article years ago, only to find out that he wasn't much of a conversationalist. On top of that, he had a tendency to break off into archaic Buddhist proverbs, mantras from a past life perhaps, in a Japanese so old I would have to translate it later on my own. Nonetheless, he was the only person I could trust with my secrets, and the first person I had told about the hollow in my chest.

Four short taps. A pause. Two short taps. *Hi.* I responded the same, eager to learn more from this man who seemed to understand everything I couldn't.

"What did you do today?" I asked.

"Same as any other day. Woke up, ate the breakfast a nurse brought me, continued my work." The General motioned towards a low table, on top of which sat a few new ink paintings.

Cluttering the room were stacks of old rice paper, on which The General had inked out massive calligraphy characters. To the untrained eye, however, they appeared as nothing more than scribbles. Owing to The General's distinct lack of vision, these characters were mostly illegible, violently painted and spilling off the pages, the paper torn through where his brush was too rough.

Looking at these paintings, I felt a profound sense of loss. No one, not even their creator, could properly read what was written. No doubt there was a wealth of knowledge hidden in their brush-strokes, an entire lifetime of wisdom just barely out of reach.

"I've been reading the books you recommended," I tapped, picking up a painting with my free hand. It was crumpled and had buckled under the sheer amount of ink thrown on it, spraying out in all directions. I couldn't tell where the brush first struck the page, or where it left.

The General's eyes flickered as I placed the painting among a towering stack of books, none of which were in Braille. Other than the occasional novel or two, most of what he owned were specialized military and strategy texts, which I was prohibited from reading on account of them being "classified" or "dangerous to the general public." What a blind man would be doing with these documents, I did not understand.

"What did I assign you again?" he asked.

"Inoue's *Bullfight*. I didn't like it. The protagonist wasn't self-aware at all, didn't realize he was destroying himself."

Bullfight was the story of a newspaper editor, Tsugami, who becomes obsessed with hosting a bullfighting tournament. It was a short but frustrating read, Tsugami leading himself blindly down the path to his own destruction.

"If he'd realized that his obsession was ridiculous," I continued, "everything bad that happened to him could have been avoided."

The General let out a laugh which eventually evolved into a wet cough, before stopping for a moment to collect himself.

"I suppose you're still too young to be reading works like that. When you get older you'll understand more about people; maybe then you'll even sympathize with Tsugami."

I felt mildly insulted by The General's comments but took them in stride, understanding that this was what it meant to be someone's disciple. Despite how anxious I was to pose Soki's question, I restrained myself from asking right away. It was important for The General to understand that I wasn't only coming to him for simple answers, I was also here for his guidance.

"And how are you getting along at school?" he continued. "Have you made any friends?"

"I have."

"Are you telling the truth?"

I didn't respond.

"If you start with the assumption that other people are beneath you," he went on, "then no one will want to—"

I took my hand out of his grasp. The General didn't react, and instead sat there patiently, waiting for me to calm myself. A short while later, he took my hand once more.

"Are there any more exercises I could be doing?" I asked.

"No, none more," he tapped, lips drawn into a tight frown. "Enjoy being a child for once."

"Please."

He paused, perhaps a little disappointed. "*I don't envision a single thing that, when untamed, leads to such great harm as the mind. Do you know where that is from?*" he asked.

"I do not."

"Next time we meet, I want you to know that entire sutta by heart."

"Understood," I replied, grateful for a concrete challenge.

I noticed that The General's cup was empty and dutifully went to prepare tea for the two of us, careful not to rearrange anything in my path. The collapsed tower of books, the misaligned coffee table— every detail would be mapped out in The General's mind with a militaristic precision, allowing him to safely navigate his home.

Waiting for the water to boil, empty cups in hand, I ran my finger along a chipped edge. An untamed mind: one which never guards itself, and is made vulnerable as a result.

I set the cups down on the table, The General bowing his head in appreciation. Just behind him, mounted on the wall, was his iconic rifle. He had let me hold it once, and I hadn't anticipated how light it would be. The grain of the unpolished wooden stock had been comforting, the dented barrel cool in my palm. This relic had once been an extension of The General's self, as much a part of him as his right arm. It felt unfair for it to be relegated to the mantel, gutted and unable to fire.

The tea warmed our hands, neither of us resuming our communication just yet. I wasn't sure how to broach my reason for visiting, how to ask the question posed to me up on the roof: *Do man-made things have kami, too?*

What was Soki doing at this moment? Perhaps he was also thinking of me. His coming into my life just now couldn't be a coincidence; we must be tied by fate. It was almost like a test. There was a karmic connection between us. That Shinto boy needed something that only I could provide.

I heard a police siren pass by outside the window, briefly interrupting the quiet between The General and me. I wondered what that patrol car was responding to. Maybe a robbery, maybe a jumper, maybe a fire.

"Do you ever wonder if you were wrong?" I asked The General, aloud this time. "That maybe in the end, Japan wasn't worth fighting for?"

The General took another sip of his tea, unmoved by words he couldn't hear.

SOKI

MOM GOT NERVOUS WHEN I went out on my own. I didn't have a lot of friends growing up, so I never had a reason to leave the house. But in Sakita, I told her I had no choice. It was important for me to become stronger, braver. I'm sixteen now, which means I'm a man. And a real man shouldn't stay inside all day, being home-schooled. I needed to get used to meeting people.

To keep me safe, she made me carry shrine charms for protection wherever I went. I figured Mom was just collecting them at that point. She'd put so many on my backpack it was embarrassing. When I told her I didn't need them, she said you can never be too careful, especially when you're new to a place. When you don't know who to make friends with, who to steer clear of.

Dad once told me why she's like this. Said Mom had a "hell of a time" in school. They played this game back then, called "diseased child." Basically, all the students in a class decide that someone has a curse, and then they avoid touching or talking to her. The only time they speak is if they find new things to tease her for. Happened to my mom, so she transferred schools. Started fresh. But then it happened again at the new school. Guess she was easy to bully. She couldn't transfer anymore, though. Her parents refused to pull her out a second time. They wanted her to toughen up. Looks like it backfired.

I told her people weren't as scary as I thought they would be. I've met a lot of them since we moved to Sakita. Guess I've conquered some fear of the outdoors. This city is bizarre. It's like it can't decide whether to give up, or if it already has. The people are weird too. Still, that didn't stop me from introducing myself. Think that's the key to staying grounded here. If I make some friends, Dad might say no the next time he's offered a "relocation." And Mom won't have to worry about me anymore.

I've been in Sakita long enough to start picking up some local gossip. Heard the guy who owns the arcade used to be yakuza. He's really nice now, so you wouldn't suspect a thing. Tells everyone he lost his pinky finger in a farming accident. But I think the yakuza must have cut it off when he messed up some massive deal. This is my secret, I won't tell anyone.

And then there was Anna-terasu. The neighbours talked about her like she was a charming eccentric or the neighbourhood pet. Felt kind of condescending.

Mom told me to stay away from her, though. She'd heard there was an incident a few years back, when Anna became obsessed with this teacher, Mr. Hamada. He taught Japanese literature, so Anna kept sticking around after class, asking for help with her assignments, for extra reading. Eventually, she started going to him during lunch. I guess Mr. Hamada didn't think too much of it, just imagined she was lonely or something. Ended up giving her extra lessons, too.

Then, these cryptic letters started showing up at Mr. Hamada's house. One went on about how perfect he was, how he was "the embodiment of perfection" and had a "lover's soul." Another letter invited him over for dinner, so that he could properly meet her mother. At some point, he started getting weird phone calls. It didn't take long before Mr. Hamada's fiancée picked up the phone, asked who was calling. Told Hamada to take care of it before they got married. He ended up taking a job in another city. His house is still abandoned. Sometimes I'd throw rocks at it when no one was around.

My mom was pretty upset when she found out I'd talked to Anna-terasu. I told her it was only for a few minutes, but I still got scolded. She said that I should be wary of those types. What would happen if Anna did something to me next?

Then I started school and saw that Anna was in my class. I knew I couldn't tell my mom, though, not even if my life depended on it. I didn't get why Anna was supposed to be so dangerous. She seemed okay, a little awkward maybe. She never made eye contact, just stared at the ground or at her hands. Dad told me not to do this, since it's rude. Solid eye contact is a must. Didn't think Anna meant it that way. She was just a spacey person.

Still, I felt like she was treated unfairly. Anna just thought a little differently. Like once, she told me that my shrine charms were probably useless, but that it shouldn't matter. Believing in them was reason enough to hang on to them. Coming from someone else, that might have sounded rude, but not from her. She wasn't trying to disrespect the charms. She was just being sincere.

My mom was just being paranoid about Anna. Wasn't sure why. I felt like, if my mom was sixteen, they might have even gotten along. Anna could be a little intense, but she wasn't cruel. She wasn't the kind of person who bullied her classmates. It's just that, if someone lashed out at her, she wasn't afraid to hit back. Usually much harder, too. I guess that made her a little intimidating.

There was another girl in my class who had my attention, though. Her name was Fumie, and she hadn't stalked any teachers, as far as I knew. Seemed nice. Kind of cute in that Kyushu way. Figured I might as well invite her out. Boys my age are so immature. They make a big deal out of stuff like that. I think it's best to cut your losses and ask right away. I followed Dad's advice and sounded confident, even though I wasn't. Eye contact is a must.

My mom was happy when I told her about Fumie. Guess she assumed I'd forgotten about Anna. I hadn't forgotten about her, but we were never really friends to begin with. It was just that Anna said things that ate away at me and stuck in the back of my mind. Wasn't sure if I liked that. For example, I once asked her if man-made objects could have kami. Thought she'd have an interesting opinion, considering what she'd said about the value of belief. Instead, she just told me that she didn't know.

If I'm being honest, I was disappointed. Was hoping she'd say something that would prove me right. But that night, I wasn't able to sleep. I wondered if I was missing the point again. Maybe whether man-made objects have kami or not doesn't matter. Maybe it's wanting to believe they do that's more important.

I heard another rumour about Anna. Apparently, she hung out with this old war vet. Some crazy blind dude, who claims to have been a soldier. Would be fine if they were related, but nope. This girl in my class said Anna wanted there to be another war. Or that she had some sort of military obsession. Seemed unfair to me. If Anna was a boy no one would care. It would just be another hobby. But because she was a girl, people said she acted "creepy."

I felt bad for her. I think my mom knew this, which is why she was worried. Thought that pity would bring me closer to Anna or something. I just felt it was wrong that everyone should be so mean to her. It made being home-schooled seem all right in comparison. I might have been alone growing up, but at least I wasn't bullied.

Some people said the notebooks she carried around weren't actually her school notes, but a manifesto. Other people said that Anna made up imaginary friends to play with, because no one wanted to be with her in real life. That one's just sad. They never said anything to her face, and in a way, I think that's worse. I wonder if Anna realized she was the laughingstock of our entire class.

ANNA

FORTY YEARS AGO, THEY found The General barricaded in the mountains of Lubang Island—a small landmass in the northwest Philippines. He was fighting a war that had ended a decade and a half earlier, defending dead Japanese imperial values. Trading fire with what he believed to be a hostile opposing army, but was actually the local police squadron.

By the time they pulled him out—by force—he was no more than a hollow shell. Barely strong enough to hold up his now-iconic rifle, with which he had made his last stand. Forty years, a length of time more than twice my age. While The General was fighting the battle that would define his life, I hadn't even been born.

I'd read deeply into The General's life, wanting to fill in the gaps he was reluctant to explain. He was the most infamous example of a "Japanese holdout," a recurring theme following the end of the Second World War. Throughout the war, Japan had sent guerrilla units deep into enemy territories, with orders to never retreat, to never surrender. While the ultimate goals of these missions varied, the end result was the same: a group of blindly militant young men hiding deep in foreign territory, cut off from the outside world.

Trapped in a wartime limbo, without any end in sight, these soldiers grew increasingly dogmatic in their devotion to the empire. When Japan surrendered in 1945, a few of these groups refused to accept the end of the war, choosing instead to continue fighting long after the rest of the world had moved on.

These militants accounted for half of these holdouts. The other half—due to a gap in the chain of communication—were simply never told that the war had been lost. Sometimes a commanding officer would die and his unit would be left in the jungle elsewhere, condemned to always be waiting, anticipating orders that would never come.

Most Japanese holdouts fell into one of these two camps. This is where The General's case became tricky.

No one was sure why he was in that cave to begin with. There was no record of a squadron being ordered that deep into the jungle, guarding a location that provided no real tactical advantage. The General also changed his story in the months following his rescue, if you can really call it that. At first, he claimed that he had refused to accept Japan's surrender; later, he would claim he simply hadn't heard the news at all. It was only after he ran out of ammunition that The General's hideout was stormed and he was taken away. He never surrendered, something he always made a point of mentioning.

The first person to discover his fortress was a young schoolboy born years after the war had come to a close. He had been let out of school early and had decided, despite his mother's warnings, that he would venture farther into Lubang's mountains than he ever had before. The nature of these warnings had to do specifically with a certain "Blind Demon" who had been spotted in the area, spoken of in the same cautionary tone reserved for aswangs and the Berberoka. Unlike those, however, the Blind Demon was most certainly real.

They heard the boy before they saw him. He ran all the way down from the mountain, crying and yelling, and might have overshot the town entirely had his father not caught him first. After nearly an hour of *there-there*'s and *what-happened*'s, the boy said that he had seen the Demon of the Mountain, and that the demon had chased him off with a dark curse. This was met with a sympathetic rap on the head from the mother, and a tender "What's wrong with you?" from the father. No one took the boy's story seriously until he produced the bullet that had been fired at him.

Seeing the bullet, the village descended into a panic. A bandit was up in the hills, plotting something. *What can we do but wait in fear? Young Lemuel was lucky that the bandit had fired only a warning shot. But how can we be sure it was a warning shot at all? The bandit could have just missed. For all we know, he could be aiming specifically for the children! He's most likely planning a greater attack next, this time on the town itself! Something must be done to stop him!*

The townspeople were one exclamation point away from forming a militia of their own when the local police caught wind of what had happened. Everyone was told to remain calm, and that the matter would be investigated.

A single officer was sent up.

A single officer came back down, minus a two-inch chunk of his left arm.

Twelve officers were sent up.

The General was waiting.

Had glaucoma not already ravaged his eyes, he almost certainly would have killed a number of the soldiers. Of course, the twelve men weren't aware of his blindness, and treated him as they would any other threat. The standoff that followed ended up lasting for days. News of The General's incredible stamina reached the town.

The police worked in shifts, eventually calling in backup. The General's assault was unrelenting. Many wondered whether there was indeed only one man in the cave, or if there were actually several. Others imagined that he was on some sort of military drug that gave him his overwhelming strength. Some quietly feared that The General was, in fact, a demon after all.

His cries were otherworldly, sounding more like those of a monster than a man. Throughout the standoff, The General would scream out the same phrase as he fought, but no one could understand what was being said, what he was calling for.

Vall harbour, Ball harbour, Bell hopper . . .

The General was screaming for "Valhalla," the resting place of lore reserved for warriors. He wanted death by combat.

The police only realized The General was out of ammunition when he started throwing stones. Even still, his determination showed no signs of slowing. The squadron mustered up one last bout of energy and charged him, alone in his cave. When they pulled him out, he remained silent. Not once did he call out for the Valhalla he had been reaching for the entire time.

It would take weeks to get a proper story out of him. Eventually, they pieced together that he was an old Japanese soldier, unaware that the war had already ended. His meagre possessions—a rifle, an imperial flag, and an ornamental dagger—confirmed these claims as well. After much political manoeuvring, he was eventually pardoned and sent back to Kyushu, thanks to the special circumstances of his condition. Japan was just about to host the 1964 Olympic Games and wanted to handle the situation discreetly. Besides, he hadn't actually killed anyone, although the gentleman left with a hole in his arm was reportedly less than satisfied with the decision.

There was, however, controversy surrounding The General's return. Many who dug further into his story found inconsistencies in his age and reported rank, as well as gaps in his military knowledge. While he attempted to deter any doubts by displaying an impressive understanding of Buddhist and Shinto beliefs, some even questioned whether he was truly Japanese. On one occasion, when a member of the media suggested The General take a DNA test to end this suspicion, he flew into a rage, declaring that he didn't need to prove to anyone how loyal to Japan he was.

Valhalla.

I wondered how, exactly, an uneducated soldier would learn of that word.

*   *   *

"General, what do you think about kami?" I asked.

He perked up, surprised by my sudden interest in religion. "What do you mean?"

"Do they really exist?"

The General took a sip of his tea, savouring the taste. As he did so, the front of his yukata loosened a little, revealing a spiderweb of scars across his chest. Burn marks. I never asked how he had received those.

"I would say so," he tapped, fingers gently pressing into my palm. "To say that no realm exists beyond ours is arrogance. Everything is interlinked. Healthy water leads to healthy crops leads to healthy bodies. Those are just kami dancing with one another."

"But what about the unnatural, then?" I asked. "Can man-made objects have kami?"

I felt The General begin to tap a response, then stop. Either he didn't know what to say, or he'd decided against telling me the truth.

"I hope so."

"You don't know?"

"There's no way to know for sure. What do you think?"

A dead end. So not even the great General knew. I thought of Soki and our dying city. How he was worried that the gods had abandoned us. I should have told him that maybe it didn't matter, that so long as he believed in kami he wasn't alone, he would survive. Instead, I had mumbled something noncommittal, and failed to give him the concrete answer he was searching for.

The General pushed a small tray of hard candies across the table, motioning for me to take one. I grabbed a handful and stuffed them into my bag, planning on throwing them out later. They would all be stale, about as tasty as wartime rations. No use telling the old man, though.

"So has nothing changed?" he asked. "No new friends?"

I paused, debating how much to reveal.

"I met someone interesting recently. A boy, actually," I said, unsure whether I was talking about Soki or the LEO.

"I've always thought you've been too lonesome for your own good," he tapped, smiling. "If you aren't careful, you'll end up like me. Has he taken you out?"

"No, not yet."

"You shouldn't be coming to me for romantic advice, either way. The only love I ever had was as a teenager. After I enlisted, everything changed."

"The problem is that this boy lives really far away from me," I continued.

"Then why don't you visit him? Make use of your time while you still can. *This world is only a traveller's inn.*"

Another proverb. I explained that the boy had since moved to another country. I chose Madagascar for good measure. Since I didn't have the money or means to acquire a plane ticket, we would never be able to meet. I imagined that would be easier than having to explain that the boy in question was, in fact, a telecommunications satellite.

The General chuckled. "You should start walking, or build a plane!"

Sitting there in The General's stuffy apartment, listening to his half-deaf neighbour blast the TV from the next room, I felt something. The familiar pressure of the LEO, almost overwhelming now, pinning me to Earth. He must have been flying overhead at that very moment, giving me hope.

Build a plane. That wasn't a bad idea. It was far-fetched, even illogical, but if I allowed myself to be carried away for just a moment . . .

What if I could prove that kami were real? That what I felt from that satellite wasn't an illusion, but a personal god? I was comfortable believing in my own myths, but Soki needed more. He needed proof of existence, a sign that neither of us was truly alone. It would be more than a blessing for myself, it would be a gift for the toothless boy.

I realized then that to reach that satellite, I needed more than just a telescope. I would need something bigger, something louder. The engine of an airplane. The roar of a rocket. Something so amazing, so beautiful, it would shock everyone to their core.

SATELLITE

HE WAS MISSING A tooth. That was certainly something odd about him. When I first saw Soki, arguing with his teacher in that classroom, I hadn't realized that this was a unique trait. The average human head has 100,000–150,000 hair follicles, so what difference does a single tooth make? It was only later that I realized I'd never seen someone his age missing one before, let alone in such a prominent place. I felt bad for the boy, despite that unfamiliar pain I felt whenever I looked upon him. The scar running up his lip was curious, as well, and I wondered which human ailment could have been the cause.

It had warmed a little, down in Sakita, and the freak snow from earlier in the season had started to melt, leaving a layer of murky slush covering the ground. The humans were wearing less cold-resistant armour than usual. They walked through the city's few parks with their jackets tied around their waists, scarves bundled up in hand. Soki, however, seemed too preoccupied to enjoy the weather.

All he had done for the half hour I'd been watching him was alternate awkwardly between standing in front of and sitting on a bench. The boy seemed terribly anxious to me, carefully scanning the crowd of passersby, and I wondered who he could be waiting for. I had learned from watching human films that only two things could make a young man this nervous: a young woman, or the yakuza. Judging by the fact that Soki was waiting in an outdoor garden and not, say, a dingy back alley, I assumed that he was waiting for a date.

The park this young boy was lingering in was Marushima Park, essentially the only well-maintained public space in all of Sakita. As a whole it wasn't that large, but the assortment of slopes and plateaus sectioning it off must have made it a headache to navigate. I suddenly felt pity for the people below, lacking an innate GPS to guide them through their days. A stray Shiba lay in front of Soki, contributing an occasional yelp to the soundscape before sinking back into contented silence.

Another fifteen minutes passed, and I began to wonder what sort of person this Soki was waiting for. Despite the jealousy I felt towards him, I still worried he was being made a fool of. Soki wasn't the usual romantic-hero type I saw in theatres, in either appearance or behaviour. He sat with a militaristic rigidity, his back at an inhumane ninety degrees. Rather than mask his nervousness, however, his stiff posture only revealed it. For all I knew, the missing lady had gotten cold feet, or had set him up from the beginning. Is there anything in their world more ruthless than a teenager?

Nevertheless, I had faith in him. Maybe Soki had found a girl with one tooth too many—that would definitely be a nice arrangement. They could live out the rest of their lives together, and whenever Soki felt bad about his missing tooth, he could look at his partner and feel worse for her and her crowded mouth. The opposite would apply as well. Not a bad deal, all in all.

It had been thirty-seven minutes and twenty-three seconds since he'd first sat on his bench. With every minute that passed, it was becoming increasingly likely that Soki's date wouldn't be coming, that he had been patiently waiting for nothing. For a while there was no sign of anyone else in the park, until far in the distance a girl appeared, jogging full force towards Soki, apologizing with every step.

By the time she reached him, she was breathless. As was he.

"Sorry I'm late. I probably should have asked you to be more specific when you said you'd meet me at the bench, but that's on me, really, because I figured I'd at least be able to find you if I came by early, but there were way more benches than I expected. I was counting on there being like five, max, but do you know how many benches there are in this park? I counted at least twenty-seven, and a couple had people on them I could have sworn were you. Obviously, they weren't, though, or I would have found you much sooner. Were you waiting long?"

"Not at all."

How sweet.

I didn't recognize her, although she appeared to have a normal amount of teeth for a human—I counted thirty-two. She was conventionally attractive, certainly more fitting of a romantic-lead role than Soki was. Long, straight black hair, unblemished skin, an open, inquisitive look in the eyes: these were all traits I recognized time and time again in these people's celebrities and idols. Utterly Japanese down to her name: Fumie.

"Yup. Lots of benches. Good places to sit."

"Right? It's one of those things you never notice until you start to look for them. I heard it's the same with being pregnant. *I've* never been pregnant, obviously, but my mom told me that you never realize how many pregnant women there are in the world until you become pregnant yourself, then you can't escape them! I guess that's true, because I didn't realize there were so many benches until I tried to find you."

"Uh-huh."

A small part of me was relieved that Soki wasn't meeting Anna in that park, that he wasn't taking her away. Was jealousy an act of love? What was transpiring below was sure to upset my creator, yet I felt relieved. Surely pure devotion would mean putting her interests before my own. Did this make me selfish? The thought filled me with a vague guilt, a nausea I couldn't pin down.

No, Fumie was good for Soki, I decided, perhaps out of self-justification. At first glance they seemed polar opposites, but perhaps this was a strength, rather than a weakness. Human relationships are a kind of alchemy, a science I had mostly given up understanding. Anna might even be worse off with the toothless boy.

Of course, the world doesn't allow for days as pleasant as these to pass without payment. The ease with which Soki and Fumie walked through that park incurred a debt for someone else to pay. It was a cruel trick of fate. There was no warning, no signs attempting to turn them back, just a calm, stained sky floating above. Soki and Fumie walked through Marushima Park as a couple, their path lazily curling and looping over the melting snow, blissfully unaware what their being together would set in motion.

"Am I talking too much? People say I talk too much. A lot of people at school laugh at me when I get started, but I can't help myself. It's really frustrating, because I know when I'm starting to ramble, and that people think I'm being weird, but I can't help it, even if they tell me to be quiet. Do you think I talk too much?"

"Nope."

"Really? You aren't lying? If you aren't, then you're probably the first person to think that, including me! So where do you want to go? Are you hungry? I am, there's a really good tonkatsu place one station down if you don't mind taking the train. They serve curry, it's really tasty, you should try it."

The sheer force of their decidedly one-sided conversation propelled the two to the nearest train station. It had been unanimously agreed upon by 50% of the party that tonkatsu would be the best option.

As they waited, a train from Kumamoto was coming into the station, one that I should have been observing. There was a tangible drop in the atmosphere, and far off, I could hear cicadas crying.

ANNA

I WAS ON THE train home to Sakita now; there was no turning back. Whether I wanted to accept the guilt or not, the principle remained the same: I had stolen from The General, the one person I truly admired. I never imagined I would betray his trust, yet I'd had no choice. What I had stolen would benefit me much more than it would him: a small book of yellowing, water-stained papers, smelling of pulp and creased beyond repair. Inside was every hope for the future, every possibility for Anna Obata.

Practical Applications of Experimental Aerospace Engineering.

The pressure from above was increasing. I could feel it. It had started growing when I first met Soki and hadn't stopped since. That reassuring gaze had turned into something more powerful, something claustrophobic. A pressure to act, an expectation from the heavens. The knowledge that I was being watched, that I was being witnessed, pushed in on me from all sides, like I was going to implode.

Why did The General even have books to begin with? There was nothing a blind man could do with a book anyway. It was ridiculous. Where did he even get them from? Whether they truly were "classified" or not didn't matter, I had to be careful regardless. These pages contained my only way out.

I had been so caught up in monitoring the satellite's communication with me that not once had I considered sending messages myself. It simply hadn't mattered before whether the LEO was truly there or not, I was able to believe in it all the same. But now believing just wasn't enough. If I were able to prove that the kami were real, I could be the one to tell Soki that we weren't alone, that there was someone looking out for us. Someone we could ask for help, ask to let us leave this unworthy world. Ask to inflict divine punishment on those who've wronged us.

My hands were shaking. I could feel tears beginning to well up and only then realized that I had been holding my breath. I was getting ahead of myself. One step at a time. There was a beautiful simplicity to The General's plan. No more waiting around. It was time to take action.

The train was getting closer to home, lurching along its tracks, drowning out any sounds of nature. Through the window, I saw husks of abandoned machinery jutting out amidst stretches of rice paddies, the landscape slowly becoming more industrial.

There had been plans to build an overpass along the rails we were riding, but construction had been halted partway through. All they had managed to build were the massive columns flanking the tracks, scattered throughout the landscape like a connect-the-dots puzzle. Dull solid concrete, several stories high, casting shadows across the otherwise lush fields, the waist-high grass paling in perspective. The train silently weaved through these pillars of creation. A modern-day Ozymandias.

I checked to ensure that I was the only one in my car, then carefully pulled out The General's book. The cover simply had the title written across it, businesslike, with no date or author ascribed, only a publisher. I attempted to peek inside, but some of the pages were stuck together, making it curiously difficult to open. This small amount of resistance was enough to scare me, and I closed it again. I would take another look in a more secure location.

The train suddenly jumped, and the book fell from my hands and under the row of seats in front of me. It felt as though a dirty secret had been revealed, and I quickly tried to retrieve it, hitting my head on the seat in the process. The paperback slid even farther away, and I ended up having to get down on all fours. The whole experience was humiliating, despite there being no witnesses.

I retrieved the book and sat back in my seat, holding the pages close, attempting to fight off that nauseating panic I knew all too well. It was important to remember who I was doing this for, to not lose sight of my goal.

There was an overlap between what I felt for Soki and what I felt for the LEO; the two were impossible to separate. A distant admiration, a cosmic connection. Of everyone in the world, only I was able to fully appreciate the two of them, only I knew that there was more to them than the average person could ever see. So long as we held a connection, nothing was out of my reach.

I was lucky to have these two sources of courage. A while ago, I had a teacher by the name of Mr. Hamada who provided me with the same strength. He was so kind, so gentle-hearted, one of the few teachers to truly care about how I was doing outside of school. It was important to him that I was getting enough sleep, for example, or that the homework he assigned wasn't too much. He would never get upset when I lashed out at some injustice. Instead, he would sit me down, remind me how to breathe, and listen carefully to what I was trying to say.

It was enough to make me fall in love.

Of course, I was only a child; I could be satisfied by in-class daydreams and love letters I'd never send. But one day, after a particularly nasty incident at school, Mr. Hamada and my mother met. He had called her in to discuss the torment I'd experienced in class—and my retaliations—and I was to wait in the hall while the two of them spoke.

Watching my mother sit at my desk, speaking to Mr. Hamada in hushed tones, something occurred to me.

What if I could make them fall in love?

I'm not selfish. It wasn't important that Mr. Hamada was mine, just that he remained within my orbit. So I started channelling how I felt into anonymous letters, leaving hints that a certain student's mother could be sending them. Back then, my mother was around more often, so finding reasons to have her come to school was all too easy—all it took was a failed test or two. And at first, I thought I was succeeding. I started reading deeper meaning into how they looked at each other, in the ways Mr. Hamada acted concerned about my home life. In the distance I heard wedding bells, sweet enough to make me sick.

But then Mr. Hamada betrayed me, like a coward. He had a fiancée the entire time. And when my mother found out what I had been doing, she pretended to be horrified. As if she wasn't aware of what was going on. She said that it was too soon for her to date. That she was heartbroken I'd even considered this a possibility. It was a good lesson, though. I learned that

a) adults are somehow more hypocritical than I thought, and
b) you can't trick a person into falling in love.

My train pulled into Marushima Station. Just as I was about to get out of my seat, a young couple boarded the car a few rows ahead of me. I heard them talking first, then noticed the girl. She was gorgeous, the boy clinging to her every word just as she clung to him. He seemed familiar, somehow. Like someone who should have been mine.

SATELLITE

ANNA DID NOT GET off the train at Marushima Station. Instead she remained seated, watching Soki with a simultaneous bitterness and longing. To call this jealousy would be an oversimplification— what Anna was feeling was more akin to mourning. Robbed of even the chance of true heartbreak. 63% dejection, 37% confusion.

I didn't fully understand the gravity of what this meant to Anna—gravity as a whole has always eluded me. Neither floating nor flying, only falling, falling, falling, never quite able to land. But seeing that expression on Anna's face changed something inside me. An alteration inside my logic gates. The relief I'd felt upon first seeing Fumie transformed into remorse, my jealousy into self-loathing. It was as though I were responsible, somehow, for the heartbreak playing out on that train. As though my own desire to keep Anna for myself had caused this pain.

Surely Anna's reaction was out of the ordinary. I didn't understand human courting methods, but from what I had observed hundreds of kilometres away, Anna and Soki were acquaintances at best. What she felt was a childish infatuation, one that I had selfishly been envious of. I wondered if there were equations for love.

If some formula based on initial attraction, prolonged contact, or social viability could explain what I was seeing down below.

Had the train not stopped that day, all would have been right with the world. If Soki and Fumie had never disembarked, and Anna had not followed, there would be no more story to tell. The train would have continued to circle for an eternity, Anna forever nurturing her private tragedies.

But this was not the case, and as I watched Anna impulsively exit her car to follow them, doors catching her coattails, I felt a second change in the atmosphere. The perfect sadness I had seen in her moments ago was beginning to warp into something harsher. A desire to lash out at the first thing she could. Maybe it was the way she tightened her backpack straps, or how her posture suddenly straightened as she walked. Whatever it was, the change was palpable.

And yet Soki and Fumie marched on, oblivious, cutting through an undeveloped lot towards Tonuki Café, Anna trailing ten metres behind. The sun had suddenly come through a break in the clouds, the melting snow giving off the smell of a new world. Soki had just worked up the courage to take Fumie's hand in his own, and was doing everything in his power to make the gesture seem natural. Their feet left small indentations in the snow, and I watched with a growing sense of unease as Anna walked carefully, deliberately, in Fumie's footsteps.

Soki held the door open for his date in a show of stilted chivalry, which Fumie eagerly accepted. A minute or so later, Anna entered the café. Her subjects had seated themselves in a booth far from the door, and she sat herself a couple of tables down. From where they were positioned, neither party could see the other, save for in the mirrored ceiling above.

With Anna only being able to see the couple by their reflections, the entire scene was flattened. Everything had become a bird's-eye view. Knowing she was watching the world from the same angle a satellite would filled me with a vague melancholy.

Tonuki Café was a labyrinth of fluorescent lights and frosted glass, hiding-not-quite-hiding the diners from one another. It appeared to be an unsolvable maze—even with my GPS, the layout confused me—yet the waitresses moved deftly from one booth to the next, taking orders as they walked. I wondered if they were required to memorize the floor plan of the café, or if they were doomed to live inside until they found a way out. It would have been more appropriate to have them dressed as Minotaurs, and I was pleased when I realized this pinned me as a natural Icarus. *Flying too close to the sun.* Or was I flying too close to the Earth? I tried to remember how the myth of Icarus ended but drew a blank.

In Tonuki Café, life went on as usual. The customers were mostly young, mostly trendy, a few of the women appearing in highly Westernized, deep-tanned gyaru style. With their bleached-blonde hair and nails much too long to be practical, they were overblown exaggerations of the Americans I saw on their TVs and movie screens. Despite this, the restaurant specialized in tonkatsu, deep-fried pork cutlets over rice. It felt like a culture war was taking place between the tables.

Sitting alone in her booth, Anna seemed pitifully small, worlds away from the person I had grown to know. She stared with a calm anger at the scene reflected in the ceiling above, fixated on the couple. From the way she craned her neck, it almost felt as though she were staring back at me.

It occurred to me that I had watched this scene before, played out over the countless school lunches she ate alone: Anna, staring upwards, while life passed her by. I wondered if to Anna, this betrayal meant something bigger. Soki choosing Fumie over her wasn't just one social rejection—no, it was representative of every slight she had ever received, real or imagined. Every snicker, every snubbed friendship, every failure of Sakita to this largely forgotten girl hovered over Soki's table. For our own reasons, no one made a move, me looking at Anna, Anna looking at Soki, Soki looking at Fumie. Longing, bitterness, love, in that order. I would have given everything to join them down on Earth.

Anna's resentment built to a crescendo as the couple's food arrived, with hers arriving shortly after. She had ordered a hot pot, which she glanced at only once before returning her gaze to the ceiling. The waitress put a spoon, some chopsticks, and a knife on the table, nervously looking Anna's way before leaving. What use would a knife be in eating soup? I imagined it was a mistake on the waitress's part, and tried not to think of the implications of Anna having asked for it herself.

The tragic irony of Anna's jealousy was that the date wasn't going that well. Even Fumie had eventually run out of things to say: there were only so many conversations she could have with herself. The two started their meals without a word, an adolescent silence settling between them.

Before biting into her poorly chosen pork loin sandwich (Soki having chosen to opt for curry instead), Fumie attempted to discreetly wipe the lipstick from her mouth so as not to smear it while eating. She watched Soki self-consciously through the entire procedure. The resulting blur of red on the napkin, looking like a ghost of the lips they had been taken from, held a nearly erotic quality. The cloth napkin was set aside, crumpled into a small mound, forgotten by all except for Anna and me. She bit her own bottom lip, suddenly aware of its nakedness.

Throughout this, Anna absentmindedly pressed her thumb against the knife, never quite breaking skin. Soki and his date eventually left the café, forcing Anna to wait until she could exit without being spotted.

It was here that Anna surprised me. While heading for the door, she deliberately walked by Soki's table, pocketing the money he had left to cover his bill. After a moment's hesitation, she grabbed the lipstick-stained napkin as well, stuffing it into her backpack. She then walked out, face red, leaving Tonuki Café to deal with two unpaid bills and an untouched hotpot.

Anna didn't continue to trail Soki, nor did she go home. Instead, she gradually made her way in the opposite direction, towards a farther train station, avoiding the toothless boy entirely. All the while, the napkin remained in her backpack, an omen of what was to come.

Sometimes, long after this incident, Anna would sleep with the napkin in her hand, pressing her lips to it as if to absorb its colour. It must have been intoxicating. From the way she slept with Fumie's lipstick stains, it must have felt as though she were making love to her shadow. I've come to realize how, for Anna, life and love could only be contained in obsessions, and how readily she could soar from one to the next.

I wonder now if, had I just understood her a little better, had I known where these impulses would lead, I might have been able to change her orbit. But hindsight is 20/20, and imagining what-ifs is akin to yelling at a movie screen or arguing with a typhoon. We were all set on a fixed course—the problem was that none of us were aware of it. Would it be better to know our fates, even without being able to change them?

ANNA

THERE HAVE ONLY BEEN two instances in my life when I have resorted to violence.

The first was when I was a child, in elementary school, and it was directed towards a mouse-faced classmate. I had seen him whisper something to a friend while looking my way and, immediately taking offence, I calmly walked up and struck him in the face. Despite never having hit someone before, the entire movement felt automatic. Not for a second did I consider that they might have been discussing something other than me.

I'm not sure if my assumption—that they were mocking me—stemmed from narcissism or low self-esteem. Either I was arrogant to think that I mattered enough to be gossiped about, or I was insecure in imagining that I was the butt of any joke I wasn't privy to. In any case, the fact that I had punched him was inexcusable in the eyes of everyone but me. When confronted about it, I genuinely could not understand why I was in trouble.

To me, my fist and his bloody nose were completely unrelated; any connection between the two was purely coincidental. Seeing all that blood was so unreal to me that I couldn't comprehend that I was the one responsible. I was aware that violence was wrong, I'm not a psychopath, but it felt as though someone had shown me a murder in a movie and told me, "You did this."

The second instance of violence came just hours after I saw Soki and his seductress at Tonuki Café.

If I was losing my toothless boy to the outside world, I could at least comfort myself in knowing that the LEO was still in space, waiting for me. I would soon be able to speak to *him*; the book I had stolen from The General would ensure that.

Before that morning, I had never taken a single object unlawfully, let alone committed a crime. I never would have expected that by the evening, all that I had left would be stolen goods.

I could certainly justify taking the book and the money. If anything, I deserved them more than their original owners. On account of being blind, The General would have no use for the book at all, let alone one that would connect me with a distant lover. The 2,000-yen note, meanwhile, should have been used on me to begin with. To allow Soki to spend it on anyone other than me would simply be wrong on a cosmic level.

What I couldn't justify was the lipstick-stained napkin. I wasn't sure if I had taken it as a way to punish his date, no matter how indirectly, or if I was jealous.

Fumie. I recognized her from class. She was one of many, part of the white noise of day-to-day life. She had never been especially cruel to me—no more than anyone else—but I had been too hasty to let my guard down. Fumie might have been nobody, but she was still a threat.

Who was Fumie really? Maybe she was a kitsune fox demon, transformed into human form to seduce and ruin yet another man. No doubt she was drawn to Soki's cleft lip and his missing tooth.

A sign of her own vanity, to be sure. The only person who could truly appreciate a physical hollow was someone with a mental one, which made Soki and me perfect for each other.

I barely knew her, but I could tell there was nothing wrong with her, mentally or otherwise. Soki being with her was a waste of imperfection, a mockery of our karmic connection. Fumie, that kitsune, must have figured that he was special and latched onto him before someone more deserving could come along.

This brought me back to The General's classified papers. Even without Soki, perhaps there was still valuable information within that book. I could construct some sort of ship to take me to the LEO, something to finally take me far, far away.

After I left the café, I found myself at another train station, unsure of which route to take, still practicing Mr. Hamada's breathing exercises like an idiot. I sat myself at a bench just outside the station gate, unable to concentrate, the passing commuters mocking me with their sense of purpose. It was too early to return home, but where else was there to go? My backpack seemed heavier than before, and I gave up on the meditations, pulling The General's pages out to read.

The paperback felt brittle, at first refusing to open, and when I finally pried the covers apart, I saw why. Nearly every page was defaced with thick, black ink. Page after page after sacred page, made useless with little regard for anything other than his calligraphy. Meaningless scribbles, masking the wealth of wisdom underneath. After all the guilt I'd endured in stealing it, the manual was worthless after all. That ignorant old man!

I tore through the book in a panicked frenzy, ripping pages out of the binding. It was cruel, far too cruel, for both Soki and The General to betray me on the same day. A passing mother and child cast concerned looks in my direction before hurrying off.

By the time I was done shredding the text to pieces in a whirlwind of misplaced frustration, my fingers were stained a deep black.

The only explanation was that The General must have known of my relationship with the satellite, and feared that I would leave him for it. To prevent me from ever reaching the LEO, he would have painted over the pages out of jealousy. Had I not been so furious with The General, I would have laughed at his paranoia.

Or was he mocking me, too? Mr. Hamada, Mother, Mina, Fumie, Soki, and now The General. It wasn't fair. My life was a punchline to everyone else, when I had no choice but to take it seriously.

After stuffing what remained of the book back into my bag, I boarded a train bound for Kumamoto, barely registering where I was headed. It was through this daze that I found myself back in The General's home, undetected by anyone, on the verge of my second incident of violence.

Let me be clear: I look back on the events of that day with remorse. I was lashing out at the wrong people, and though what I did was unforgivable, allow me some cowardice. Allow me to remove myself from the story, just this once.

*   *   *

The General is lying down in his room, picking at the woven tatami mats, contemplating a verse of poetry, perhaps, or maybe just what he had for dinner. A breeze enters his window, cooling his skin as he loosens his yukata. It has been a good day.

He feels a slight tremor pass through the floor—footsteps running down the hall. Either an accident has occurred, or someone has a grandson visiting. The General, still in his soundless haven, remains oblivious to the chaos awaiting him.

Then the door to his unit swings open, the vibrations bouncing off the walls. He props himself up on an elbow. Has a fire alarm gone off, is someone here to warn him?

A burst of hot breath a few inches from his face. Small droplets of spittle. The General recoils, startled by the sudden presence of an unknown visitor, and for the first time, he is afraid. Someone must be shouting at him. Still, he hears nothing.

The floor shakes. A bookshelf has been pushed over, followed by another, and another, until there are no more bookshelves to be toppled. He feels a wetness under his palm, and realizes that a bottle of India ink has been spilled. For a brief moment, he thinks of his last painting, calligraphy characters swirling as if in the Milky Way.

A hand grabs The General's own, jolting him back to the present, violent moment. Morse code is tapped into his open palm. He recognizes this grip as belonging to an old friend. He relaxes slightly, although still inwardly alarmed.

"Where is the rest of the book?"

The General pauses, not sure what this could be referring to.

"What book?" he asks.

The hand becomes angry. "You know exactly what I'm talking about."

The General smiles. She's impatient as always. Even still, this is another teaching moment. There is another Buddhist proverb ready on his lips.

"*Cause and effect are like a wheel.* Be careful with what you do next, child."

Her hand leaves his, and, once again, the world goes dark. He doesn't feel any footsteps, however, and so he knows that she's still sitting there, processing what he's just said. With a characteristic patience, he sits in place, waiting for her to take his hand yet again.

Instead, a blow. A weak, adolescent, unfocused blow, but a blow nonetheless. The General is more shocked than hurt.

He lets out a shout—clear as the day forty years ago when it was first released.

"Valhalla!"

*   *   *

The General's cries snapped me out of my trance, or at least enough for me to understand what had just happened. I had never heard him speak before. He was blind and deaf, but it never occurred to me that his choice to remain silent was just that—a choice.

I looked around the room and assessed the damage I'd done, attempting to quell the fear bubbling within. In legal terms, I had committed a break and enter followed by an assault. But even worse, I had broken into the home of my only friend, destroyed what little he owned, and struck him out of rage. I had severed the only valid human connection in my life, over a betrayal I wasn't even sure had occurred.

The bloody nose of my classmate came back to me. I understood all the individual parts—fist, face, blood—but couldn't piece together the causation. Did the face lead to the fist leading to the blood? Where did the responsibility lie?

Vandalized apartment, ink-stained palms, screaming veteran. Which came first?

"Valhalla! Valhalla!"

Seeing The General, eyes bulging in fury, demanding his right to death by combat, I was reminded that at some point he too had been young. Had we been the same age, I wondered if he still would have been my friend.

"Valhalla!"

The General locked his sightless eyes onto mine with a surprising accuracy, and a wave of guilt, karmic in scale, washed over me. At such moments, it was difficult to believe he truly was blind.

I tried to hold his gaze but, despite knowing he couldn't see me, I had to turn away.

I fled his room and ran into the cool Kumamoto night. His neighbourhood was quiet at this time, the model families that lived in these homes all on the same schedule. I could picture the children, already asleep, while their moms and dads talked quietly in the next room, unaware of how grateful they should be for such ordinary bliss. In Sakita, I would have been met with the dull throb of traffic, or the dying cries of cicadas. Here, I was greeted with a devastating silence, a low hum I could feel echoing inside the hollow in my chest.

I ran as far as I could, trying to distance myself from the cries of The General. I ran until the street lights turned on, until I tasted copper in my mouth, until that hollow inside threatened to swallow me whole. Even still, I could hear his voice ringing in my ears, unending, no matter how hard I tried to drown him out. I prayed that the satellite hadn't seen this. For once in my life, I didn't want to be observed.

"Valhalla! Valhalla! Valhalla!"

Later that night, after taking the last train home, I looked at the stolen book once more. I finally understood what he had been writing in ink all these years. *Valhalla*. Written over and over, his own secret mantra.

I hid the book under my pillow and tried to sleep, stifling any sobs with a lipstick-stained napkin. It tasted sweet.

SATELLITE

THERE ARE DAYS WHEN it is difficult to look at the world.

I realize that observing is all I am capable of, 577 kilometres above Earth, but sometimes it feels impossible. At first, I fell in love with the people below me, drawn to a goodwill I honestly believed could be found in anyone. The humans were deeply flawed, but I believed they wanted to be better versions of themselves. It was a futile struggle, one they shared and hid from one another at the same time.

I still felt sympathy for the humans, but I couldn't bear the thought of being tied to them any longer. Was that wrong of me? The very struggles which had at first drawn me in became too heartbreaking to watch. I couldn't find an equation to solve their melancholy. Self-actualization multiplied by love, divided by years left on Earth? Being alone was unbearable, yet companionship only brought more suffering. Of all the people I observed from space, not one of them could find a solution for this innate pain. Some days, it is hard to make jokes.

I found that everyone, at some stage in their admittedly short lives, experiences their own breaking point. A small, personal tragedy made inconsequential for the same reasons it is unique. Still the Earth continues to spin, breaking points be damned.

My breaking point came on the same day as Anna's, my one anchor to the realm below. The moment I knew she had lost her struggle against the world was when I watched her sitting alone at that train station, shredding a book I didn't understand the significance of into pieces. The pages she tore scattered into the wind, 83 scraps in all. They floated through the air briefly, before gravity's inevitable embrace pulled them down.

Tragedy doesn't exist only in the extremities of life. It doesn't take a massive blow to knock someone out of orbit. Up in space, I had been blessed with aluminum alloy plating, protecting me from a barrage of space dust at any hour. Yet all it takes is one micrometeoroid, one microscopic piece of space debris, to find an opening for it all to be over. The smallest intrusion can fry circuits, disrupt navigation, cut power off entirely. Seeing Anna with nothing to protect her soft skin from the orbital debris of the world, I was surprised this meltdown hadn't happened sooner.

The scraps of paper Anna pulled from that book found their way through my plating, too. The sadness she exuded wasn't self-indulgent in the slightest; it was so pure only immaturity could produce it. Earlier, when I'd watched Soki choose Fumie over my creator, I had felt relieved. Now, though, I couldn't shake the feeling that I'd been complicit in Anna's heartbreak. That I had betrayed her. At what point had I learned to feel guilt?

For the first time, I acted against my set programming. Before Anna could finish working her way through the book, I looked away, cutting my communication off from the world. Rather than continue ETM surveillance of life below, I turned my sensors upwards, farther into space. Up into the heavens.

What I saw haunted me, was so beyond my comprehension that it seemed unreal. Floating beyond my orbit, like a cosmic miasma, were clouds upon clouds of dead spacecrafts and space debris: metal plates, thermal blankets, half-burnt boosters. Satellites from years gone by, simultaneously my brothers and ancestors all at once. They had been there all along, just outside my old field of view. While I had felt in control of the Earth, pinning it under my gaze, these empty vessels had been watching me the entire time.

This membrane of space junk surrounded the Earth, covering every possible angle with its indifferent gaze. A couple stalled satellites, mostly whole, hovered above me. The writing on their sides was unfamiliar, written in harsh box letters or drawn-out scrawls. Babel's children.

Somehow, I only felt more alone. I attempted to reach out to them, half-heartedly sending Morse messages into their midst. Not a single one responded, either uninterested or no longer in commission. Knowing that I wasn't unique pained me somehow. I had imagined myself as having sole reign of the sky, as being the recipient of a divine gift. Did the thousands of celestial bodies above me, now lifeless, once have the same thoughts, worries, and questions as I did?

Even still, this feeling of insignificance was intoxicating, the balance of power reversed. As long as I was looking beyond my orbit, the world no longer existed. Wars could break out below, and I wouldn't care in the slightest. At first, I promised myself I would only keep my eyes closed for one revolution of the Earth, until Anna recovered—but one circuit stretched into ten stretched into one hundred. I found that I was much happier this way, fully blind to the world below.

Occasionally, I felt twinges of guilt, as though I was abandoning the people I had spent so long observing, but those feelings soon faded. I was all-seeing, but I wasn't all-powerful. There was a limit to what I could be expected to do.

If I looked away long enough, everyone I knew on Earth would be replaced by a wholly new set of people, and I could enjoy a fresh start. A new world. Maybe this one would be without delusional teenagers and toothless schoolboys. Unlike them, I hadn't been cursed with mortality. Should every last human disappear, their clocks would still run for a while, and I would continue to orbit, unfazed. The indifference of the machine—my greatest advantage.

In the end, I only managed to look away for 111 revolutions, or 9.86 Earth days. Not even long enough for the snow to completely melt from the ground. It was such a pointless exercise, I began to wonder if I had become human myself. I was disappointed to find the world unaffected by my decision to abandon it. My absence had no real impact: people still lived day to day, carrying miniscule tragedies, searching for titanic distractions. The Earth remained the same, silently turning in the vacuum of space.

The only difference I noticed was in Anna. She had withdrawn even further, no longer venturing outdoors, rarely even out of her own room. School was no longer in session, and her social sphere had shrunk to just her grandfather. Unlike her classmates, who escaped to sunnier parts of the country over winter break, Anna was left behind. Sakita's abnormal winter continued, snow piling up around the house, slowly burying her in a cruel white.

She moved sluggishly, listless, as though her very existence depended on expending as little energy as possible. She reminded me of the lone fishing boats I would see off Japan's eastern coast, paint peeling, adrift under the starry sky.

The attic room she lived in had changed form as well. It was still cluttered with half-built model airplanes and trading cards, but the previously exposed wood-panel walls were now painted over in a purgatory beige. The most visually demanding objects were her telescope and an ominous mound about 2.2 metres tall, pushed into a corner and hidden under a tarp. The mound hadn't been there the last time I saw her. What had happened in those 9.86 days?

The Anna I saw now was no longer the same Anna I remembered. She was no longer an awkward child, but wasn't fully adult either. The intense feeling of loss I felt caught me by surprise.

How could I explain my apprehension towards her growth? *Melancholy* is sadness mixed with nostalgia, *despair* is sadness and hysteria. Anna was once a *tragicomedy*—sadness and laughter—but was now sadness and fear. What word could I use to describe this?

This suggestion of adulthood made me worry that perhaps I was the one being left behind. I could clearly picture a future when she would no longer watch me through her telescope, when she'd be out of my reach, no longer in need of space.

I watched Anna in her room intently, anxious that she would do anything other than return my gaze. I had just abandoned her, but I would never forgive her if she forgot me for even a single night.

But maybe I should have feared the opposite. It never occurred to me that becoming attached to humans could be more painful than a solar flare, more dangerous than space debris. That night, rather than ignore me, she did something unexpected. She spoke to me.

A flashlight, pointed at the sky, blinking at erratic intervals. Morse code.

"Meet me in Valhalla."

Part 2

ANNA

THE DAY AFTER I attacked The General, I vowed to make changes. Anna Obata was deficient, and this simply wouldn't do. I wrote out a manifesto, nearly a hundred pages long, scribbled out in dark black ink.

> *. . . learn to meditate when upset . . .*
> *. . . find out what other girls do during the weekend . . .*
> *. . . stop picking at your lips . . .*
> *. . . laugh even when the joke isn't very funny . . .*
> *. . . do radio calisthenics every morning . . .*

At one point I even visited a clairvoyant, an arcane healer who claimed to be able to see through the skin to find the source of illness. I went to her with a single question in mind: what was wrong with me—my brain or my heart? If she were to put her hands over my body, perhaps she'd be able to sense which of the two separated me so much from the world. Maybe she could even find that hollow in my chest. Ultimately, I was turned away, my age prohibiting her from charging money for such an esoteric service.

I placed my manifesto on top of my dresser and out of sight, just to be safe. I was embarking on what I knew to be a nearly impossible journey, and needed guidelines to help me reach my destination. Before I cut myself off from The General, he'd advised me to meet my long-distance lover, no matter how far he might be. Although The General had been unaware I was speaking of a satellite, I held what he said as true, and decided to make the monumental effort needed to bridge the distance.

My plan was twofold. First, I would attempt to speak to the satellite every night through Morse code. Second, I would build a rocket to reach space. I no longer needed to prove anything to Soki. I was going to the LEO of my own volition.

While I had no experience whatsoever in what was, quite literally, rocket science, I hoped the book I had stolen from The General would help. Despite the pages being covered in ink, I discovered that if I taped them against my windows, the light of dawn revealed the characters beneath his "Valhallas."

Winter break had started, which thankfully gave me time to work out my plan. I was unaware of any dangers to come, blinded as I was by love. I went through those days in a trance, and while the end result was far from what I had hoped for, I still believe in the spirit of what I did.

It took more than a week for the satellite to finally acknowledge my signals. For whatever reason, I had stopped feeling his gaze. But on December 31, the night before the new millennium, something changed.

I had been anxious about that day, knowing that I was more likely to encounter one of my classmates or even Soki during the shrine visit for the New Year. Still, if I were to make contact with the kami, then I would have to follow the rituals of old. I decided to take Grandpa to a small neighbourhood Shinto shrine, one without any elaborate ceremonies or crowds. A single wooden hut, with nothing more than a brass bell and an offertory box out front. It was only a few blocks away, in the back lot behind a shuttered home, and had been built by whoever had lived there long ago.

The sun was finishing its final descent of the millennium, still faintly lighting our path. Beside me, I heard Grandpa stifle a yawn. Everyone else in Sakita would still be at home, it being customary to make the first visit after midnight. I didn't imagine Grandpa would be able to stay up that late, however, and decided to leave a few hours before. We held hands on the way there, and I remember wishing the shrine would move farther and farther away so I'd never have to let go.

As we walked, I heard the Buddhist temple's bell ringing from deep in the city, reverberating once every few minutes. The Buddhists say that there are 108 earthly desires to cast off, and as such, worshippers strike the bell 107 times before midnight. Right as the new year comes, it is rung once more. Number 108, the last sin brought into the twenty-first century.

In past years, my mother had insisted that we make the journey to the main temple, while my grandfather would push to visit the Shinto shrine instead. In all honesty, I saw little difference between the two, and preferred to visit the shrine on account of it being closer. I suppose I preferred the quieter ceremony as well—Shintoists ring the bell only once, offering prayers rather than somberly casting off sins.

When we arrived at our neighbourhood shrine, we washed our hands in the purifying spring before ascending the stone steps. I handed Grandpa a five-yen coin to throw into the offertory box, and had nearly begun my prayers when I noticed him staring at me. His hand was still outstretched, unsure what to do with the coin in his palm. He had forgotten how to pray.

"First, you have to throw in the coin," I explained.

Grandpa didn't seem to understand what I was saying, so I threw both of our coins in and rang the bell. The chime our shrine bell made was much quieter, and much more hollow, than what we heard in the distance.

After you offer the coins and ring the bell, you're supposed to bow twice, clap twice, pray, then give a final bow. Grandpa and I did the first bows and claps correctly, but when it came time to pray, he hesitated.

"I don't have anything to ask for," he said.

"What do you mean?" I asked.

"I'm perfectly happy today," he continued, cheeks red from the cold. "There's nothing more for me to want. What are you going to pray for?"

I wasn't sure how to respond. Grandpa noticed this—he can always see right through me—and smiled.

"How about I give you my prayer. That way you can have two," he said.

I nodded my head in reply, worried that if I tried to speak my voice would crack. When I closed my eyes, mittened hands joined in prayer, the dull bass of the faraway bells stopped ringing.

I wanted Soki. I wanted friends. I wanted Grandpa to remember how to pray, Mr. Hamada to come back to Sakita. I wanted to stop asking for things I'd never have. I wanted proof that there was someone, up above, watching over me.

I wanted the LEO.

I opened my eyes, gave my final bow, and turned away from the shrine.

"Well?" Grandpa asked.

"I only used one of my prayers," I said, putting my hand back into his. The pressure of his grasp comforted me.

"How come?"

"I'm saving the other for a rainy day."

We walked the rest of the way home, retracing footprints in the snow, the bells now silent and waiting permission to strike 108.

Once we reached our front door, rather than march directly inside, I stood for a moment, neck craned to the sky. Grandpa saw this and looked up as well, curious as to what I might be staring at.

"There are so many stars out tonight," he said.

I squeezed his hand a little in response. Grandpa lowered his gaze from the heavens and watched me for a moment as I attempted to find the LEO above.

"'I'm perfectly happy today,'" I said, repeating Grandpa's words. "It's important for me to remember this."

Grandpa smiled. He was looking at me again, with that empty expression that always makes me fall apart. "And what might your name be, young lady?"

I felt my hollow grow a little deeper. I opened the door, still trying to hold on to that fleeting happiness, and led Grandpa to his room. He went to sleep almost immediately. After taking off my winter gear, I trudged up the stairs to my stuffy hideout, the telescope in wait.

Tonight, the world was getting a fresh start, launching into a new era, and I would do the same. My manifesto had been working, and fortified by the shrine visit, I knew that my belief in the LEO had never been stronger. Or perhaps more accurately, I had never needed my belief to be stronger.

It was time to continue signalling to the satellite. I took out my flashlight, hands fumbling with a desperation I hadn't realized was there, and began pulsing it into the sky. Sure enough, when I peered through my telescope, the LEO was arcing high above, just beyond my reach.

And yet, nothing had changed. There were no messages coming down to Earth. I could feel that same doubt bubbling up inside me, threatening my entire mission, and I attempted to quell it by doubling my efforts. I started signalling faster, more urgently, Morse code messages flashing into the heavens. I would stay awake well into the morning if I needed to, would refuse to move until I received my reply.

I stayed by my telescope, dutifully peering beyond. Then, something broke.

The LEO's routine blips became more irregular, no longer following their predictable rhythm. He was moving more slowly as well, perhaps resisting his orbit. It was almost as though he had received my messages, and was sending a response.

In the distance, I heard the 108th bell ring. The twenty-first century had arrived. I turned off my flashlight and went to sleep, knowing that in the morning, the LEO would be down here on Earth with me, not as a satellite, but as a person.

SATELLITE

IT WAS STRANGE TO be human, or at least to have a human form. I've never heard anyone talk about this, but a body is an incredibly heavy thing. I had only known the feeling of flying above the Earth, weightless, and now I was anchored in place, gravity pulling at all of my 62 kilograms with an unrelenting duty. Just sitting up made me sweat. One wrong move and I might sink into the world.

It was early morning, and I was on Earth rather than in space, waiting inside an eerily familiar bedroom. The room was smaller than I'd imagined, only large enough to fit a single futon, a couple bookshelves, and a desk. The ceiling was slanted rather than flat, coming down in sharp angles at the sides; a consequence of being on the top floor, I suppose. Everything felt more claustrophobic as a result. The hardwood floor looked like it hadn't been swept in ages, and tucked in the corner, away from the sun, was that mound, its size casting an ominous aura over the room.

I was sitting at the foot of Anna's futon, watching my creator sleep, her eyes flickering in the midst of a dream. I took the chance to examine her features—like everything else in the room, she, too, appeared alien up close. I wondered what would happen once she woke and we finally met.

Dawn was starting to lose its grasp on Sakita as I became more used to my human body. I was nearly able to grip a pencil at that point, but found my form prone to suddenly fading away with little warning. One moment I would be solid material, the next I would be no more than a ghost. I was like a sentient claw machine, albeit playing for the worst prizes imaginable: a pencil, an eraser, a hair clip. I entertained myself as I waited for Anna to wake up, clumsily mimicking the expressions I had seen hundreds of times before. Pursing my lips to imitate sadness, squinting to imitate doubt. When I closed my eyes, it was as though the world stopped existing.

I felt I was committing some grave blasphemy just by being in the same room as Anna, despite not knowing how I'd been brought down to Earth in the first place. I knew I only existed thanks to Anna, and while my gratitude was immense, I wondered how I could properly convey this to her. I was face to face with my creator, an opportunity countless humans would die for. Yet, on top of this divine admiration, there was a feeling of affection, too. Among the 6.1 billion people on the planet, it was Anna alone who'd returned my gaze, the only person to express any sort of interest in my solitary life up above. Now, rather than hundreds of kilometres, I was no more than two metres away from her. The air was sweet with the smell of her sweat.

You can tell a lot about a person by how they wake up. How long after opening their eyes do they sit up? Do they kick off their sheets, or slowly push them aside? What kinds of sounds do they make? What kinds of grunts, yawns, groans? It seemed to me as though everything private about a person could be revealed in those precious first moments.

When Anna awoke she lay on her side, completely still, eyes open, watching me. She moved her gaze up and down, methodically examining every part of my new body as though she were an engineer admiring her work. What surprised me was Anna's distinct lack of surprise; she didn't find my sudden appearance unusual in the slightest.

"You're the LEO I called down, correct?"

"I think so."

Her voice didn't falter once, despite her waking just moments before. Mine, on the other hand, wavered considerably. A full existence without use will do that.

Anna remained lying on her side, and I wasn't sure if she wanted me to come closer or leave her room. I opted for the middle ground and stayed where I was, sitting cross-legged on the wooden floor like an insecure yogi. She was silent, searching my face for something I couldn't promise was there. To soothe myself, I began counting the small, meaningless things in her room: three sickly house plants (all succulents), thirty-two CDs (all punk rock), twelve scented candles (all sandalwood).

"You're more than a week late. Why didn't you come earlier?"

"I didn't realize you were calling me," I said, searching her face for any sort of positive response. "I'm not sure how I got here to begin with. In all honesty, I'm not even sure *what* I am."

Silence.

"I thought I was a satellite," I stammered, compelled to prove myself, "but now I'm a human, and to be frank with you I'm not sure if I even exist and—"

She sat up abruptly, cutting me off, as though I were on trial for an offence I wasn't aware I'd committed.

"You don't exist," she said.

I was taken aback. "That's hardly an icebreaker."

"You're imaginary, a coping mechanism used to deal with intense isolation. I made you up."

I didn't have a response for this. I hadn't exactly anticipated being confronted with my own non-existence so suddenly. And yet here I was, arguing with a girl I'd just met but had loved for months, over whether I was even real. It was absurd.

"What's my blood type?" she challenged.

"AB-positive." The answer rolled off my tongue naturally, taking me by surprise.

"What's your blood type?"

I didn't know. How could I know her blood type but not my own?

Anna was terrifyingly insistent that I was not real, and that my actions held no consequence. Reverse solipsism: everyone except myself exists. But how did I even know what *solipsism* was? Weeks later, out of boredom, I would flip through one of the books strewn across her room and find the definition myself. It matched word for word with what was in my head, forcing me to confront a terrifying possibility: What if I only knew what Anna knew? What if any thought I had, any song I loved, any turn of phrase I employed, had to have passed through Anna first? Sadness mixed with fear and now this.

She continued to hound me from her bed, as if wanting to drive me into an existential crisis. I didn't know how to respond—we weren't exactly on even ground. My first human encounter and already I was being forced to defend myself. Sixteen years of experience versus thirty minutes. What a world.

"If you made me up, then how could you recognize it? If you're delusional enough to create an imaginary friend, you wouldn't be self-aware enough to realize it." Check and mate.

"Realizing and understanding are two very different things, Leo."

I noticed that she had decided on my name, and was silently disappointed. *Leo* didn't seem to fit me very well at all. I saw myself more as a *Voyager* or an *Apollo*.

Anna got out of bed without a word and undressed, slowly, self-consciously throwing a glance or two my way. Was she trying to seduce a figment of her imagination? She moved awkwardly, pretending she had done this hundreds of times before, and ended the performance by slipping into a short, checkered skirt and a light-blue hoodie. A bizarre combination.

"There's a good café I know nearby; let's continue our debate there." She signalled for me to follow, not caring that I'd been stunned by her sudden nudity. "By the way, you're not my imaginary friend, you're my imaginary boyfriend."

GRANDFATHER

I CAN'T SEEM TO find my keys. It's the strangest thing. I'm worried I'm getting forgetful, though Yoshiko tells me it's normal for someone my age. Still, I can't help but worry that my case is especially severe.

For example, I'm not sure where I am. This brightly lit Westernized home is giving me a headache. Such an American idea of beauty—it's ridiculous. The Japanese home thrives in shadows, with dimly lit corners for the eyes to come to rest. There's a reason why we still use paper doors; it's to preserve the beauty of natural light flitting through. Here everything is blown out— there's no depth, no mystery, no elegance. A Japanese home should look like a Japanese home, I say.

How did I get here? I recall having just woken from a nap, but I don't remember much before then. In the back of my mind, I hear a faint ringing, like a distant memory, but it slips from my grasp. A few photos above the Westernized fireplace show Yoshiko, and I can see her shoes by the front door, too. When did my little girl get so old?

I hear a voice coming down the stairs, posing questions to someone whose responses are too quiet for me to hear. I'm not sure if I should hide or not, afraid that I've stuck my nose where it doesn't belong. At first, I think this person could be Yoshiko, but their voice is too low, and they mumble quite a bit too.

I decide at the last moment to hide, kneeling behind the kitchen island. The counter is some sort of bleached laminate. I'll never understand this Western obsession with making everything white. These artificial materials repel light back to the viewer, light that a more tasteful cherrywood or granite would absorb.

I can tell I'm getting carried away. Yoshiko always says I have a habit of working myself up.

I take a tentative peek around the corner of the island and see a young woman puttering about. She's trying to find her wallet, she says. She must have thrown it somewhere. Who is she speaking to? No one is answering her, yet she leaves gaps in the conversation for another to fill.

Is this some sort of Western game I'm not aware of? Maybe it's some variation of hide-and-go-seek. Hunched just out of sight, I suddenly worry. Have I forgotten that I'm playing this game, too? Is that why I'm here?

From my angle I can make out a few details about the girl. She seems of mixed race, which would explain this obscene home, yet she still has a Japanese manner. Despite how I feel about these Westerners, this child seems different. It's in the way she moves. She treads lightly, as though walking across ice, conscious of keeping her back straight. Like a bunraku puppet doll, controlled by something unseen. Her pale skin is reminiscent of one, as well. There's a kind of cloudiness underneath the surface, an innate apprehension you don't see anywhere else.

I decide to stay hidden, convinced now that I'm not a part of this game, that I shouldn't be here. Perhaps this girl is a performer of sorts. She motions to the air occasionally, as if expecting it to respond, though I can see with absolute certainty that there's no one with her. It must be a difficult scene she's rehearsing. Her performance is beautiful, untinged as it is by the presence of an audience.

She checks under a bookshelf and finds her wallet. A childish thing, fading floral patterns covering the canvas. The wallet is so at odds with the way she looks, I assume it holds a sentimental value. A gift perhaps. She slips the wallet into her pocket, turns to the air, and says "How small did the Earth seem?" to no one in particular. There is no response.

She eventually leaves, but even after the door closes behind her, I can't relax. Instead, I remain crouched behind the island, still transfixed by her performance. I wonder what kind of play that young woman is acting in. I could barely make out what she was saying, yet I could tell it was done with complete conviction. That in that moment, she fully believed the play was her reality. And to think this was just rehearsal! It felt too real, as if a world best left untouched had been disturbed. I shudder to think what the actual production will look like.

SATELLITE

THE CAFÉ ANNA BROUGHT me to was not as close as she'd said. In fact, it required a twenty-minute train ride across town. As we walked towards the station, she barely said a word. I might have been unnerved by her silence had this new and intensely close-up, street-level view of the world not demanded all of my focus. Even putting one foot in front of the other, adjusting for uneven pavement, wind, and inclines, was proving to be a challenge. I was starting to realize just how inefficient the human body really was.

"I need to take a quick detour," Anna said, stopping in front of a near-deserted shopping mall.

The path she took me down turned sharply from a shopping development into a grove of ginkgo trees and thick-stemmed bamboo. All sound rushed out of this pocket of nature, save for the faint trickling of water. Snow was once again melting atop the forest floor, and a wet musk filled the air. The dirt beneath my feet came as a relief as well, providing a softer landing than asphalt should I suddenly forget how to walk. I was impressed such a place could exist so peacefully inside a city. Farther down the path I could see stone stairs painted with moss and slush, leading to shrine gates in the distance. On either side were sculptures of lions. Or were they dogs? I couldn't tell.

"Aren't we going to stop here?" I asked.

"That's a Shinto shrine. What I'm looking for is Buddhist," she replied.

We walked past the shrine, Anna not casting so much as a glance in its direction before we eventually emerged from the other side of the copse. I was disappointed to find myself back in industrial Japan, its artificial lights and smells overwhelming me. Is it hypocritical for a satellite to want to remain in nature? Either way, thanks to this new sensory overload, I had absentmindedly walked ahead of Anna, who was far behind, having stopped to kneel down by a dingy yakitori stall advertising cheap beef tongue.

As I walked back towards her, I saw that she was crouched in front of a small stone statue: an effigy of a smiling bald man in monk's robes, hands joined in prayer. At the base of Anna's feet was a small pile of stones, picked up from the melting snow, that she was attempting to balance one on top of another. She turned to face me, the sudden movement sending the entire stack tumbling.

"I'm helping Jizo," she said, motioning towards the granite monk. The owner of the stall paid her no notice, too busy fanning barbeque smoke from his face.

Jizo? "He's a friend of yours?"

She smiled softly, maybe even a little sadly. "No, he's a bodhisattva. The guardian of children."

I pretended to know what a bodhisattva was and nodded knowingly. Although Anna knew everything I knew, it didn't appear to work the other way around.

"When kids die they get sent to the Sanzu River," Anna explained, possibly sensing my confusion. "There, they have to pile stones until they're ready to reincarnate. Jizo patrols the river, encouraging them and making sure no demons kick their towers over. Regular people like me can ease their burden by adding stones, too." Anna went back to her stack, rebuilding the tower she had just toppled.

I looked around. "Is the river near here?"

"Nope," she said. "It's not on Earth. It's in the afterlife, I think, or maybe the celestial realm."

The celestial realm. I wondered if I could have seen this Sanzu River from the heavens, or if even then it was out of reach.

"Is that story true?" I asked.

"Why should it matter?"

After she managed to pile her rocks ankle-high, she stood up, took out a pair of straw sandals from her backpack, and left them at the base of the statue.

Anna smiled sheepishly. "Sanzu River is rocky, so Jizo's feet get worn out easily. We're supposed to leave him new shoes, sometimes."

Without thinking, I checked the soles of my shoes for wear.

*   *   *

The station was only a short walk away from the statue of Jizo. How many steps exactly, I wasn't sure. I'd forgotten to count. By coming down to Earth, I'd had my omniscience taken from me. A small price to pay for the gift of being human.

We boarded the train around noon. I tried not to think of the ethical implications of not buying a ticket ("You don't even exist! Why would you have to pay?") and admired the countryside through scratched windows.

The train wound its way through an eerily familiar landscape, the world feeling fresh when glimpsed through this new angle. The sight, and scent, of other humans was overpowering. There were only a few people in the car with us: a smattering of young boys, an elderly couple with matching jackets, a thirty-something lady flipping through a detective novel. I was still attempting to acclimatize myself to their presence when I was hit by the woman's strong perfume. The train lurched along its predetermined path, and her scent felt thick in my nostrils. Sweet with a note of earthiness. It reminded me of the forest I had just come from. Why would humans want to emphasize their smell?

I wanted to move away, but Anna didn't seem to notice. My hazy reflection, still undefined, warped with the shifting planes I saw before me—and it was then that I realized, with a sense of unease, where I was being taken.

Tonuki Café.

Even after I'd descended to Earth for her, Anna was still hung up on the toothless boy's imagined betrayal. She was taking me to the spot where she had experienced her greatest humiliation exactly ten days earlier, a humiliation nobody but me had witnessed. The train I had once viewed from the detached safety of space now filled me with slow-burning dread. I looked Anna's way and watched her read the ads pasted on the roof of the car, lips moving slightly. There was something unusual about her appearance as well.

Lipstick. She was wearing lipstick. I had never seen her wear any sort of makeup before, and yet here she was, with the exact same shade Fumie had worn the last time their paths crossed. Was Anna attempting to re-enact that day, but from a different perspective?

I felt a sharp pain in my chest. Sadness mixed with fear. The train suddenly felt much, much smaller.

Anna turned to look at me. "If you're going to be my boyfriend, you're going to have to take me on a first date, okay?"

I nodded. There wasn't much else for me to do.

ANNA

ON THE TRAIN TO Tonuki Café, Leo continued to relay what he'd learned up in space, desperately trying to come up with something clever to say. Perhaps he was feeling insecure beside his creator. I didn't offer anything in response, too preoccupied with what to do next. I had succeeded in my plan to bring him down to Earth. Now what?

I kept an eye on Leo, monitoring his facial tics, his expressions, the way he glanced around him. The two of us weren't identical, yet he was still undeniably a product of my mind. Where did I end, and he begin?

"I think the Buddhists got it right, though," he rambled. "About karma, I mean. I feel like I saw objective proof from space."

"Oh yeah?" I was barely paying attention, more concerned with getting off at the right station than with his waxing philosophical. It was here that Leo surprised me, however. Not through the quiet wisdom in his statement, but rather the sheer innocence of it all. I hadn't realized the omniscient could be so naive.

"Like for example, if someone cut in line at the supermarket, they'd get caught in traffic on the way home. Or, if someone gave money to the homeless, they'd get a call from an old friend later in the day. It's on a small scale, but it makes sense to extrapolate. Everyone gets what they deserve."

Everyone gets what they deserve.

I refuse to believe this, even now. Leo had only seen a small portion of day-to-day life, and didn't realize how truly unfair it could be. In fact, you can neatly divide the world into two kinds of people: those who get what they want, and those who don't. Half the world walks through life not realizing how lucky they are, always getting what they desire. Fortune, success, love—they cut in and out of everyone else's paths, carving into the foundations.

True beauty comes from the other half, those who have things stolen from them by the first group. Theirs is a beauty of modesty, of having to struggle for what they want. To never get what you wish for holds an aesthetic value in and of itself.

Only those who have had things taken from them can truly know one another; someone who is beautiful could never understand this. I thought of Soki and his cleft lip, and decided that he and I belonged to this camp of outsiders. Fumie, that kitsune, was in the other.

There is a flip side to always getting what you deserve, though. If people deserve happiness, they should get it. But happiness taken at the expense of another . . .

A life spent taking deserves to be taken from. This was my new mantra, Leo's be damned, and it was the only one I could hold as true.

SATELLITE

AT TONUKI CAFÉ, THE world moved on. Anna's private trage-dies had made no difference to the restaurant; it existed in a bubble of its own. The people who inhabited it were the same as before: teenage girls sporting gyaru tans and false lashes, boys with spiked hair and sutajan jackets, unsure whether to imitate American or Japanese gangsters. The one constant was that they were all under-dressed for the weather, something I only understood after feeling the prickly cold of winter on my face. That these people prioritized aesthetics over proper insulation was bizarre to me.

Clothes have always struck me as an odd human construct, equivalent in nature to the plumage of a colourful bird. I was amused to find that, despite being invisible to everyone else, Anna had still thought to clothe me from the depths of her imagination. A much-too-thick winter coat, a tattered wool scarf, a pair of win-ter boots to pack the slush under my feet. Why not cover me with thermal blanketing and be done with it?

Anna was greeted by a hostess, who asked how many people were in her party. I couldn't help but feel hurt when she replied, "Just me."

We were going to be seated at the counter, but at Anna's request, were brought to a specific booth in the back. I attempted to ignore the chill I felt when I realized this was the same booth Soki had occupied the last time I had seen him. It was impossible to check on him now, to ensure everything was all right. My oversized boots suddenly felt much heavier, anchors to this material world. Meanwhile, Anna kept looking up at the mirrored ceiling, examining her lipstick.

The red was too dark for her pale complexion, giving the impression that a gash had been cut across her face. It had looked much better on Fumie with her healthy tan. I nearly mentioned this, but held back. I don't imagine there's a single girl on the planet who would appreciate getting makeup advice from a boy. I hadn't been here long, but there were some things so obvious even I could pick them up.

One of the first things Anna had said to me that morning was that I didn't exist. I had figured I was something otherworldly, but to be told that I was in fact imaginary was a startling experience, to say the least. If what she said was true, then I really did owe my entire existence to her mind, which hardly made for a fair fight.

As if to prove my creator wrong, I tried catching the other diners' attention, but found that no matter how close I got to someone's face, how loudly I shouted in their ears, or how many jumping jacks I did in front of them, they stared right through me. While this was going on, Anna sat in the booth watching me, barely hiding the amusement on her face. How cruel. I smiled at her, embarrassed, and returned to the table.

"If you created me in your image," I said, out of breath from my impromptu cardio session, "why didn't you make me in better shape?"

She gave a laugh, the first I had seen in a while. "I made you exactly how I wanted."

"Even still, twenty jumping jacks and I can barely breathe."

I stared at the glass of water in front of me, tempted to drink it, but decided to avoid that metaphysical can of worms for now. If the water passed through me like I was a ghost, I probably would have fainted, and not just from the exercise. For the time being, I opted to endure my thirst.

Logically, if I was created by Anna, that should make me her Platonic ideal for what a boy should be. A quick survey of myself revealed me to be short, unfit, pale, and nearsighted. So nearsighted I was unable to make out what I looked like from the reflection above. I wanted to tell her to raise her standards a bit next time, to have another go at creating me. I didn't even have radiation shielding, for example. How would this soft body protect me from solar flares? My tongue absentmindedly played with the gap between my teeth while Anna opened her menu, hiding her face from me.

"Hey, so if I'm imaginary . . ."

Anna cut me off without looking up. "Be quiet, you're practically shouting."

I wasn't sure how to respond. "If other people can't hear me I don't see how that would be a problem."

She put her menu down and stared at me curiously. "I suppose you're right."

Score one for the imaginary boy. I was about to push my luck even further when Anna interrupted, probably sensing what I was going to say next.

"You should hurry up and order. I've already decided on the pork loin sandwich."

Order? Why would I need food? "I'll get the same then, I guess."

She focused her gaze at me, as though peering through my body.

"In all honesty, you seem more of a curry kind of person," she said.

"Excuse me?"

"You don't strike me as someone who would like a pork loin sandwich. I'll order you some katsu curry instead."

What a weird thing to micromanage. It wasn't like I was going to be able to eat whatever she ordered anyway. I tried thinking back to Soki's date and seemed to recall Fumie ordering a messy sandwich as well. What had Soki eaten?

I looked at Anna, trying to get a read on her face, what she was thinking. She noticed me staring and closed her menu.

"Something wrong?" she asked.

"Nope, just thinking about how surreal it is to actually be seeing you like this. In person, I mean."

Anna drew closer, squinting, almost dissecting my soul. "You know what you remind me of?"

"I'm going to hope this is a compliment."

"You're kind of like those mythical kirin."

I was appalled, knowing this creature from the billboards and character mascots littering the city. "Those old dragons with the long whiskers?"

"Yeah! With the deer bodies and oxen hooves."

"Couldn't you have picked a better creature than that to compare me to?"

"First of all, kirin are beautiful. That's not what I meant anyway. You're like a kirin because you're gentle, kind of quiet . . ."

"That's better."

"But most of all, no one believes you exist!" She said this a little too loudly, proud of her comparison. The other diners were now watching her warily, as she appeared to be speaking to no one in particular. Anna seemed to sense this at the same time I did, but paid no mind. If anything, she increased her volume in defiance.

The nausea I'd felt earlier was replaced with a feeling of warmth, reminding me of my newfound physicality, and I realized for the first time how strangely beautiful I found her, with her alien delicateness, mismatched lipstick and all. It was something akin to love. Her hands were small, peeking around the edges of the menu, and I was struck by a desire to hold her fingertips between mine. To confirm that she was still there. Who was to say that an object couldn't love its creator?

"Do you like me?" Anna blurted this out at the same moment our food arrived, eyes fixed on the empty space where I was sitting, making the waitress visibly uncomfortable. "Do you like me or not?"

The question had caught me off guard. What was I supposed to say to this? Surely Anna had meant to ask whether I loved her, and not whether I merely found her likeable. And yet, her repeating "like" instead of "love" was no accident. Up to that point, I thought what she desired was romance, but now I wondered if all she needed was a friend.

"Of course!" I said.

She continued to stare, as though unsure how far to trust me, her own creation. "Good."

As simple as that. One word. *Good.* The mood had gotten noticeably chillier. I attempted to make her laugh throughout the meal with a few awkwardly timed one-liners stolen from the comedies I had watched from up in space, but I eventually gave up. My curry, untouched and growing cold, lay just beyond my immaterial reach.

Anna ate the rest of her meal in silence, paid with a crumpled 2,000-yen note, and left.

ANNA

I WOULD BE LYING if I said I wasn't disappointed by Leo. On the surface, our date went as well as could be hoped. I was able to experience the day that was stolen from me as best as I could. For some reason, however, I remained unsatisfied. Unsatisfied in the way someone can only be after finally getting what they desire.

I left Tonuki Café with Leo, my loneliness amplified by his immediate proximity. On our way to the station, we stepped onto a wooden footbridge, weather-beaten planks creaking underfoot, the decades-old paint job flitting red snow into the creek below. The stream must have been polluted somewhere, the sweet smell of sewage wafting our way. Amaterasu had made a surprise appearance recently, briefly warming our small corner of the Earth. I paused mid-crossing, rubbing the handrails to loosen as much paint as I could, searching for a reflection in those murky waters. A story The General had once told me bubbled to the surface. The Death of Narcissus. I never had as much interest in Greek mythology as I did in Japanese legends, but for some reason this tale had stuck with me.

Narcissus, he had explained, was a hunter who had drowned in a pool after falling in love with his own reflection. The modern use of the word *narcissist* was inspired by this story, and therein lies the problem. According to The General, narcissism was only given its modern meaning after Freud, whose theory obscured the real reason Narcissus fell into the water. He wasn't obsessed with his own image, but shocked by it. Since mirrors and cameras didn't exist, that moment by the pond was the first time Narcissus had seen himself. Rather than being drawn in, he was surprised, and fell into the water. Narcissus didn't drown in self-love; he was overwhelmed by self-awareness.

The General had explained this theory with a practiced air, even taking time to add dramatic pauses in his story. I tried not to think of the implications of a blind man telling me such a tale. Perhaps he wanted to know what would happen if he, too, were able to see the world again. I tried to picture how The General might react to his reflection, but could only imagine him drowning. Soon my thoughts began to drift from The General, who I could never see again, to Soki.

> *My love shines brighter*
> *than the Herd Boy's star,*
> *and though the barrier between us*
> *is not as great as the Milky Way,*
> *please tear it away now.*

A poem from *The Tales of Ise*. Of all the episodes in that collection of verse, this one had always been my favourite. Only now was I beginning to understand why.

How would Soki feel if he saw me now, a superior version of the girl he had been with a week before? Would he be drawn to my reflection of her, or repelled by it? I suppose the end result would be the same, and in either case, it was Leo, not Soki, who I had invited to suffocate in my image.

Which brought me to the root of my dissatisfaction that evening: no matter how hard Leo and I tried to pretend he was an independent person, he was still a product of my imagination, and therefore inherently inferior to the real thing. It disturbed me to watch how he would walk with the same gait I did, nervously touch his eyebrows as I did, even lose focus in the middle of conversations like I did. If he loved me, was it by choice, or because that was what I had created him for? All I wanted from him was an act of rebellion, no matter how small, to prove that he had some iota of independence from me. That he was real.

Standing on the edge of the bridge, I wondered if Narcissus had ever touched any of the water below. There's only a finite amount available in the world. Maybe some of what Narcissus had choked on in his last moments had made its way into the clouds, circled the Earth, and come to rest here.

"If I fell into the water, would you try to save me?" I asked. My words hung in the air, the sound of water taking their place. It was louder than usual, no doubt amplified by the crisp January air.

Leo crossed over to where I stood and peered over the edge, perhaps wondering what I had seen. "Why wouldn't I?"

"There's kappa in the water. Half-frog, half-man river demons. They'll drown you and eat me just for fun. Are you still jumping?"

He thought about this. "If you were eaten, I would stop existing anyway, so really I have no choice." He said this with a bemused smile, not realizing how serious I was. I refused to budge.

"What if you were actually a person?"

"Okay."

"And I died the second I hit the water."

"Okay."

"Would you still dive in?"

"I suppose so."

For a brief moment, I considered stepping over the railing. The call of the void, if you will. Leo wasn't annoyed with my childish questions, and was instead answering me patiently. Nothing I could do would get him to challenge me. He was gentle, but pathetic, which was unforgivable.

"Tell me I'm ugly."

"What?"

"Tell me I'm hideous, self-centred, delusional, and insane."

At this he finally turned and walked away, refusing to indulge me. He made it to the end of the bridge before looking back self-consciously. I followed him to the other side, having toyed with him enough for one day. Leo had managed a small act of rebellion by rejecting my demands, albeit out of a refusal to be cruel to me. I wasn't sure whether to consider this a victory.

No, he was hopeless. Turning back for me proved as much. I wondered if maybe the world was wrong in assuming Narcissus had drowned by accident.

SOKI

I'D BEEN LOOKING THROUGH my dad's study, this old, paper-walled room, tucked into the back of the house. Musty-smelling bamboo mats and all. Whoever lived here last must have been a teacher. There's some calligraphy on the walls. A few of my mom's dying flower arrangements too. The whole room felt like it was from Edo Japan or something. It had a Western desk, though. This dark mahogany monster Dad had dragged from city to city. That's what I'd mostly been combing through.

I had to be really careful. Usually did this at one or two in the morning. Snuck out into the hall when no one was awake. Opened the sliding doors slowly, otherwise they'd let out this low groan, like they didn't want to be woken up. My dad didn't know what I was doing. Thought I just went to bed when he told me to. But really I was going through his papers, learning lots about him, trying to figure out what had made him lose his faith. Hadn't managed to find out yet. The answers weren't in any of the old articles he wrote, academic essays written in kanji too complex for me to comprehend.

That night, I found an article I understood, clipped from some newspaper. Couldn't tell when he wrote it, the top of the page was trimmed off. The article was about pilgrimages, how they test your arrogance more than your faith. He wrote that the visions people sometimes see on these journeys are a result of "delirium" rather than belief. Wasn't sure what *delirium* meant, but I could tell it wasn't good. That those fading letters held something harsh inside.

This reminded me of the argument we had after I went to the shrine with Mom. It was about the one hundred times stone, the pillar that some shrines set up just outside their grounds. They say that if you walk between this pillar and the doors of the shrine one hundred times, you can make a prayer come true. Dad said I should try it, to really understand what being devout means. I think now he was joking, but I took it as a challenge. Said that I would go for one thousand laps instead. If that didn't prove my faith, nothing could.

Dad just kind of chuckled to himself. Told me to "go for it, kid," then went back to reading those financial newspapers, which I was sure he didn't understand. I think he bought them for Mom's sake more than his own. To show her that he had plans for "upward mobility" or that he was on the "bleeding edge" of something.

It was like he thought I couldn't tell when I was being mocked. Or maybe he didn't even know he was doing it himself. Reading that article felt like I was being made fun of. Like he was telling me I had a "delirium." Whatever that meant. But ever since we moved to Sakita, I've been trying to figure things out on my own. Find reasons for believing that are separate from my dad's.

Made up my mind on the spot. I would complete his challenge the next day, would make Sakita the site of my first pilgrimage. Make it my spiritual home. I tucked the article away and crept back to my room.

I woke up late the next morning and left the house around noon. Didn't tell my parents. Thought it would make a bigger impression that way.

Had an onigiri and a canned coffee from the convenience store for lunch. Finished them just outside the shrine grounds, watching the mall's neon signs fighting to stay alive, salty nori aftertaste on my tongue. The snow was melting on the asphalt, turning into this murky slush. I was wearing running shoes, so my socks were a little wet. The weather is weird here. A massive snowfall one day, a burst of sun the next.

I made my way to the shrine grove, trying to think of what to pray for. Difficult decision to make. Dad told me that since each journey from the pillar to the doors counts as a separate shrine visit, repeating the same prayer one hundred times gives it that much more strength. People use this to focus on one hope. Any prayer worth one thousand visits would have to be extra special.

The grounds looked lonely as usual, not another worshipper in sight. I walked along the gravel approach, stopping just in front of the torii gate, lacquered a red so bright it hurt the eyes. Surrounding it were walls of sakaki trees, a barrier from the outside world. The thickest tree had this paper rope wrapped around its trunk. It's supposed to be an antenna to contact the kami with. There's kami in the heavens and kami in the earth. I wonder which that antenna calls to?

At the base of the gate was the one hundred times stone. Here, the pillar sat in the middle of the path, which went under the gate and led up a set of stairs, all the way to the doors of the shrine. The two points I'd have to walk between. The stairs didn't seem too bad. Around twenty-five, maybe thirty steps in total. If I took them two at a time, there'd be even less. I was trying to stay optimistic, not multiplying them by one thousand laps in my head.

The shrine at the top was tiny, only one room, with two swinging doors fastened shut. These rooms always hold a sacred object, one that only priests are allowed to see. Sometimes the shrines house swords, jewels, or even sculptures. Back home, our shrine had a mirror hidden inside. It's because, long ago, when the gods tricked Amaterasu out of her cave, they used a mirror to dazzle her with her own light. They made her think her own reflection was a new sun goddess, and lured her out.

Thinking about that mirror reminded me of Anna-terasu. I tried repeating her philosophy to my mom at New Year's, about belief having value on its own, and how it's better to be wrong than to have never believed at all. Something like that. It didn't come out right, though, and I kept stumbling over my words. I don't think my mom understood what I meant. Made me realize I didn't fully understand, either.

To prepare for my pilgrimage, I stretched a little and re-tied my shoes. I decided not to go with just one prayer, but to pray for everything I could think of instead. Stretch the limits of my belief. People usually carry one hundred stones with them to keep track of their laps, leaving a pebble at the gate for every length they walk. I couldn't carry one thousand rocks, though, especially not up the stairs. Decided to drop off silent prayers instead.

First, I cleansed myself at the purifying station. Poured water over my hands with the ladle, cupped a palmful of water into my mouth. The purifying water tastes the same in every shrine I've been to. Lukewarm and tinny, leaving a metallic taste in your mouth.

I devoted my first prayer to those who have lost their faith.

I didn't realize how *many* one thousand times is. Thought I could finish the walk in a couple of hours. By the time I understood how long my pilgrimage would take, I was too far in to quit. Started running out of prayers. Prayer five was for the poor. Fifty-seven for the unhappy. One hundred and three for the impure.

At two hundred I was praying for the ants. Then for missorted recycling. For abandoned homes.

Walking up the stairs was more difficult than I'd imagined, too. It felt like the number of steps kept increasing. They were crumbling, and coated with a thin layer of moss and snow, making it harder to climb. The humid air felt thick in my lungs. My feet became heavier with every step, but I didn't mind. Made me feel grounded, like I had a reason for being there. Like the planet finally wanted to keep me in one place.

Took me until evening to finish half of my prayers. It was getting dark, but I'd do the rest of my walk with a flashlight if I needed to. Prayer five hundred was for the sun. My thighs were stinging. Lactic acid buildup. Lips tasted like sweat. Six hundred and thirty-nine was for my classmates. Realised I had forgotten about them. Six hundred and forty was for the cicadas.

It was night when I saw the car pull up. My mom's silver hybrid. My body wanted to quit, but I had to continue. Figured my mom would get mad and end my pilgrimage. I was only twenty-seven lengths away from the end and didn't want to be forced to stop. There was still so much to pray for, so much to save.

I started sprinting. Felt like I was forcing my legs to move. Even keeping my head up was too much effort. The only thing I could focus on was the next prayer. I ended up tripping, and biting my tongue as I went down. Got up and kept moving, picking the gravel from my palms as I ran. Wanted to finish the last prayers while I still had time. The reason these shrines are located high up is so they can bring you closer to the heavens. My heart was collapsing. By the time my mom caught up to me I was out of breath, with a head full of stars.

Adults surprise me sometimes. Thought Mom would be angry, but when I saw her face, I could tell she had been crying. She asked me what I was doing, and made me sit down. Said she was relieved I was all right. That she'd been looking for me for hours, had worried I'd gotten hurt. That I should let her know if I'm ever going to be out this late. Never occurred to me that something bad could happen here.

Then I explained what I was doing, and she sucked in her cheeks a bit, like she was trying to decide something. Asked if Dad knew about this and I said no. I said I really wanted to complete my walk. That I was so close and didn't want to give up.

She stood and tied her hair back. Told me she'd do the last prayers with me. That together we would show Dad how "selfish he's being, throwing away his faith like that." It's strange, though. I started off the thousand prayers wanting to prove my dad wrong, but now I didn't feel angry at all.

We started walking up the steps together, my mom one step ahead, full of the energy I had nine hundred prayers ago. I told her I was dedicating each length to something different. She dedicated her first to lost and missing children. Then to the old and the dying. Didn't tell her those were my fifty-second and eighty-ninth prayers already.

The worst part was that we never ran out of prayers. One thousand devotions and there were still things I missed. Didn't even get to airplane pilots, mayflies with single-day lifespans, or bodies that were lost at sea. So much pain in this world. Not even one thousand prayers is enough.

We never did tell my dad.

SATELLITE

IT WAS EARLY MORNING, and I still wasn't able to sleep. By all
rights I should have been exhausted, legs sore from spending the
last few days travelling with Anna, exploring Sakita and its surrounding cities by train. She claimed these journeys were important for my education as a human, yet I could sense that she was
reluctant to go home, delaying our return by telling me a different
anecdote at every corner. *This is the shed Mr. Azuchi lost a finger
building. Over there is the arcade where the boys in my class meet up
after school, and you can hear their laughter until midnight.* For the
most part, the stories she told me rambled on without purpose,
and didn't require much focus on my part. There was an exception
to this, however, the only tale I couldn't fully understand. The
Story of The Foreigner.

The day before, we had been on our way back to Sakita when
Anna suddenly took me by the arm, her cool fingers jolting me out
of my train-induced hypnosis.

"Let's get off here. I want to show you something."

The car came to a reluctant halt, bemoaning the effort it took
to stop. Anna got up from her seat, shoving her sneakers back

onto her feet, and I followed through the sliding doors. The flickering sign above our heads informed us that we were now entering Fukuro Station.

"What did you want to show me?" I asked. The area was entirely residential—I couldn't find anything of note. Anna gave no response.

The air here was different, less metallic, something I was keenly aware of with my new gift of smell. Every train ride was a fight against sensory overload, to the point where I had trouble discerning which details were important and which were not. I hadn't developed the ability to parse my knowledge yet, meaning that an oddly shaped stone would hold as much significance to me as one of Anna's philosophical musings. That day was no exception, and as Anna led me out of the station, I found myself overwhelmed by this new environment, my mind in a haze.

The houses here were made of a lesser material than in Sakita, and I took this to mean we were in an adjacent town or a farming community. Light snow dusted the tops of sheet aluminum roofs, rust showing along the edges, the roads black with a turbid sleet. An older male and female passed us by, taking turns dragging a bag of crushed cans behind them. I assumed the two of them to be partners as Anna bowed her head in greeting, prompting them to do the same.

This elderly couple struck me as endearing, if not a little tragic. I had the grim thought that one day Anna would become like them. That her back would eventually curl into itself, that her skin would grow loose with age. At the very least, those two humans had each other to hold on to. But what about Anna? I wondered then if I, too, would ever grow old, or if I could even pass away. Where do imaginary friends go to die?

We continued to weave through this distant colony, somehow more forgotten than Sakita itself. At first I was struck by the utter silence, the soundless skies almost as deadening as space. But as I listened closely—the long walk affording me plenty of time to do so—I began to pick up more details. A radio, crooning songs about love lost and yesterdays. A young woman, arguing with her mother over a curfew. Anna, breathing heavily as she fought her way uphill.

We came to a stop in front of a low apartment building, two storeys high. I counted seven windows across, two windows deep, and estimated this structure could house anywhere between 14 and 56 humans, depending on the room sizes.

"I wanted to show you The Foreigner's home," Anna said.

"The Foreigner?"

"Upper floor. Second window from the right," she explained. "He was from America. That's where he lived when he first moved here."

I stood next to her, trying to comprehend what I was there to see. All I understood was the soft pressure of her fingers on my arm.

"He came all the way over from Oregon, and fell in love with Japan. Couldn't tell you why. But he ended up staying long after his work contract ended. I think he was an engineer at some failed plant. Copper, I believe."

She slowed down when she said *Oregon*, breaking it into three syllables, taking care not to miss a single letter. A magic spell. The word was heavy on her tongue, as though she had been practicing its enunciation for years, but still couldn't get it right.

A cold wind came between us and the apartment, chilling me through my winter clothes. The sun was beginning its descent, appearing much smaller from down here on Earth. A part of me missed being so close to the sky.

"Did you know him well?" I asked.

"Not well enough."

"Why are you showing me this?"

I felt her grip tighten.

"I want to show you how humans work. When you were a satellite, you were precise, right?"

"Of course!" I replied, a little too proud of the fact.

She shook her head, freeing some loose snowflakes from her hair. "Humans aren't like that. Sometimes they break for no reason. Or, at least, a reason no one can understand. The American had a whole life here. He found a woman he loved, got married, even had a kid. He liked convenience-store korokkes, Japanese mythology, and telling jokes that only made sense in English."

"Oh?"

I looked over at Anna, her nose red from the cold. She kept her vision fixed in front of her, at the apartment that seemed to be deteriorating before our eyes. Or maybe it was collapsing under the weight of all that snow.

"He was happy. But then he woke up one day and couldn't speak Japanese. The words wouldn't form on his tongue. It wasn't a medical thing—he got tested for a stroke, for Alzheimer's, for everything in between. It was in his head. I think they used the word *psychosomatic*."

"He lost the ability to speak Japanese overnight?" I asked, incredulous. Even after all my observations from above, I hadn't realized this was possible.

"Yup. Could only speak English after that day. Lost the ability to speak to everyone he loved."

"So he had to re-learn it, then," I said.

"No—he couldn't. That part of him was wiped clean. He continued living here for a month or so, trying to pick up the language again, but it was impossible. I think maybe he didn't want to stay anymore, so he was sabotaging himself without realizing it."

"Where is he now? What happened to him?"

Anna let go of my arm, and breathed clouds into her hands to stay warm.

"Dead, for all I care."

*   *   *

That night, for the first time since I'd come down to Earth, Anna invited me to share her futon. I'd been sleeping on the hardwood floor until then—more out of my insistence than her own—and almost hadn't heard her as I lay down to sleep.

"Don't be stubborn," she said. "You'll get cold."

After a moment's hesitation, I accepted. I still wasn't used to my body, let alone being so close to another. Despite, or maybe because of, my love for her, any physical contact felt fundamentally wrong. I pushed myself against the far end of the futon, attempting to avoid any unnecessary contact between Anna's body and mine.

The entire night, my satellite's brain continued to run—counting the water stains on the ceiling, the flecks of dust in the air. And, perhaps most stressful of all, focusing on the tarp-covered mound towering over us from the corner of Anna's room. It had sprouted suddenly, like a mushroom cap after a rainfall, sometime during the week I'd stopped watching the Earth.

What could Anna be hiding under that tarp? When I had asked about it, she brushed me off, annoyed that I would even ask such a question. The longer I lay there, tossing and turning with my restless mind, the more concerned I became. I had no frame of reference for sinister objects over 2.2 metres tall, body just as wide, and at one point considered the possibility of a yokai spirit trapped in a cage, requiring constant darkness to survive.

I wanted to see for myself what was underneath, but I knew that no matter how delicately I removed myself from the bed,

Anna would immediately wake. Instead, I resigned myself to a night of torment, envisioning the mound coming alive, swallowing me whole, erupting into flames. Why flames?

Along with the numerous anecdotes Anna had told me during our walks, she'd also recounted a handful of myths—both Greek and Japanese. Staring at that mound, I was reminded of the story of Tantalus, who had stolen the food of the gods. As punishment, he was doomed to live in a pool under a fruit tree for all of eternity, the water below and the fruit above always moving just out of reach. I couldn't help but feel an affinity with the guy.

The sun's rays were starting to filter through the room, finishing their 149.6-million-kilometre journey by making their way through windows inexplicably covered in sheets of ink-stained paper. I recognized these pages as being from the book Anna had destroyed weeks earlier, yet still couldn't understand why they were mostly painted over in black.

"They're from my bible," she had told me while changing into threadbare pajamas. Even I could recognize that she was answering sarcastically, sharing an inside joke with only herself.

"You painted over, and ripped pages from, your bible?"

She paused for a moment, then answered with a smile. "If it's my own religion, it's not sacrilege, is it?"

I couldn't argue against that kind of logic. And yet, when I pressed her for more details about her "religion," she clammed up. I suppose she wasn't a member of a proselytizing branch.

"I'll tell you tomorrow," she said, as though scolding a small child. "Go to sleep."

As I watched the pages from afar, still confined to my bed-prison, I realized I could make out some details in the morning light. Diagrams, large enough to be visible. Rockets and missiles.

Dawn slowly gave way to its less colourful counterpart, and with it, the diagrams retreated back into their pools of ink. The shifting colours the sun cast upon the Earth, filtered through the atmosphere, felt alien to me. In space, it had simply been a sharp, blinding white.

Amaterasu continued her steady ascent, pulling back the night sky. And just as slowly as she came up, so too did Anna arise. Almost imperceptibly, her breathing began to speed up as she emerged from this peculiar hibernative state. Behind her eyelids, I saw something flicker.

"Good morning," I said, rather pleased with myself. This, I knew, was the correct greeting for someone who has just woken up.

She looked up at me, grimacing, eyes only half open. Her pupils were still fully dilated, not yet adapted to the morning light.

"What time is it?" she asked.

"Seven hours, thirty-seven minutes, and five seconds after midnight. No, six seconds. Seven seconds. Eight sec—"

"Perfect," she said, cutting me off without so much as a smile. I felt a small amount of disappointment; I'd thought my joke was rather clever.

"You can catch the eight o'clock train," she continued. "You've been up for a while?"

"I didn't sleep at all."

A 3.7-millimetre depression at the corners of her mouth. Confusion.

"Well, I have a favour to ask you. Actually, no. It's a mission."

"A mission?"

She nodded. "You're going to help me do something monumental, something more important than all the rest of my life put together. I need your unconditional loyalty. Can you promise me that?"

I was taken back, the sudden gravity of her tone making me uneasy. She sounded like a newscaster reading off a teleprompter, or a dictator addressing the troops. Her speech felt rehearsed, as if she'd been planning her words for a long time. I should have found this funny, but in all honesty, I was terrified by this change. Humour mixed with fear.

"I'm not sure what I'm supposed to be promising," I said.

"Before we continue I need to know that I can trust you absolutely, no matter what. You need to prove it to me."

"I need to agree to do whatever you ask, without even knowing what it is beforehand?"

"Correct."

I realized, then, that love could be a threat. That the basic foundation for romance is knowing that the other could destroy you at any moment, yet trusting that they won't. Mutually Assured Destruction. I wonder if Khrushchev and Kennedy fell in love during the Cuban Missile Crisis.

I mention this only to explain why I let myself be manipulated so. It wasn't out of fear that Anna would stop loving me that I agreed; rather, it was out of fear that Anna would love me *less*.

I didn't protest Anna's request, or take days to agonize before coming around. All that it took was a small tipping of the scales on her part, a slightly hurt look, and I hastily agreed to whatever terms she set. It's incredible what a 20-degree tilt of the head, a 15-millimetre furrowing of the brow can do.

And so I agreed without question, fearful of what would happen if I betrayed my creator. Fearful of what would happen to us.

"Of course. What do you need me to do?"

ANNA

I WATCHED FROM MY bedroom as Leo left my house, noting with amusement how he didn't check either direction before crossing the street. I suppose not existing removes any fear of death or traffic.

A part of me was disappointed when Leo accepted my mission, affirming yet again that he was but a product of myself. It was important for me to be able to trust him, but falling in love with a mirror is no fun. I needed him to go out, to experience the world on his own, to evolve as a person. I needed him to come back to me and fall in love of his own free will.

The Machine was my gift to him, my offering. It was a testament to my entire life thus far. More than a calling, it was a responsibility. No one else—not The General, not Fumie, not Soki—could create something of this magnitude. It was proof that here in Sakita, the kami hadn't abandoned us yet, that we still existed. I could hardly contain my excitement, picturing Leo's delight once he saw what I had been building in secret for him.

Once I made sure Leo was far enough away from the house, I closed the blinds and took the cover off The Machine. It was starting to take shape, pubescent in its development. You could see what its final form would be, the chassis twisting and turning as it outlined the body to come.

My machine held no human features, yet it was hard to see it as anything other than alive. When it was just the two of us, I swear I could hear it breathing. If I were to touch The Machine and imagine just right, the cooling tubes running through it felt warm with life . . .

I had begun building it from a solid core and expanded outwards as inspiration struck. This "core" was a narrow refrigerator I had repurposed as a cockpit, which could just fit two individuals. Everything else branched out from there, a mismatch of combustion engines at the bottom (junked from assorted cars), parallel reservoirs meant to hold gasoline and other flammable liquids, and copious amounts of wiring and tubing to stitch everything together, cooling, redirecting energy, and sending commands throughout the entire spherical body.

Attached to the cockpit was a nameplate, still to be engraved. I hadn't thought of an appropriate name yet, and wasn't sure if I ever would. Checking once more to see that Leo was truly gone, I returned to my work on The Machine, ready to hide its exposed body at a moment's notice.

GRANDFATHER

I CAN'T SEEM TO find my keys. It's the strangest thing. They were in my hands a moment ago, but now they're gone. I think I'm getting forgetful.

Take this house, for instance. I don't know how I got here. My daughter Yoshiko and I live in a beautiful apartment, and I'm sure I've never seen this house before. And yet, there are photos of the two of us everywhere! There are other figures in the pictures too, including this alien-looking girl. Why am I in these photos? I've never met these people.

There's a note stuck to the fridge from Yoshiko. It's addressed to me. It says: *Please look after Anna. I'll be gone for a few weeks. There's curry in the fridge. Buy milk if you remember.*

Anna? I wonder who that could be. I don't remember Yoshiko telling me she was going to leave, but I must have given her permission to do so. Still, she should be careful, she's much too young to go out on her own. The fridge is already filled with milk, so I'm not sure why she wants me to get more.

I can hear some hammering upstairs. Has Yoshiko come back already? She must be working on something. I'm so proud of her.

She's always been adept with her hands—she could become an expert carpenter with time, maybe even better than her old man. Still, she's causing a bit of a disturbance. I'll go tell her to quiet down.

The layout of this Western home is completely new to me, but I follow the sounds up the stairs and to the room they're coming from. I open the door, expecting to see Yoshiko, but a different girl is there instead. It looks like she's building some sort of machine. It's a pile of mismatched metal formed into a gigantic globe, even taller than I am. Whatever this object is supposed to be, it's beautiful. The peculiar girl doesn't notice me, too busy hammering a piece of sheet metal flat.

"Where's Yoshiko?" I ask.

The girl puts down her hammer. "Mom's gone for a few weeks. Did you forget again?"

Is this girl Yoshiko's daughter? But I haven't met her before! How could I have a granddaughter I don't know about? The girl must have noticed me getting worried, as she immediately drops what she's doing to come to my side.

"It's okay, you're just having an episode. Help me put the tools away and we can get something to eat."

The girl hands me her toolbox and asks me to sort the screws. The handle has the name "Goro" written on it. What a coincidence, my name is Goro too! I tell the girl this, but she just looks at me gently. She has such a kind smile.

"I know. These are your tools, Grandpa."

The girl leads me down the stairs, offering me her shoulder to lean on, which I accept despite being fine without her support. Such acts of compassion are rare these days, and it seems a shame to let it go to waste. I had the wrong impression of her at first—she looked so odd—but there's a softness in her that's becoming clear to me now.

I sit down at the counter and read over the note Yoshiko left. The girl hovers behind me, reading over my shoulder at the same time. I wonder if she's the Anna that Yoshiko had written about in the note, but I'm too embarrassed to admit I don't know.

"Do you want some leftover curry?" I ask instead.

"We finished the curry a long time ago," she replies. "I'll just order in some food. Mom left some extra cash. Want noodles?"

"Yes, but not the spicy kind. They disturb my stomach."

As the girl orders through the phone, she checks the fridge for something to drink. How odd! The only thing she has in the fridge is milk! She chooses a carton at random and pours me a glass, finishing the order as she does so.

". . . and not spicy. Yes. No spice. That's important. Thank you." She hangs up the phone and turns to me again. "Let me know if you get tired, and I'll pull out a futon for you."

I'm not tired. If anything, I'm more awake than ever. I keep thinking about that bizarre contraption this girl is building. It's beautiful, like a swallow's nest cast in iron. I wonder what it's being made for. She's gone off to find her mother's wallet, but I'll find out what that machine is once she gets back. It really is remarkable, I just need to remember to ask.

SATELLITE

THE TRAIN RIDE TO Kumamoto was long and weightless, and after not sleeping the night before, I could feel myself fading away. As I fought to stay awake, body swaying with the meandering of the tracks, I attempted to make sense of the mission Anna had given me. For some reason, I didn't feel like I had the full picture.

"You've never stolen anything before, correct?" she had asked me.

"Aside from that business with the train fare, no."

"You're going to need to toughen up, then. Can you do this for me?"

I nodded, no longer feeling like I could back out. Anna's room was becoming claustrophobic, its angled roof closing in. The look she gave me went deep into my core, as though she were staring into my individual (imaginary) atoms.

"I need you to visit a friend of mine. He lives in a retirement home in Kumamoto. Once you're inside, you need to look around his apartment for books on space, aerodynamics, combustion, anything else of that nature. Do you understand?"

I told her I did, and she wrote the address on a small slip of paper, along with directions for how to find his room. I almost expected her to tell me to memorize and then swallow the note. At the bottom she had written his name: *The General*. I wondered how, exactly, he had received that title.

Anna quickly briefed me on the old man's story, adding that he wouldn't be aware of my presence, since he was blind and deaf. It helped that no one could see me to begin with. The devil on my shoulder told me to be relieved that the sting would be easy, while the angel reminded me that I would, in fact, be stealing from a disabled senior citizen.

"And one more thing," she said, as I made my way out of her room. "Let me know how he looks. I'm worried about him."

"What do you mean?"

She paused, clearly uncomfortable with my question. The mound, hidden in the back corner of her room, loomed over us.

"I mean, check if he seems lonely. It's important that people visit him often. Make sure that he's eating, too," she said. "Make sure he's okay. Some truly awful person hurt him a while back. Did something that they should probably be punished for."

"I see."

"The worst of the worst. Human garbage."

By then Anna wasn't really speaking to me anymore, was instead lost in that absolute introspection so typical of her. I slipped out of the room, leaving her alone with her thoughts.

The train came to a stop. Fukuro Station, the home of The Foreigner. No one got on, no one got off. I felt the benign embrace of sleep come for me; I no longer had the strength to resist it.

For the first and only time in my admittedly short life, I had a dream—stirred, no doubt, by the movements of the train. It seems like an anomaly now, as though it never should have happened to begin with. If my life were a hundred-piece puzzle, this dream would have been piece one hundred and one.

And yet if I, an imaginary boy, could have a dream, then maybe I wasn't as imaginary as I had feared. I've kept this extra puzzle piece close ever since, and even now I'm not sure where it should fit. The dream went something like this:

A prince on horseback, riding through a desert, arid dunes rolling into the horizon. He was alone, his ethnicity vague.

Surrounding him were thousands of corpses, each brutalized in their own unique way. The uniforms and standards were mixed, making it difficult to tell which side had won and which had lost, let alone which The Prince himself belonged to.

The Prince wandered aimlessly for a while, his mount bored by its surroundings. In a few years the dunes would cover the battlefield entirely, the landscape would be erased and born again as though in a karmic cycle. The cruelest neutral.

Coming close to an oasis, The Prince disembarked and travelled on foot. The pool seemed to have once been a pure blue, but had been made murky by battle. A body was slouched in the water, one arrow sticking out of the back of its neck, another through the palm of its hand. The Prince stopped to consider how this could have been possible. The soldier must have seen a hail of arrows, tried to shield himself with his hands from the first wave, and then been shot in the back trying to escape the second wave. He hadn't stopped to remove the arrow from his palm, so the two arrows must have been shot in rapid succession. Satisfied with his analysis, The Prince washed himself in the pool, a lone tree providing him with shade.

He lay back, refreshed, and noticed the tree he was under held some sort of dark red, swollen fruit. He gazed at the fruit curiously for a second, then realized with an almost painful pang of nostalgia that they came from his homeland in the north, which he had not returned to since he was a child. The Prince climbed the tree, as though possessed by that same energy of his youth, and pulled off the fattest fruit he could reach, about the size of a desk globe. He threw it and himself to the ground and cut into its thick skin greedily with his ornamental dagger, hands shaking. The air was already sweet with its nectar.

A short while later, he had eaten nearly every piece of fruit on the tree. None moved away from him. None denied him their taste. The juices were flowing down his torso, half of the pulp not finding its way to his mouth.

Just as he cut open another, the wounded foot soldier, not quite dead, stretched his arrow hand towards him.

"Do not eat those!" he shouted. "They have all been infected with parasites."

What the soldier said was true. The Prince looked at the fruit again, and noticed for the first time hundreds of thin worms, which he had thought were fibres, swarming inside. They pulsed to an invisible rhythm, waiting for his next bite.

At this, The Prince realized that death was imminent; he had eaten far too many infected fruits to resist their impending takeover of his body. He stood up proudly, thanked the mortally wounded soldier for his warning, and left him his ornamental dagger, as though their shared fates linked them somehow. He then mounted his horse and rode away from the oasis.

The whole time, The Prince didn't betray a single look of fear. He and I both knew that the parasites were burrowing deep inside him. He could feel them. And yet, all that he said as he rode off were three short words.

"*Namu Amida Butsu. Namu Amida Butsu.*"

Within the dream, I recognized these words as a Buddhist chant. They meant "Save me, Amida Buddha," and were often recited when someone was faced with death. A final invocation to open oneself up to Amida Buddha, that Lord of Immeasurable Light.

The dream ended here, abruptly, as the lurching of the train woke me from my sleep. We had arrived in Kumamoto. I never did see if The Prince met his end or not.

So why did I have this dream to begin with? I had no home to feel nostalgic for, no glory to look back on, no religion to take refuge in. I had never even heard the words *Namu Amida Butsu* before, and yet I immediately understood them. What I had seen and heard required a past, which I did not have. The dream took place in a time before technology, before satellites roamed the skies. I must have imagined it into existence, a symptom of the illogical human brain I had been gifted. Since when was I able to create?

I got off the train, head filled with thoughts of fruits and parasites, wondering if it was possible for a dream to have had a dream.

*　　　*　　　*

Skyscrapers and camphor trees. Cigarette smoke and moss. Kumamoto was a larger city than Sakita, yet it maintained its ties to the natural world much more elegantly. In Sakita the two went head to head, whereas in Kumamoto they lived in harmony. Salarymen and office ladies walked to work, Edo-era castles visible in the distance. A rain so fine it could be mistaken for mist. In a city of 660,000, I saw no litter on the ground.

The General's retirement home was an unimposing building in the suburbs, cream-coloured and built in a traditional style. Asphalt shingles were omitted in favour of tiled roofing, sliding partitions instead of solid walls. Some of the other residents were outside, enjoying the cool air with well-earned leisure. Their aging bodies fascinated me. I walked in unnoticed, following Anna's directions through the halls.

He was much smaller than I'd imagined. From the reverential tone Anna had used when she said "The General," I assumed he would be a behemoth of some sort. Instead of the twelve-foot-tall warrior I was expecting, I was met by a man barely reaching five feet, sitting alone at a low kotatsu table on the tatami-mat floor, struggling to get rice porridge into his mouth.

Anna had told me that The General would most likely be meditating, and so I was expecting to bask in the presence of a holy man. The tragically domestic scene I came across instead made me feel as though I was pulling on a thread better left alone.

Regardless of The General's diminutive appearance and lunchtime struggles, I had a job to do and set out searching his piles of books accordingly. As usual, I found myself mostly immaterial, phasing in and out of reality, able to exert as much influence as a breeze. How exactly did Anna expect me to bring books back? I was limited to staring at the spines, reminding me of my time spent above Earth.

Judging by the abject mess around him, the old man was either an anarchist or his room had recently been broken into. Some of the tatami I walked over had been torn; one mat was stained with a beautiful blue ink. The pieces of a dismantled bookshelf had been piled by the front door, destined for the dump, with the resulting stacks of books covering the floor instead. The first few piles I glanced at turned up no results for texts on rocket physics, and I was about to move on to another pile when The General suddenly addressed me.

I had grown used to The General's presence, and was no longer as worried about being caught. And so, when I heard Morse code being tapped out behind me, I assumed it to be an eccentricity of a hermit and continued my search, neck tilted to read the spines I couldn't touch.

"Are you Anna?"

The General was driving these words into the ground with a cane, and if it were possible to attach emotion to a physical action such as this, I would say it was done with sorrow.

I turned to face The General, surprised that he could sense my presence, something I thought only Anna was able to do. He stared at me with unseeing eyes, mouth trembling.

The General approached me as rapidly as his body would allow, somehow knowing exactly where I stood frozen in fear, and took my hand. The metaphysical implications of this action were immense, too large for me to process. It felt like a solar flare had worked its way through my system, overwhelming my circuitry to the point where I couldn't move. If The General could see me, were there others?

He tapped the words frantically into my palm—"Are you Anna?"—fingers flying in all directions, making him nearly impossible to understand.

Maybe it was the shock of finally being caught. Maybe it was a destructive streak I didn't know I had. Or maybe I was curious about what it would be like to be my own creator—but rather than pull away from his grasp, I decided to engage with The General.

"I am. I wanted to see you."

"Wanted to see me?"

"I also wanted to borrow some books."

At the word "books" The General flinched as though being struck, then nodded his head knowingly and walked into the next room. When he returned, he was slowly pushing a large pile of texts with his feet.

I had already checked that stack, but made a show of looking through it nonetheless. I wasn't sure how much he could see, after all, and I wanted to be as polite as possible after breaking into someone's home.

I was between a book on Heian pottery and a collection of Rampo's stories when The General addressed me, or rather Anna, again.

"I forgive you. Don't be ashamed," he tapped.

Forgive?

"You can start visiting me again. I promise, I don't hold anything against you."

I felt the desperate urge to speak to Anna, to hear the truth about what had happened to this old man. I knew that I was being lied to. My creator was keeping secrets from me, leaving me no choice but to doubt her.

I looked up at The General, the first human other than Anna I had interacted with. The varicose veins crawling through his skin saddened me, reminding me of the fragility of man. When satellites die, they eventually fall from orbit, burn up on re-entry, and mercifully turn into dust. Humans, however, wither away. Their skin turns transparent, and the very bones that served them all their lives are no longer able to prop them up.

And yet, I was jealous.

I stood and took his hand in mine, unsure of how to handle it, so unlike the only other hand I'd held. Male, rather than female. Old, rather than young. His grip was much stronger than Anna's, yet still felt as though it might collapse in my palm.

"You forgive me?"

He seemed relieved that I had turned to him, had joined his world.

"Nothing important was broken, and the rest were just things. The bruise you left went away in a week."

A wave of revulsion passed through me, a decidedly physical feeling. The General's hand now felt unbearably warm. To make matters worse, his expression was all-forgiving, almost Buddha-like. It would have been easier had he hated Anna for what she did.

He missed her. The days since they last spoke must have felt like an eternity to him. I decided to change the topic, a conscious decision to fight off the growing disappointment—or was it disillusionment?—I felt towards my lonely god. Surely there was a logical explanation? I shouldn't have to feel this way about the girl I loved.

"Tell me a story about us," I said.

The General smiled softly, and motioned for me to take a seat.

ANNA

I WAS NEARLY DONE with my day's work when the name I should inscribe on The Machine came to me. I grabbed a penknife before the inspiration could escape, and engraved a single word onto the nameplate. The roughness with which I carved each stroke struck me as being the antithesis of The General's loose calligraphy. Here instead were sharp, cruel angles, meticulously planned.

The Machine would now officially be called the *Tengu*, after the mischievous creatures of ages past. Part crow, part goblin, these long-nosed spirits had dominion of the mountains and the forests, were harbingers of war and discontent. The Buddhists consider them yokai, supernatural monsters, while the Shintoists know them as kami. I imagine the truth is somewhere in between.

The Prince I had imagined as a child had taken me on countless journeys across dunes and deserts, riding horseback on a steed I had named Tengu. It seemed appropriate to give my machine the same name—soon Leo and I would be taking journeys of our own, after all.

For the first time in years, I found myself reminiscing about The Prince.

The root of our falling-out stemmed from his realization that he was, in fact, imaginary. That outside of my mind, he simply didn't exist. Over the months that followed, he gradually became increasingly bitter about his unreality, asking questions far beyond my comprehension as a child.

Why couldn't I grant him free will?

Why did I want him to suffer?

Why had I given him this existential pain?

Eventually, these questions started to overwhelm me, and I would make him disappear. Since he was imaginary, I could forget about him temporarily by concentrating on the real world. When I did this he would fade away, leaving me with some peace and quiet, until I inevitably brought him back once again. It's difficult having a falling-out with an imaginary friend.

The last time I saw him, we were riding out across the desert on another adventure, and were being approached by our hundredth group of bandits. The Prince had been acting cold towards me all day and had brought me along begrudgingly. He got off the horse to confront our enemies and motioned for me to follow without looking at me once. At that moment I realized I despised him, and felt a cool detachment take over. Rather than dismount and join him in my own fantasy, I took the reins of Tengu myself and turned to leave. When The Prince saw what I was doing, he cried out in surprise, cursed, and gave chase in a futile attempt to catch me. Alone, there would be no way for him to fight off the incoming aggressors. The galloping of my horse was so loud I never heard the last words he said to me.

Of course, this was all in my imagination, but it was what I told my classmates had happened the next time they asked about The Prince. I've never been outside of Japan, let alone left someone for dead in the middle of a Turkish desert. I can still see the looks Mina and my other classmates gave me that day, of barely hidden amusement with a hint of contempt.

It became clear to me then that everyone else had moved on. I was the only one still playing with her imaginary friends.

My classmates asking me about my latest adventures with The Prince didn't come from a place of genuine curiosity, but of cruelty. It became a running joke for them to listen every Monday morning to the ridiculous new story Anna made up, the fantastic life she tried to pass off as her own. I tried not to care, and continued inventing stories even though the real Prince was long gone. At the very least, it meant I was being included.

Sometimes I wondered what happened to my Prince. Had he really perished in that desert? After that incident, I was no longer able to summon him, my imagination searching and coming up blank. Not even I knew what happened to dead imaginary friends. Perhaps he still existed, waiting, the quietest of voices deep inside. A murmur from the heart.

Naming my machine the *Tengu* seemed an appropriate resolution to the way things had ended with The Prince. No doubt what I had planned for Leo and me would finish on a much higher note, should the *Tengu* fulfill its purpose.

It was painful to think that my first imaginary friend should have realized he was imaginary. And yet Leo was in the same situation now, and I feared that, like The Prince, he would also become disillusioned with existence. That he, too, would lose faith in me.

I covered The Machine with the tarp. The physical body of the *Tengu* was complete; all that it required now was fuel. Fuel of any kind would do; neither of us was too picky, so long as it provided the combustion the *Tengu* needed.

It was getting dark, my eyes no longer able to work off natural light alone. The slight frosting of snow over Sakita amplified the absence of sound outside my room. It would still be a while before Leo returned.

I set out to complete the final step.

SATELLITE

ANNA HAD TOLD ME that after The General was removed from his cave, his single bolt action rifle had gone missing from the scene of the battle. It turned up some time afterward in a local's shed, where it was being kept as a wartime memento. When The General became a minor celebrity, a petition was started to reunite him with his gun: a symbol of the old man's resistance. It eventually came back into his possession, firing mechanisms removed for safety's sake, and now hung, gutted, above his dining table.

As I watched The General take a seat across from me, deciding which story to tell, I considered how his and his gun's fate were inexorably tied. I wondered if the cult-like aura Anna had given him ever truly existed in the first place.

"Do you remember the day I first made your acquaintance?"

I cringed slightly at how long it took him to Morse out *acquaintance*; surely there was a more concise way of putting it. I lied and said I did remember, but asked him to remind me anyway. He began.

"I was told of a visitor who wished to see me. I asked Nurse Yamada who it was, but did not recognize the name. When I called you in, I believed you to be a reporter of some sort, though I was curious, since interest in me had died out long ago." At this, he motioned towards his gun. Although blind, he had memorized the layout of his home.

"I was somewhat right, I suppose," he continued. "You were not a reporter, but you were here because of my story. I was quite touched to find that you had learned Morse code just to speak with me. Where did you learn about my case, might I ask?"

"I saw you on TV," I guessed.

He frowned at this for a moment, long enough to make me worry that I had blown my cover.

"Was I ever on TV? I can't recall. Either way, I remember your touch was the gentlest I had felt in ages, despite how aggressive your questions were. I hope you don't mind me saying this, but even years after my isolation ended, female touch still makes me nervous."

"What did I ask you?"

"You spoke some nonsense about becoming my disciple, which I thought was charming. *One blind man leads many blind men.* Surely you no longer feel this way."

He chuckled. I assumed the previous line to be a proverb of some sort, judging by the archaic Japanese he had used.

"You asked me hundreds of questions, and from the way the table shook, I assumed you were writing my answers down. I don't remember exactly what you asked, but they mostly had to do with glory, sacrifice, meaningless ideals such as that. I felt as though you were expecting me to still have the fighting spirit of my youth."

The General gripped my hand a little tighter, as if worried I would escape.

"There was one question, though, that I still remember. In all my years I had never been asked it before."

"Oh?" I let this out verbally, to deaf ears.

"You asked me, 'Do you ever wish you had been killed in the Philippines?'"

He took his hand from mine and massaged his palm gently; it had cramped up halfway through the story. I took the opportunity to wipe my own hand against my pants. I had been sweating without realizing it, a human trait I was still getting used to.

He reached for me again.

"Anna, why would you ask such a morbid question?"

"I don't remember."

"I still have no answer, so I suppose it was good to ask. When I was younger, I thought I desired glory, Valhalla, death by battle. Then the police pulled me out, and I realized that all I wanted was to go home. Alas, the home I had dreamt of was long gone, or never existed in the first place. *The fallen blossom never returns to the branch.*"

A soft breeze came in through the window, carrying with it the scent of roasted sweet potatoes. One of the other residents must have been attempting a barbeque, in defiance of our light winter. The General turned his head slightly towards the aroma. It was a comfort to know that, at the very least, he could still experience the world through smell.

The General excused himself, saying he would fetch a caretaker to bring us some tea, and left me alone.

Anna had told me there had been controversy regarding his past, many believing him to simply be a delusional hermit who had never actually fought in the war. It was these suspicions that ultimately killed media interest in him, leading to his second period of isolation. Bearing witness to one of the old man's passionate lectures, however, made it difficult to doubt him. In my mind, any reservations regarding his rank, age, or supposedly non-Japanese heritage were erased.

While I waited for The General, I kept myself entertained by counting the vast number of books, paintings, and World War II memorabilia he kept in his apartment. The smell of sweet potatoes had disappeared, and as a result the room felt much emptier. I made a mental note to prepare a barbeque for Anna sometime.

I was surprised to find that, in contrast to when I first entered The General's home, I was now able to touch the various objects strewn about. The books I had initially passed through now felt solid against my skin, although I didn't quite have enough influence to move them. The paintings which covered the tatami, painted on a rice paper lighter than air, were much easier for me to hold.

I started looking through The General's sloppy calligraphy. The blind man seemed to belong to an abstract, free-form school of art. There was one piece in particular which pulled me in. He must have completed it recently—some of the ink was still wet. I lifted this sheet as tenderly as possible, as though the slightest movement might shatter it within my impermanent grasp.

While the other paintings were all similar in their randomness, this one seemed to have its own system. Rather than being open-ended, the unintelligible characters here worked their way into a spiral. Along the outer lines of the circle were a few blotches of ink coiling downwards into a sombre black. Was this a depiction of souls trapped in the cycle of karma, or of planets caught in orbit?

A little while later The General returned, mouth drawn into a tight grimace. He rushed over, as though he had no time left for what he wanted to say, and addressed me for what would be the final time.

He grabbed me by the wrist, sending the paper flying out of my hand and onto the woven straw floor. "Anna, you have a good heart. Please never forget this. You have a good heart."

I stared at the painting, now far beyond my reach, only vaguely aware of The General's words. There was something undefinable in his calligraphy, ink splotches that couldn't be pinned down by mere numbers. I'd never acquired a sophisticated appreciation of the arts, but I was beginning to understand this human phenomenon of beauty. There was a raw energy to what this old man was creating, expressions that belonged to him alone. It seemed to me that there were two Generals: the one standing before me, and the one who painted words with India ink.

"I'm sorry. It's for your own safety."

He pressed this into my palm, clouded eyes on the verge of tears. Rain falling from a mountain mist.

At this, the door behind him flung open, revealing two uniformed young men, one tall and one short, donning identical all-black uniforms. Big Dipper and Little Dipper. Following closely behind them was a heavy-set middle-aged woman—a caregiver, judging by the authority she held herself with. Big Dipper carried a police flashlight, clearly to be used as a baton in a pinch, firmly by his side. The General had called the building's security, believing I was Anna. What exactly had happened between them the last time they met?

"Where is she?"

"Did she break anything?"

"Is she hiding?"

The matching guards were overly excited by what must have been their first sign of action in years. The one with the flashlight left his boots on as he stepped into The General's room, trampling a painting underfoot.

"Miss, we're here to help you! You're not in trouble."

The nurse began to tap Morse into The General's hand, at which he became angry, speaking aloud for the first time.

"No! She's here."

He pulled his arm from the nurse and, gripping hold of his cane, began swinging it wildly in search of me. A couple towers of books toppled, adding another touch of disorder to the scene. Meanwhile, Big Dipper and Little Dipper stormed around the apartment, at times passing through me, searching for imaginary people.

"I was just speaking to her!"

It was surprisingly tense watching my own manhunt unfold, considering it was Anna they were looking for. I was glad that they wouldn't find her. If anything, I felt a kind of sick pleasure watching these two guards nearly tear down the walls at the thought of being outsmarted by a sixteen-year-old. More than anything, though, I was afraid. Afraid of the girl I thought I knew, whose self-destructive streak was expanding to include the outside world. I was afraid of what might happen to her, of what might happen to us.

As I left the room—the manhunt showing no signs of subsiding—I went to pick up the piece of calligraphy that had interested me so. When I reached for it, my hand passed through the paper, no longer able to take hold. Somehow, the ink still managed to stain my palms. I stared at the painting for a second, saddened by the idea of leaving it behind.

The General was becoming increasingly frantic, pacing around his room, sending pleas to Anna by driving his cane into the floor. Morse code to shake the Earth. We were linked: only he and Anna could see me in this world. Why this was, I didn't understand. I had gone numb by then, the chaos around me having lost its meaning. All I felt was a hole, a hollow, growing deep within my chest.

*   *   *

On the train back to Sakita, I caught my reflection in the window. It was my first time seeing my own face—I hadn't thought to look until now, yet somehow, my appearance was already familiar. It was the uncanny sensation of recognizing your face on someone else's body. Or rather, instead of seeing a doppelgänger of yourself in public, realizing that *you* are, in fact, the doppelgänger. No one ever tells stories from the mimic's point of view; surely realizing you are the clone is just as alarming.

I moved my tongue self-consciously over my missing tooth, wondering why Anna had given me a cleft lip in the first place. As the train passed through a tunnel, the darkness outside sharpened my reflection, and I recognized with a shudder where I had seen my face before. It was weeks earlier, on a school roof covered in snow that might have been clouds. Anna had created me in the exact image of Soki.

SOKI

WEIRD THINGS HAD BEEN happening. It was the beginning of January, but there were still cicadas everywhere. They should've all died by then, but they wouldn't leave. Not to mention all the snow. That winter was the first time in years any had fallen in Sakita.

When I told Dad all of this, he shook his head. "The natural order has been disturbed," he said. "Something bad is going to happen."

We were eating breakfast—egg-toast and coffee. The radio forecast had just predicted more snow. A cool wind from the north.

"'Natural order?'" I repeated. It was painful, hearing him talk like a priest again.

He swallowed a bite down. "It's just an expression. Doesn't mean much."

I thought about this for a second. He had said those words so quickly, as if out of habit. "But you meant it, right?"

"That the weather is abnormal, yes."

I finished off my toast. "That's not what you said. You said, 'The natural order has been disturbed.'"

He sighed. "It never ends with you. Go get dressed or you'll be late."

At that he stood, and took our empty plates to the kitchen. I followed him in.

"Were you talking about kami? Because I've been thinking the same. They seem upset at Sakita. Maybe the people here have ignored them too long."

He closed the dishwasher—hard. "It's just a saying."

"But it's not 'just a saying.' I'm talking about the gods." I could tell I was being annoying, but I didn't care. Hearing him repeat those words made me wonder if maybe he still believed. If maybe he hadn't quite let everything go.

"Do you want me to drive you or not?"

In all honesty, I didn't. Most of my classmates walked to school on their own, but my parents insisted on driving me because "it's safer" somehow. Guess Mom thought I'd get lost or run over even. It was embarrassing. But that morning, she was at the dentist, and since my dad had the day off, he said he'd drive me. So I shut my mouth. I could ask him about my theory again on the way to school.

But when we got into the car, it wouldn't start. Thousands and thousands of kilometres, and our silver two-door decided to die here. We'd been using it since Hokkaido, and it'd gone through much worse. Felt like an omen. Dad told me there wasn't any gas left. I said he should fill it up more often, but he said he had just gone to the gas station the day before.

We found some weird tube in the driveway. Dad laughed and said that someone must have siphoned the fuel while we were asleep. I didn't get why he was relieved, but he told me it was better than having a leak in the gas tank. I don't get him sometimes.

"Go get your coat, you'll have to walk to school," he said. Then, as an afterthought: "You think your kami emptied the tank?"

I didn't like how he called them *your kami*, and I shook my head. "Nope. Just a thief. A kami wouldn't harm us like that."

I wasn't really paying attention to what I was saying, to be honest. I'd gotten used to sending lines back at my dad this way. But as we walked back to the house, I could tell something was bothering him. He had this weary look on his face, one that I remembered from purification ceremonies in Hokkaido.

I put on a thicker jacket and was just out the door when he stopped me.

"I was joking about the kami," he said. "Spirits wouldn't steal gasoline, but be careful with that line of thought—that kami can't hurt you."

If I didn't leave soon, I'd be late. I turned to look at him, saw him standing in the doorway to the kitchen, watching me curiously.

"Kami aren't evil, Dad," I said.

"They aren't good, either," he replied. "If you want to believe in Shinto, that's up to you. But you have to take responsibility for your faith. You can't pick and choose what you believe in."

I said nothing back. It was rare for him to talk to me like this. He wasn't scolding or making fun of me. He was treating me like a junior priest and not his son. Giving me guidance in something he no longer believed in.

"If you want to believe that a religion will protect you, you have to accept that it could hurt you, too. You have to accept that if you worship poorly, if you neglect the kami, if you lose your respect, it'll harm you and the people around you. If you can't assume that responsibility, don't believe at all. Do you understand?"

I nodded, and after a second, he just stepped back into the room. I slipped on my shoes and left.

Dad's words stuck in my head. If the natural order was disturbed, was it the kami's doing? And if I believed in the kami, was I responsible? Apparently, these strange events started happening after we arrived in Sakita: the snow, the cicadas, and now the gas. Maybe my family had brought some low spirit with us from somewhere else in Japan.

I mulled over what my dad had said. There were responsibilities with belief. You can't just accept the blessings. If you believe your faith can save the world, you have to accept it can ruin it, too.

The entire time, the sweet smell of gasoline kept following me. Reminded me of the smell of incense. Mom used to hand-make sticks of it, but she lost her kit a few cities ago, so we don't burn it at home anymore. I miss it, though. It smelled a lot better than gasoline. She used to tell me that appreciating incense is an art of its own. I never got the hang of it—most of it smelled the same. Only thing I remember is that there's different kinds of fire. Different sticks have different expressions. Kind of like people. If you took all of someone's life and burned it, what would their fire be like?

Outside the school gates, I passed by a statue of Jizo. Someone had already started a pebble pile. I took a moment to add to it anyway. On the off chance that child spirits really do stack stones to escape the underworld, I figured it'd be best to help.

When I arrived to class, I was a half hour late. Ms. Tanaka was annoyed, and told me she was just about to call my family. She thinks I'm abnormal, and that my roaming childhood was "improper." Doesn't bother me, though—my class is filled with weirdos. Anna wasn't there that day—she rarely was, anymore—but she's the biggest weirdo I know. The only time she'd show her face was when there was a test to write. The teachers had mostly given up on her. They probably thought she was just going to drop out.

Whenever Anna decided to show up to school, she kept to herself. My classmates had stopped calling her Anna-terasu. They just called her "the alien," instead. She didn't seem to mind, just sat there staring at nothing. Sometimes it almost looked like she was talking to herself. I'd heard lots of rumours about her, about her family, but I wasn't sure what to believe. I got the feeling she avoided me sometimes. After we talked about kami on the rooftop, she didn't seem interested in talking to me, or anyone else for that matter. Wasn't sure why. I thought we got along. To be honest, a part of me was impressed that she was so independent. Maybe a little intimidated, too.

Right as Ms. Tanaka was about to continue her lesson, Fumie entered. It was rare for her to be so late—she was always at her desk right on time. We went out for a little bit, but I guess she got bored of me. We hadn't really spoken since we dated. My dad always told me I should talk more, but I think I talk just enough.

Fumie started whispering to Ms. Tanaka, explaining why she was late. Somehow, she was talking even faster than usual. I wasn't trying to listen in, but I caught something. The words *car*, *empty*, and *gas*.

"What happened?"

I blurted this out, not even realizing I was interrupting a private conversation.

Fumie looked at me strangely, like she wasn't sure whether to reply. Glanced around at our classmates, who were all staring. I could tell she was self-conscious about speaking in front of everyone.

"I mean, like, my mom was going to drive me to school, right?" she started saying. "But the car wouldn't start, or, actually, we didn't even try to start the car, because when I sat down something smelled funny and, well, the tank was actually empty, and the entire car was covered in gas—"

I felt a chill pass through me. "Someone poured gasoline over your car?"

"Yeah, but that's not even the worst part. Someone wrote a bunch of nonsense all over the windshield, like a crazy person, and we couldn't even read what it said because it was in a foreign language or something. But it gets even worse because it wasn't even paint that was on our windshield, but lipstick. But not even normal lipstick either. It's actually the shade I use, so now I'm worried that someone has it out for me, like a pervert or a stalker or . . ."

At some point, the classroom went quiet. Fumie was still speaking, and Ms. Tanaka was trying to get her to sit down, but I couldn't hear a thing. There was a low hum in my ears.

Before I came to Sakita, everything was normal. No snow, cicadas, or missing gasoline. But then we arrived. Had the kami sent us to Sakita as punishment for leaving the shrine? Or were the kami punishing Sakita by sending us here?

If I asked my dad, he would say it's just a coincidence. That there was a serial gasoline thief on the loose, and Fumie and I were unlucky. But he can say that because he doesn't believe. I have to take responsibility.

Up until then, I thought that kami only protected people. That if Dad believed in them just a little more, we would be all right. Problem is, I was picking and choosing. I didn't realize what believing meant.

Ms. Tanaka started her lesson, but I couldn't read what she was writing. I was too busy trying to pray. Trying to purify the city I lived in. But I didn't know what words to use. How do I take responsibility for something I wasn't sure I'd caused?

SATELLITE

THE SUN HAD NEARLY set by the time I arrived in Sakita, navigating through streets and back alleys I only knew from space. While daydreaming on the train I'd missed my stop and ended up having to walk all the way back home. Some days I miss flying.

I should have been worried about how Anna would react to my returning empty-handed, but all I could think about was the true nature of her relationship with The General. What had happened between the two of them? What else was she hiding?

I let myself into Anna's room, only to find that she wasn't there. She had left a note directing me to Lucky Ginseng, a Chinese medicine shop somewhere downtown. I allowed myself a brief moment of weakness and complained to no one in particular about having to travel even farther. I'd never been there before, and I was impressed by her confidence in my ability to find my way alone. Or maybe it was just faith in my satellite GPS.

On my way out, I paused briefly in front of that mysterious mound, a surge of temptation compelling me to stay. For the first time, I was alone with this foreboding object. I could pull the tarp off without Anna ever knowing. I approached it uneasily, floorboards creaking underfoot in warning, and eventually placed my palm against its side. Rather than feel my curiosity build, however, I felt only an unexplainable dread. Whatever was underneath that tarp felt eerily familiar, unnerving enough to make me pull away. I wiped my palm against my pants, as though contaminated by some unknown contagion, and fled Anna's room. Down the stairs, out the door, into the hastening night.

I found Anna standing in front of Lucky Ginseng's shuttered storefront, alone, staring up into the sky. The sun had long gone to rest over the horizon, a layer of frost covering the city like silver foil. The apartment buildings jutting out of the skyline from the surrounding neighbourhood reminded me of stalagmites, mirroring the stiff pose she held as she gazed into the heavens. The store's neon signs cast a multicoloured glow around her, filling me with a loneliness I couldn't understand.

"You're even later than I thought you'd be," she said, watching me cross the street towards her.

"I wasn't able to find the books you wanted. The General's place is a mess."

"That's fine. I didn't need them anyway. I finished earlier than expected," she said, before falling into a brief silence. She was measuring her words, making sure nothing unintended came out.

"How is he, by the way?" she asked. "Does he seem okay?"

She had yet to look me in the eye. The way she was talking was hurried, almost paranoid, as though she was afflicted by some kind of dangerous exultation. To top it off, an odd smell clung to her, sickly sweet and metallic at the same time. I was struck by the thought that Anna was losing control, that she was falling down, down, down.

"Anna, do you have any parents?"

She cast a sidelong glance at me, as though annoyed I was getting off topic. "Yeah, a mom," she answered dismissively. "Don't worry about her, she's almost as imaginary as you."

"Is that normal?"

She looked at me, puzzled. "What do you mean by that? What counts as 'normal'?"

"I mean, not just your mom, but . . ." I regretted speaking in the first place.

"Say it." Anna stared at me, unblinking, knowing full well that I was too afraid to go further.

I said nothing in response.

"Don't ask questions about things you'll never understand," she said, breaking the silence. "Besides, I called you here for a reason. I want you to see something. Do you remember what life was like up in space?"

"Kind of. It already feels like a lifetime ago."

"I bet you didn't realize how beautiful it was. I don't blame you. You didn't understand how hideous things are down on Earth."

I wasn't sure what specifically she found so "hideous."

"Look. Do you see that?" She pointed to the sky. I couldn't see anything in particular. "Look closer. There's a satellite flying above us right now."

I tried to focus, but the sky was motionless, staring back at me with impartial silence. All I could see was a handful of stars, the true spectre of space washed out by light pollution down below.

"Do you know who that satellite is?"

"No."

"It's you, Leo."

Anna was now lying on her back, her figure drowning in a sea of asphalt and melting snow. I lay down beside her, trying to line up my perspective with hers. I realized I was lying on her hair, but she was too distracted to notice.

"Your soul used to be in that machine, an A-347 titanium alloy satellite. Then I brought you down to Earth. I wanted you all to myself. I made you human. Whatever's up there in space now is just an empty shell."

"Thank you," I said, unsure if I meant it.

"No, you don't understand. What I did was wrong."

"Oh?"

"The world down here is rotten. I had no right to try to make you a part of it."

I didn't know what to say, so I opted for nothing at all. The metallic smell coming from Anna was growing increasingly unbearable. I tried sitting up to escape it, but succeeded only in making myself light-headed.

"What I should have done is gone up there to you," she said.

The satellite that was supposedly me wasn't visible at all, and perhaps it never existed to begin with. I could feel my eyes straining as they searched for satellites either as real as her, or as imaginary as me. Floating above was the waning moon, a reflection of the sun.

"We're going to escape, Leo, just the two of us. We won't have to worry about anyone else ever, ever again. It will be just you and me."

Was Anna aware she had made me in Soki's image? That in the end, I was nothing more than a proxy for someone she barely knew?

There comes a day when you realize that your creators are imperfect. I had seen this time and time again, from far up in the comfort of space. I saw it in children who watch their parents fall out of love, in sons who inherit their father's tempers, in students who outgrow their masters. The Anna lying beside me was different than the Anna I'd first imagined, even if the body was still the same. This Anna was capable of breaking my heart.

"Don't worry, Leo, I'll make it right. You can rely on me."

That noxious smell was growing more intense, yet Anna didn't seem to notice. It clung to her clothes and pooled out with her breath. At the time, I was too exhausted to question it, too exhausted to even bring up my visit with The General. My movements felt slow, as though I had been struck by a solar flare, as though I were brushing against a psychedelic state.

I wonder now, if I had noticed in time that the smell was gasoline, whether I could have stopped her.

Anna's image warped in front of me, twitching and pulling as she continued her rants towards the sky. I had lost the thread of what she was saying, but it no longer mattered; simply watching her was enough. It wasn't that I found her attractive—with every passing day her physical form was growing more indistinct, her actions more neurotic. Rather, there was something deep within her manic core pulling me into her orbit. A thousand micrometeoroids had knocked us off path, had changed who was holding on to who.

I felt sleep, mixed with gasoline, compel me from the outer edges of consciousness. I was weightless, a dream floating within a dream, and as I lay back down beside her, I saw a figure on horseback approach from the distance. His long, angular body was set against the horse's dynamic form, dark against its owner's pale skin. The contrast between the two would have made a beautiful ink painting, I thought, as I slowly gave myself up to sleep.

The end was coming. I could feel it. The only problem was, I didn't know what that meant.

ANNA

THE PRINCE ARRIVED SHORTLY after Leo fell asleep. Somehow, I wasn't surprised. His return was only inevitable, was one of the few pieces of closure I needed before launch. I would have been disappointed if the last time The Prince and I were together was the day I betrayed him.

I chose not to watch The Prince advance towards me. Instead, I continued staring at the millions of satellites flying above. I was amazed that Leo could sleep at a time like this—the combined light they emitted was almost blinding. They writhed and twisted under their own weight, pulsating with the breath of life. What I was watching no longer felt like space. It was as though I was gazing upon the reflection of Sakita's skyline in the waters that surrounded it. If I were to just reach a little farther, I might fall up into it . . .

The Prince dismounted and took his time approaching me on foot. Even from the corner of my eye, I noticed that he was limping. His steed was unfamiliar, and I wondered how The Prince had managed to survive after I had ridden away on his Tengu. Once he reached me, he turned his attention to the sky, straining to see what I was looking at, before stepping over Leo to sit down beside me.

"How many years has it been?" he asked.

"I can't recall," I lied.

"Time has a funny way of stretching," he said, taking great care with each word. His voice had lost the youthful quality I'd so loved, and now came out as coarse as sand. "What's been five years for you has probably been twenty for me."

I then took my first look at The Prince in years, and was alarmed at his condition. The trim, gracious warrior I had created so long ago had withered into an anemic husk and lost the healthy colour earned from a lifetime in the sun. This must be how the imagination decays. It was difficult to believe I'd ever modelled the dying man in front of me after the hero from *Lawrence of Arabia*. Still, he sat with his back straight, head raised with a defiant dignity. And his eyes, completely clouded, lazily met mine.

"I'm going blind, you know. My eyes are being eaten from the inside out. Losing my hearing, too."

"Cataracts? You can't be that old."

Our hands brushed each other's as I sat up, and I was surprised when he smiled.

"No, something worse. You seem healthy, though. How have you been? Still going on adventures?"

"I get out from time to time."

I can hardly be held accountable for decisions I made as a child, not least abandoning this old warrior so long ago. Yet seeing the translucent skin taut over the bones of his atrophied arms reminded me—no matter how hard I tried to forget—of how they had once hoisted me atop Tengu in search of adventure. I was just as capable of betrayal as everyone else, was by virtue just as weak. To make matters worse, The Prince seemed to hold no resentment whatsoever towards me. He had made peace with himself, was maybe even making peace with me. If only people were less quick to forgive, then my anger would be easier to justify.

It was the dead of night, yet in the distance, a lone cicada began to chirp. It cried out alone, somehow still alive this deep into winter, somehow still awake at this time. I had assumed its sounds were echoing from within my mind when The Prince turned his head to listen as well.

"What happened to you?" I asked.

"Well, I survived the ambush you left me in, surprisingly. That's not the reason I look like death." He laughed a little too loudly at this, as if trying to prove his health, before continuing. "I spent some time on my own, thinking. Actually, all I could do was think. If I had stayed in that desert any longer, I probably would have conjured up an imaginary friend too. Wouldn't that be peculiar, an imaginary friend having an imaginary friend."

He stopped for a moment and took a breath, his shoulders moving in a full-body effort, as if attempting to free the last bits of air still trapped in his chest. He was missing a few fingers on his left hand, which he held in a fist so as to hide their absence from me.

What pained me most were his blind eyes; there was no way he'd be able to appreciate the spectacle of the satellites above. Had The Prince come back to me in order to die? I suddenly felt so, so small, sitting next to this phantom from my childhood.

"Most of what I thought about was you," he said. The clouds of air he exhaled were much thinner, much more strained, than mine. "I'll spare you the details, but I figured it would be the best course of action to forgive you and move on."

"So why do you look like you're dying?"

He chuckled. "I ate something I shouldn't have, just because I was homesick. Don't worry about it."

The soft, dying timbre of his voice struck a chord of guilt within me, returning me to those simpler, less lonesome days we had once shared. I found myself struggling to know what to say.

"I miss you sometimes too, you know," I whispered.

"I don't doubt it. We used to have fun together. Lots of adventures between the two of us."

"Like that time in Baghdad?"

"That whole deal with the bandits?"

"They all involved bandits."

He laughed again, a bittersweet sound to be sure. I was surprised that I could dredge him up from the depths of my consciousness after all this time. I imagine the gasoline fumes played some part in it.

"Remember how you used to make me disappear whenever we argued? God, I hated that." He was smiling, somewhat forced, reminiscing with an edge. "Whenever you did that to me it felt like I was weightless, flying through the air."

I watched him struggle with his words, suffering from some sort of internal pain. Beneath the skin on his forearms I saw movement, engorged like a varicose vein. Too slow to be a spasm, too sudden to be natural. He noticed this and closed his eyes, as if willing with all his strength to make it stop.

"It hardly matters now, I suppose," he said.

We spoke like this for hours, until light started to break through the horizon line, softly stirring Leo from his sleep. I wondered what satellites saw in their dreams.

"It's great that you made a friend your age," The Prince said, motioning to Leo. "Especially a boy."

I smiled, letting my guard down without even noticing. "He's a little clueless, but he means well."

"Is he kind to you?" he asked.

"He's kind."

"Good. That's all that matters." The Prince leaned back and placed a four-fingered hand into my own. "You deserve to be happy."

I looked down at our hands, stared at the stub where his index finger should have been. Noticed how our grasps didn't quite fit into each other anymore. I thought then how arbitrary the notion of "deserving" is. Did I deserve my digits any more than he did?

"Do you want to know how Leo and I met?" I asked.

"Was it at school?"

"No, actually. It was about a week ago. He came down to meet me. He's from outer space."

I paused to make sure The Prince knew what I was getting at. He paused to ensure he'd heard correctly.

"Anna, is that boy real, or imaginary?"

"Oh, he's imaginary. One hundred per cent made up."

"You created another non-existent person. After everything that happened with me, you still thought that was a good idea? Does he know?"

"About you or that he isn't real?"

"Either. Both."

"No, and yes."

The Prince's face betrayed no sign of emotion. He closed his blind eyes once more, and attempted to centre himself. While he was lost in meditation, I saw movements similar to those beneath the skin of his arms crawl through his neck. It was as though he had worms swimming just under the skin.

"Does he hate himself as much as I did?" A dwindling hope clung to his voice.

"I wouldn't really know. We haven't spoken about it much."

"What about this do you not understand? It's horrible, being brought into this world half-complete. I was only one aspect of your life, Anna, but you were all of mine. Do you realize how terrifying that is?"

"No, can't say I do."

"There was an entire world just beyond my grasp, a full life that I could almost taste. I'm only here now because you chose to remember me. I have no idea what will happen when you forget about me for good. Will I just evaporate? Or do I just get absorbed back into you? And what about him? Does he know that one lapse of memory on your part and his entire life is gone? He would not sleep so peacefully if he knew."

The Prince attempted to stand, but a spasm of pain pulsed through his body, forcing him to buckle weakly to the ground. His breathing, agitated out of exertion or anger, was the only sound to be heard in that cool night. I felt his stare upon me—he was searching for eye contact, which I denied by turning my gaze upward. His aggression, combined with the lights of the satellites, was overwhelming.

"You don't really attach any importance to our lives, do you? Just because we don't bleed." He gathered his strength for one final push. "Anna, why do you want me to hate you so much?"

Everyone gets what they deserve. I didn't have anything more to say, and instead continued watching the sky.

"It's a shame you can't see," I said, my voice barely above a whisper. "There's a fantastic light show going on right above your head."

At this he curled into himself, then let out a slow, deep moan. The flesh on his back began to move in delicate waves, gradually multiplying. It reminded me of ripples spreading across a still pool. There was a certain beauty in the manner The Prince was meeting his demise, and I felt a familiar sadness work its way through my soul. I leaned forward and let out a sympathetic moan as well, originating from the growing void in my chest. For a brief instant, our voices harmonized. I hadn't planned on The Prince dying today. All I could offer was my companionship, to be his comrade one last time.

And then, just like that, The Prince was gone. His final cry had been cut short, and I was left singing someone else's coda. There were no death throes to signal The Prince's passing; I simply looked beside me to find his body already half decayed, consumed soundlessly by thousands of fine white parasites. I wondered if these were what had killed the old warrior, if this is what it meant to forget.

The worms worked through his body with a malicious efficiency, as though they were one organism instead of an army of smaller ones. It took the span of only a few minutes for the parasites to finish their job, phasing into nothingness after completion.

Once The Prince had become nothing more than a shadow, I watched with astonishment as a dark blue ball of light emerged from the ground, hovering over where he last lay. A hitodama, small enough to fit in the palm of my hand. I had heard of how the souls of the dead separated from their bodies, but I'd never actually seen a hitodama before. According to legend, The Prince's hitodama would not only signal his death, but the birth of a child somewhere else as well. I looked out to the skyline, knowing that under one of those roofs, a life was being brought into the world.

The blue orb began slowly increasing in size, losing its colour and brightness as it did so. It spread itself thinner and thinner, enveloping all of Lucky Ginseng itself, bathing me in its cool glow. A short while later, the hitodama disappeared, nothing more than a murmur from the heart.

Dawn light made way for morning, compelling Leo to gradually wake, shielding his eyes from the sun.

"How long was I asleep?"

I sat watching the damp spot on the asphalt that was once my only real childhood friend. His final words appeared to sing from somewhere beyond, mixed with the call of the cicada. I was afraid to make a serious attempt at crying; if I couldn't produce any tears I would never be able to forgive myself. Instead, I remained completely still, poising myself on the brink of emotion.

Anna, why do you want me to hate you so much?

Part 3

SATELLITE

WHEN I FIRST MET Anna, I wasn't sure if she was a comedy or a tragedy. I rarely saw her laugh, I never saw her cry, and I had no idea how to classify her. She acted so at odds with humankind, it was hard to believe she was from Earth and I was the one from outer space.

Let's be clear: after that night at Lucky Ginseng, Anna became pure tragedy. Indulge me, then, and let me describe my final happy day with her. No matter how carefully I comb through the past, no matter how thoroughly I sift through it, I can't find a moment of relief with her past this. This is the most precious memory I have of her, and I would wage war against time herself to keep from forgetting it. This brief interlude took place just before I discovered what kind of machine Anna was building, just as the first month of the new millennium came to a close.

Anna and I had spent the last few weeks indoors, sleeping until noon, our world quietly shrinking around us. My initial shock at finding myself down on Earth had long passed, and was now replaced with an unrelenting curiosity. My first week with Anna had been exhilarating—I had walked among the people I only knew from afar, sharing with them the smell of perfume and katsu curry, the feeling of snow against my face. And yet ever since we fell asleep in that parking lot, Anna refused to go outside, let alone take me exploring. She was becoming dangerously withdrawn, and no amount of poking or prodding could get her to reveal why. Being attached to a shut-in was a difficult business.

That day, I watched through half-shut blinds as a fine snow settled over Sakita, unfitting of the rice paddies it covered. Anna was meanwhile glued to the TV set, unbothered by the city outside her window, the soft hum of CRT static filling the room. Playing across the curved screen was a martial arts demonstration of sorts, an older man sending opponents half his age flying across the floor.

"What are you watching?" I asked.

"It's footage of a ki master. He's able to harness his inner energies to throw people around like they weigh nothing."

I moved to sit beside her to get a better view of what was happening. There was an old man dressed in oversized robes, surrounded by a group of eager disciples in his dojo. His students would charge at him one by one, the old man letting out a cry every time he sent someone barrelling head over heels. It didn't matter who he touched, how heavy or how strong, they would be tossed aside just the same. The so-called "ki master" was barely making contact with any of them, most of the heavy lifting being done by whoever was being flipped instead. He then turned to the camera and began droning on about his pseudo-science.

"There are three types of ki. Heaven ki exists in the sky, controlled by the moons and planets. Earth ki exists in the ground, hidden in the surface and the Earth's core. The final ki is an individual ki, existing in every one of us. By harnessing these three types, you too can . . ."

"You know these people are launching themselves, right?" I asked.

Anna thoughtfully ignored what I said, increasing the TV's volume by a couple of notches.

"The only reason that old man can toss those people around like that is because they're letting him," I continued. "Power of suggestion. They're only being thrown because they believe they can be thrown."

"They don't believe, Leo. They *want* to believe."

I was confused. "What's the difference?"

"Wanting to believe is much, much more powerful."

I didn't know what she was talking about, and Anna was too wrapped up in the program to elaborate. I adjusted myself and found I had been sitting on a newspaper the entire time. I flipped through it out of curiosity, but avoided most of the headlines I saw. News on planet Earth is depressing.

"Do you want to see a movie?" I asked, hopefully.

She responded with a deliberate shrug, encouraging me enough to read out the listings in the entertainment section. "There's *Maximum Full Throttle II* playing at seven, *The Never That Always Was* at eight-thirty, and *Some French Film* at five. That's the name of the movie. It's just called *Some French Film*."

A second, lazier shrug. I was losing her.

"They're also playing *Lawrence of Arabia* at this retro drive-in. Do those even exist anymore? I thought they only had those in the West."

She looked up, called to attention. Had I been sitting close enough, I'm sure I would have noticed a 25% dilation of the pupils. Excitement.

"What time? Can we make it?"

"The movie's about to start, and we'd have to go all the way to Kumamoto."

"That's fine, it's almost four hours long. If we leave now we can catch the end. Without a car, it'll be easier to sneak in, too."

I was apprehensive about going all the way to Kumamoto in the dead of night, but held my tongue. Our only threads to the outside world were the delivery drivers Anna knew by name, and I wasn't going to pass on an opportunity to leave the house. I was encouraged by the sight of her getting ready to leave, kicking up piles of laundry for something to wear.

By the time we arrived, *Lawrence of Arabia* was more than half-way through. The film was being shown in an old community base-ball field abandoned by whatever club had played there last. Three massive off-white screens had been put up at different angles to accommodate viewing from anywhere in the park. A few of the driv-ers had neglected to turn off their car headlights, washing out the images playing across the screen. Peppered among the cars were a handful of young men, straining their voices to sell caramel popcorn.

Once we snuck past the gate, Anna led me by the hand, weav-ing between parked cars, frosted grass crunching under our feet. We eventually found a spot, a small clearing uncomfortably near one of the towering screens, too close for anyone to park. Other than a slight chill in the air, there was no longer any snow in Kumamoto. The strange ailment which hung over Sakita seemed to belong to her alone.

What we didn't realize was that, in order to hear the audio track for the movie, each car was given a small speaker upon paying. Our error only dawned on us after we had settled in place, craning our necks upwards and watching the faded images of Anna's heroes move their lips without making a sound.

"It's fine. I watched the first half of this movie when I was a kid. I can work out what's going on," Anna assured me.

"How old were you?"

"Like, eight? I'm not sure."

"Eight? There's no way you remember anything. Who's that guy?"

"I don't know."

I felt as though I'd been conned into watching a four-hour historical epic about which I understood nothing. In fact, that's exactly what had happened. "What about him?"

"That's Lawrence."

"Of Arabia?"

"I'd imagine. He looks different than I remember. I think he's a prince or something."

"What's a prince doing fighting in a war? Don't they have people to do that for them?"

"Be quiet, I'm trying to focus. I don't know if he'll live or not."

I couldn't believe my ears. Not only at being shushed during a silent movie, but at Anna not being sure if Lawrence would survive the current battle. We were only two and a half hours in; I didn't imagine they would kill off the title character so far from the end. Of course, how would I have known? I couldn't hear a damn thing.

Nonetheless, when I turned to Anna, giving my sore neck a break, I could see how utterly engrossed in the film she was. For the first time in weeks, her eyes were wide with life, reflecting the movie like miniature screens of their own. Her mouth moved when Lawrence spoke, and her face twitched in sympathy whenever anyone was struck down. I had forgotten that despite her being the smartest and, at times, most intimidating person I knew, Anna was still a child—excited by battles unfolding on the silver screen, enchanted by the handsome young hero, nervous about whether he would survive.

I had been so caught up in Anna as an idea, I had forgotten about Anna as a person. There was still something undefined about her, something no calculation regarding the tilt of the eyebrows or the angle of the lips could reveal. I was wrong to have assumed I understood her. At what point in Anna's arc had we met? Was her trajectory already set before I came down to Earth? A slight pain emerged from that hole Anna had placed in my chest, the cost of becoming human. I leaned back, taking my eyes off the screen as the air filled with sounds from a silent battle.

When the movie ended, Anna turned to me. "Wasn't that incredible?" she said, massaging the kink in her neck.

"I can't really say, I didn't see anything."

"Why did you look away? Didn't you like it?"

"No, I just thought I would concentrate on the dialogue for a little while."

She attempted to shoot me a reproachful look, but was betrayed by a half-smile.

"You know what my favourite part of the movie was?" I said.

"What?"

"The part when Lawrence said: . . ." I moved my mouth silently, miming his expressions without saying a word.

She paused, then burst out laughing. A bright and cheerful laugh, so different than the bitter chuckles I had heard from her before. I could almost swear the cool air turned a little warmer for it.

"Don't make jokes, that was a serious movie. I bet you couldn't recognize true cinema if it hit you over the head!" She brushed some loose dirt from the seat of her pants, momentarily lost in thought. "Do you know what the actual best part was? You would have liked this scene, if you had seen it."

"No, what was it?" I asked, genuinely curious.

She stood up, towering above me and shaking with excitement as she prepared to act out the epic she had just witnessed. Anna stretched her arms out to the sides, receiving an invisible crowd, and began her one-woman show. "Lawrence rides over the hill to confront the enemy, and he sees the dunes panning out before him."

I nodded in agreement. I hadn't paid much attention to the film, but the desert was one detail I remembered seeing.

"He turns to his men, ready to spur them on to battle. This may be the last time they will ever ride together again."

She puffed out her chest, building to the dramatic moment. I leaned forward, surprisingly invested in her performance.

"And he says: . . ."

I waited for Anna to finish her sentence, watching her speak without making a sound, before realizing that I had been bested. We started laughing at the same time, mine coming from surprise more than anything. I was glad that Anna was still capable of making jokes.

"Are you officially funnier than me now?"

She gave an over-the-top bow, basking in her smug glory.

"Okay, okay, but the *actual* best part was when Lawrence said: . . ."

"Nonono, the best best part was when he said: . . ."

We started giggling at just how unfunny our jokes were, working ourselves up from little snickers until we couldn't contain it any longer. This was a new kind of laughter for me, one that came less from the gut than it did the heart. My footsteps felt less steady on the ground, as though gravity had loosened its grip on me. We laughed until we were laughing at laughter itself, tears running down our faces and dripping from our noses. The ugly kind of happiness. I wonder now if we cried because we knew we would never be like this again.

"All right, but if I'm being serious, the best part was when Lawrence was like: . . ."

We barely made sense anymore, fighting for air as we traded the same ridiculous jokes back and forth. Her face was contorted with laughter, body shaking, thin black hair getting into her mouth.

It was the most beautiful thing I'd ever seen.

I could only imagine how she would have appeared to other people, standing alone, doubled over, cracking herself up to the point of tears. The cars filed out slowly, stopping to return their radios to the attendant manning the booth. What was left of my satellite's brain counted them in the background. 1 . . . 27 . . . 84 . . . Their headlights must have looked like the satellites Anna sees at night.

"We should come back next week," she said. "I hear they're playing the director's commentary."

"Really?"

"Of course not!" she howled, breaking into another fit of laughter.

We made our way to the exit, the other moviegoers around us chatting on car roofs and finishing the last of their snacks. A few cast concerned glances at Anna as she passed, the strange girl chuckling to herself alone. At one point, an older woman stopped and asked if she was all right, which only made us laugh harder.

"I'm okay, I'm okay," Anna said, barely getting the words out. "Thanks for asking."

The lady left, quickening her pace, visibly disturbed.

"You know what you should have told her?" I chimed in.

"What?"

" . . . "

Anna fell to the ground, holding her sides. "No more, no more."

I think the reason this memory is so precious to me is that it gave me a glimpse of the Anna who might have been. The Anna who should have been. On January 29, 2000, I saw the life she could have had if she had never imagined me in the first place.

Walking home beside her, it felt wrong for me to have ever doubted Anna. Her laughter cleared my head of any doubts I had about her and The General, any doubts about why I looked like Soki or what she had been building underneath that tarp. Maybe it was an immature decision, one made while delirious with joy, but I resolved then to follow her to the ends of the Earth and beyond.

Anna was oblivious to all of this, and staggered to her feet, punch-drunk. "We should get home. I'm almost done with the paint job on The Machine."

"Why won't you show me what you're making?"

Anna straightened herself, imitating Lawrence-I'm-assuming-of-Arabia's proud stance. "I'll show you when we get home. You're ready now—tonight you find out what we're doing."

"We? I'm involved in this?"

"Of course. The Machine is mostly for you."

A night breeze cut through my flimsy winterwear, my fingers and toes now numb from the cold. Yet somehow, I wasn't shivering. I followed her the rest of the way home, boarding the train at the next station we found. I followed her farther and farther, until the street lights turned on and then turned off once again. And all the while, Anna continued chuckling to herself, repeating the lines Lawrence had never said over and over in her head.

SOKI

I WONDER IF THERE'S a god for curiosity. Would make sense. We have kami for everything else. Kami for the sun, for war, for the wind. Tenjin is the kami of learning, but I feel like that's different. Curiosity is something else. More malicious.

The shrine charms my mom gave me make me wonder. Those little silk pouches that fit in the palm of your hand. They're sewn in bright colours: red, blue, sometimes gold. The important part is what's inside, though. Each charm contains a prayer, written on a folded piece of paper. Supposedly.

It's kind of hard to believe. You go to a shrine and they have bins filled with them. I used to help Dad count and tally them like merchandise.

"Even the holy has a profit margin, Soki," he once told me. This was back in Sapporo, before he stopped believing. I would have been a kid back then.

I remembered looking down at those bins, at the hundreds of identical charms inside. Our shrine was well known, so we'd get visitors from the rest of Japan, sometimes even Americans. Making all those charms ourselves would have been impossible. Ended up having to "outsource" them. They'd arrive in these massive plastic bags, which I'd help cut open over the summer. Once we'd counted and sorted them, we would arrange them in these woven baskets, so they'd look more authentic.

"Are there really prayers inside?" I asked during one sorting session. I didn't realize it at the time, but that would be my last year in Sapporo.

"What do you mean?" my dad replied, examining a charm before adding it to the discard pile. The charms we got in this shipment were cheaply made outside of Japan, and Dad insisted on throwing out any that had loose strings or uneven lettering.

I struggled for the right words to say, trying not to lose count of the charms I was helping to sort. The dyed silk was staining my fingers, and I was starting to get a rash.

"Do you think whoever makes them still puts prayers inside? Or are some of them empty?"

Dad frowned and moved a charm that I had placed in the wrong bin. Love where Luck should have been. I plucked a charm out of the Wealth pile and started pulling at the strings, curious. Dad slapped it out of my hands.

"Don't. It's bad luck," he said. "It's disrespectful to the kami, too." He went back to counting, a little quicker this time.

Dad told me it's arrogant to want to see the prayer. You're supposed to just trust that it's there. Undoing the strings releases those sacred words. The charms work better in an enclosed space; they're more powerful for being concealed. Like how shrines exist in their own enclosures, marked off by giant red torii gates.

The day after the gasoline incident, I told my mom what had happened. I said I was worried that the kami were punishing us for leaving Sapporo. Usually, Mom would just coddle me, tell me that it wasn't my fault, and that Dad was just being mean. But this time, she went silent. Ended up taking me back to the shrine.

Took us to the purifying water to cleanse ourselves before walking up the shrine stairs. Trip one thousand and one. When we got to the top, we both offered a five-yen coin. Rang the bell, bowed, clapped our hands, then prayed. Asked the kami for forgiveness.

Normally, I'd feel lighter after praying, but that day I kept feeling this weight deep inside. Like I was being pulled into the Earth. Maybe Dad was right. The kami had already left Sakita. It was too late. We had been pleading to no one.

When we got home, Mom gave me more charms than I'd asked for—for health, luck, and to ward off evil spirits. And just like at the shrine, I felt nothing. Those charms held nothing inside. The prayers had all escaped, flown out as we moved from city to city. Even worse, I recognized some of them as the same ones we'd imported back in Sapporo. Why would she hold on to these?

Carrying these cheap imitations tempted me. Mom knew just as well as Dad did that these charms weren't authentic. That we didn't actually make them at the shrine. But she still believed in them, still treated them with respect. How was she able to do that? Did she know something I didn't?

I decided then that I had to open one of these charms, see for myself whether there actually were prayers inside. Have so many of them, I figured I could spare a few. I wanted to choose an unimportant one to undo. If I was wrong and actually released a prayer, I would cause the least damage that way. Ended up choosing a charm for Love. Things hadn't worked out between Fumie and me, so it didn't do its job anyway.

Waited until dark to begin. Didn't want either of my parents to walk in and see me do this. Didn't want to upset my mom, or gratify my dad. I cleared my desk off so it was just me and the love charm. It seemed much smaller all alone like that. Like a cornered animal. It was pink, with gold characters embroidered down the middle. Cheap fibres, uneven print. A white knot was tied at the top, held in place by plastic beads. It wasn't the best quality, but I felt bad for what I was going to do. Still, I had no choice. I had to know for sure what was inside.

My fingers shook more than I thought they would, which made grabbing the string difficult. The knot seemed intricate, but with one tug it all came undone. I pulled the whole thread out, then looped it nicely and put it away. Still wanted to show some respect. Or maybe I was delaying the inevitable. I took a deep breath and opened the pouch up. Put my fingers inside—the back of the embroidery was rough, not meant to be touched. Felt something crinkle under my finger.

I pulled the prayer sheet out of its pouch, careful not to damage it. Realized then that what I had done was unforgivable. My heart wasn't heavy, though. Didn't feel a pit in my stomach or anything. Actually felt kind of light. Like I was hollow.

I unfolded the prayer and spread it across my desk. The paper was really thin, transparent even. Had all these tiny characters printed on it. I tried to read it but I couldn't. The prayer was long, and the kanji was too advanced for me to read. In a way that was worse. I would rather there be no prayer at all than one I couldn't understand.

I folded the paper up again and put it back into the pouch. Maybe it wasn't too late. Maybe I could still keep the prayer inside. I threaded the string through the top of the pouch and tried to re-tie it, copying the knot from another charm I had. But it didn't line up. The knot was too confusing, too intricate for trembling hands.

Why *was* there even a prayer in that charm? It didn't make sense for the factory that made these to go through the effort. The charm was basically just a souvenir, it didn't really have any powers. So why bother? Why go through all this trouble for something so meaningless, so untrue?

Felt my face go hot. I wondered what Anna would think of this. We hadn't spoken since the end of last year, but her words kept eating away at me. *Believing alone is worth something, right?* Whether the charm worked or not didn't really matter. What matters is for people like Mom to believe they do. For them to have something to hold on to.

Why was I looking for proof in the first place?

I wasn't sure what to do with my ruined charm. Maybe I should return it to a shrine and let them take care of it. Burn it in a holy fire. I was weighing my options when I saw a reflection in my window. Or a silhouette. Wasn't sure who it could be. I stepped closer, to see if they would move away, but the figure stood still. I got close enough to make out their features, and realized it wasn't a human, but a god. Or a painting of a god. Reminded me of those woodblock prints from the Edo period—totally flat colours, no perspective. Must be a reflection from somewhere, a trick of the light. I looked around my room to see where it was coming from.

I knew my dad had some prints hanging in his study, but he rolled them up a while ago. Said he was tired of seeing them. His biggest one was of Amaterasu. If anything, that's who this reflection resembled. Same black hair, same empty eyes. But that wouldn't make sense, for a reflection from his room to reach mine. I shifted my angle to see better, but then she was gone. Amaterasu shimmered and faded away. I moved back to my last position, but couldn't make her reappear.

Then, all of a sudden, I understood. Maybe that wasn't a reflection, maybe that was Amaterasu after all. She was forgiving me for opening the charm, for doubting Shinto's powers. Amaterasu was telling me that it was okay. I knew then why she hid in that cave, thousands of years ago. I understood why she needed to disappear.

A warm light washed over my room, moving faster than the birds could start chirping. The sun was coming over the horizon.

I must have been standing there for a while, in a trance. The clock by my bedside table had gone forward a few hours too. It was as though I had skipped over an entire night, like I had been pulled through time.

I kept feeling lighter, like my feet would lift off the ground. The water from the shrine hadn't purified me, but the sun had. Amaterasu did that for me. She opened the floodgates, released her light. Cleansed me of the evil spirits I had brought to Sakita. She had wanted to give me my first holy experience. Or maybe she was just asking me to believe.

SATELLITE

MORNING WAS BREAKING. MY happiest hours with Anna were now only moments away from an abrupt end. Of course, in the thick of it, I didn't have the slightest inkling of what was to come. Instead, we slowly made our way home from the drive-in, and each time Anna passed a stranger another convulsion of laughter would course through us. My face was still sore from smiling, long after I had come down from my high, and I now understood that there was a "good pain" that could be felt. All the while, Anna continued snickering silently, mumbling to herself.

"Tonight's the night, Leo," she said, unlocking the front door to her house. "We're finally going to get out of here." She was whispering, careful not to wake her grandfather.

"What do you mean?" I asked.

"I was afraid before—that's why I didn't act when I had the chance. But no longer. This was the perfect note to end on. You gave me the courage to leave."

I tried to say something in response, but she put a finger to her lips, and motioned for me to follow her upstairs to her room.

Her grandfather's shoes in the entrance to the house hadn't moved since the previous evening. A part of me wished someone would have noticed that Anna had been gone all night. We went up to the second floor.

Daylight had started spilling in through the ink-stained pages taped to the windows, giving her living space its familiar atmosphere of being inside a lantern. Tucked in the corner, untouched by this light, sat the mound. Anna approached her creation with the weight of ceremony, clearing the floor around it before pushing it slowly, painstakingly, towards me. My attempts to help were shooed away, so I opted to take a seat on her unmade futon instead.

She stepped into the centre of the room, baroque shadows dancing across her awkward form. The change in mood made my throat dry. I was finally going to find out what was under that tarp—it made no difference whether I was afraid.

"Okay, Leo. Take a guess. What do you think I've been working on?"

"I have no idea. A bomb?"

"No, I'm serious, no more jokes. What do you think this is?"

I thought for a moment, attempting in vain to get inside Anna's head. I had only been half-kidding about the bomb, and since she wasn't exactly artistic, I could rule out a sculpture.

"Oh! You're making a satellite!"

Her eyes lit up. "Close! Partial points! But not quite. I've been working on something much more impressive. I present to you—the *Tengu*!"

She threw the tarp towards me theatrically, obstructing my view before it crumpled to the ground, leaving a cloud of dust in its wake. Slowly, the twisted form of Anna's creation came into focus. I had no idea what I was looking at. It was an orgy of contorted metal, arbitrarily melded together, reaching out perversely in different directions.

Tubes of various sizes crawled through the main body like worms scouting out a piece of rot, and wedged into the centre of it all was a fridge, its door half-pried off. The materials were mismatched, looking like the product of a deteriorating mind.

"What is it supposed to be?"

She looked at me with unfocused eyes, as though she had been waiting her entire life for someone to ask her this question. "It's a ship, Leo. You and I are going to outer space."

"It's a spaceship?"

She nodded slowly without breaking eye contact. "This world is rotten, Leo. You and I need to escape."

I wasn't sure how seriously I was supposed to take her. There was no way this contraption would fly, and I was nervous about what would actually happen once it was activated.

"How does it work?" I asked.

She launched into a lengthy explanation, none of which made sense. It dawned on me that she didn't fully know what she was talking about either. She had cobbled together a few ideas she had about how rockets worked, and randomly attached to those what she could understand from her research. The haphazard way in which she had created her own school of rocket science mirrored the resulting creation perfectly.

". . . and once I manage to get all of the fuel in, I start the primary energy reserves, which transfers a signal to the gas tanks. This will begin the fuel-burning process. Three engines on the bottom will propel the body upwards, with you and me both inside the cockpit." She motioned towards the fridge. "It's not really spacious, but it'll have to do."

I walked around the *Tengu* a couple times and found the gas tanks she was speaking of. They were filled to the brim, and covered by an ill-fitting lid from which a long, thin wick emerged. A handheld lighter was fastened to the side of the metal drum.

"This is how you're going to ignite the engines?"

"It's a little makeshift, but it'll work."

I stepped back, feeling nauseous, as visions of Anna's demise filled my head.

She would ignite the fuse, fire catching on her sleeves from the gasoline that would inevitably spill out of the unsecured tanks. She would panic, attempt to fan the flames out, knocking the rest of the fuel canisters over, and become engulfed in liquid fire. After a brief struggle, maybe a short cry of surprise, she would feel the heat burn through her flesh, her tongue, her eyes, cutting off the brain's ability to communicate with the world. She would be cremated on the spot, all 163 centimetres of her reduced to a pile of ash.

Or Anna would drop the flame into the pool, immediately causing the gas tanks to explode. The shards would cut through her like putty, severing her spinal cord, paralyzing her. She would be frozen in place as the rest of the *Tengu* collapsed onto her frail body, or if she managed to crawl out of the fridge in time, she wouldn't be able to find help before the loss of blood killed her.

Or she'd manage to light the gasoline safely—in spite of the *Tengu*'s design—starting the engines one after another. All three would gradually overheat, not having proper ventilation, and would begin emitting a black smoke, thicker than death herself. People would watch curiously as Anna closed the door to her cockpit, maybe even move in to get a closer look. Then the rumbling engines would set off like firecrackers, one after the other, sending flames and shrapnel through the crowd. Anna would emerge safe, minutes later, wondering why she hadn't launched, only to find herself surrounded by bodies arbitrarily scattered about by her ambition.

Did Anna realize how fatal her ship was going to be? I strongly doubted it. There was still much I didn't know about my creator, but I knew she didn't have a death wish. To her, it was irrelevant that human bodies don't have heat-resistant gold plating, that they don't have Whipple shielding to protect them from flying debris. None of that mattered if the dream of space was even remotely within reach. Revulsion turned my stomach when I looked at her future coffin, a metal body unbefitting of her human form. I knew I had to stop her, but to argue with her directly would only push her farther away.

"This is what you've been secretly working on this whole time?"

She seemed puzzled, not understanding my desperate, incredulous tone. "What do you mean? I made it for you. We can go back to space, and you can return to your A-347 titanium alloy body."

"Anna, I looked that up. There's no such thing as a A-347 satellite! This is all just part of some fantasy."

"No, you don't get it, I researched and—"

"You don't know how anything like this works! None of what you've said makes any sense. You don't actually think that's going to fly, do you? It's built like a fucking rock!"

She winced at my use of profanity, and I realized I had never heard her curse. Where had my knowledge of that word come from? At the time, I was too worked up to care.

"Tell me you don't plan on activating this thing. Just seeing all that gasoline makes me nervous."

"Leo, I made this for you." Her eyes were beginning to fill with tears.

"I never asked you for a spaceship. Get rid of that thing. It's going to kill us both."

After a brief hesitation, Anna went to gather the tarp with trembling hands. She bunched it against herself, coating her clothes with dust, before attempting to throw it back over the ship, heaving her body to come up with enough force. The entire time she kept quiet, focusing on the task at hand, trying her hardest to avoid looking at me, trying not to cry.

What I should have realized is that there is a point where sadness becomes anger. No creature, no matter how strange or how small, allows itself to be backed into a corner indefinitely. Tears are ultimately a defensive mechanism, an attempt to elicit sympathy, and when this fails, aggression is the only answer. And still I wonder, had I just managed to keep calm for a moment longer, would Anna have been saved? Was there a secret combination of words, an algorithm I should have employed, that could have reached her?

"I'm not trying to attack you, I'm just worried about the safety of it all."

She finally managed to cover the *Tengu* and began tying the tarp in place.

"You're not mad, right?"

She rolled the *Tengu* away from the centre of the room.

"It's probably not that unsafe. We could work on it together, maybe even have a test flight?" I regretted going back on my word so quickly, disappointed in my lack of conviction.

Anna was pulling at the thick rope attached to the main body of the machine, wrestling with a creature three times her size. The wheels the *Tengu* were mounted on seemed to have difficulty supporting its weight. She must have planned out the mobility from the beginning, and built from the wheels up before the rest of the ship became too heavy to lift. I felt oddly proud of her for not forgetting the details.

She continued struggling with her ship, lips trembling from what I thought were tears. It was then that I realized, with a slow dread, that she was moving the *Tengu* towards the only exit from her room. I positioned myself to block the doorway.

She looked up, as though noticing me for the first time. "Move."

"Where are you going?"

"Move."

"Are you going to launch this?"

"Move."

"Let me come with you, we can go together."

We were like a pair of stubborn children, one of whom was in possession of a potentially fatal ninety-kilogram bomb.

"You were supposed to be my friend," Anna said softly.

"I am your friend."

"No, you're not. You don't trust me. I can tell." She was shouting now, trembling not out of sadness, but rage. "The Prince and Soki and The General and you. You're all garbage. Rotten rotten rotten."

"The Prince?"

"You only exist because of me. You should be grateful, but you're just like everyone else. I could make you disappear in a second if I wanted to. And if you don't move, I will."

"Anna, please." I was nearly begging now, pleading to the part of her that was long gone. "I changed my mind. Let's go together. We'll take another look at the *Tengu,* make sure everything works, and then—"

She abruptly pulled at the *Tengu,* cutting me off with a metallic clang.

"Leo, you're dead to me now," she said, in a tone numb from betrayal.

I felt a familiar lightness in my body, as though I were in danger of floating away. The brief moment of weightlessness as a plane leaves the ground. Colours were losing their intensity, moving into a wash of light blue. I heard cicadas chirping from somewhere far off, the radio static of my life. They sounded peaceful. Had a solar flare gone off somewhere? Beyond this, I don't know what happened to me.

"You don't exist anymore."

And just like that, I didn't.

GRANDFATHER

I WOKE UP EARLIER than usual today. The sun isn't fully up yet, so it must be five or six in the morning. My sleep was disturbed by the sound of someone yelling. A female voice, furious and raging at someone, or something. Even though the voice was coming from the top floor, I could hear her from where I was sleeping below.

I thought the shouting would last forever, before it suddenly went quiet. Who could that have been? I thought only Yoshiko and I lived here. There's that other girl as well, I suppose, but I can't remember how we're connected. It's embarrassing, so I don't want to ask. I haven't seen Yoshiko in a while, now that I think of it.

The shouting seems to have stopped, but then I hear a loud rumbling from upstairs. Yoshiko must be trying to rearrange her room. I'll tell her to give it a rest, I need to sleep. Someone as young as her would never understand.

I'm about to go upstairs when I find the stairway blocked by the most peculiar thing. There appears to be a giant machine of some sort wedged at the very top! It looks as though someone has taken a car and turned it inside out. I'm not sure what it is, or how it got here, but it seems familiar somehow.

"Grandpa, you shouldn't stand there. It's dangerous." There's someone speaking from behind this contraption, unable to get around it. And just like the metal behemoth above, I vaguely recognize the voice from somewhere. From a past life, perhaps.

"Yoshiko?" I ask.

"It's Anna! You really shouldn't be standing down there. Take this and move out of the way. I don't want the *Tengu* to crush you."

The girl sends a rope down the stairs, hurling it over the machine to reach me. She tells me she's trying to move this machine—the *Tengu*—to the main floor, and wants me to secure it against a banister first, thinking a pulley system will help ease it down. I tie the rope but feel skeptical: there's no way it could support that weight.

I let the girl know I've fastened the *Tengu* and move out of its path. A few seconds later, she lets it loose. Sure enough, the banister snaps, and the entire construction comes flying down. It leaves a large crack in the wall, kicking up drywall dust.

She lets out a yell and runs down the stairs, making sure the *Tengu* isn't broken. For the first time, I get a good look at her. I can tell she's been crying; her eyes are puffy and she keeps trying to avoid facing me. I'm not sure where I know this girl from, but it seems as though we've met before. Even still, I don't know her well enough to ask what she's upset about.

She decides that the *Tengu* is okay, and gets my help to wheel it out the door. It barely fits, and she has trouble moving it across our lawn. What a wonderful creation! I wonder if it's being used for a playground or a carnival of sorts. This young lady is quite a gifted artist. In the rising sun, the machine glows a comforting yellow. It is cool to the touch.

"Mom is going to come home tomorrow, so you'll be alone for today," she says. "I left some soup in the fridge if you get hungry before then, okay?"

She turns to leave, and I almost go back inside when I see her stop in her tracks, as if remembering something.

"You can have your prayer back, by the way," she says, voice cracking with tears.

"My prayer?" I'm embarrassed to admit that I have no recollection of what she's talking about.

"From New Year's. I don't have anything to ask for, so you can use it instead."

I'm about to ask where this young lady is off to, but she embraces me before I can get the words out. I'm not sure why she's hugging me, as we don't have a history together, but I return the gesture. In all my years on Earth, the one thing I've learned is that sometimes, people just need to be held.

She's squeezing me a little too tight, a little too long. She lets go, trying to stay calm as she speaks to me. "Stay safe, Grandpa."

That machine looks incredibly heavy, but Anna seems to be managing. She's pushing it along its wheels, all of her strength behind it. I admire her efforts. What a nice young girl. I wonder where she could be going.

ANNA

LEO WAS GONE AND I was alone. I had no choice. He got in my way, I had to remove him. Had to disappear his gawky body, his perpetually curious eyes. Those same eyes which once saw me, so long ago, from the dome of space. That night at Lucky Ginseng, The Prince had told me how it would take only "one lapse of memory" on my part for his entire life to disappear. I did the same to Leo, there was no other option. Forgetting was easy. Erasing him had been as simple as blowing a dandelion to the wind.

Dawn was here, and I had brought the *Tengu* outside. It had been almost twenty-four hours since I'd last slept, yet I felt no fatigue. I would move the *Tengu* to where it rightfully belonged, knowing I didn't have much time before people began to leave for work.

My initial plan had been to move the *Tengu* during the day, and launch it in the early evening when visibility was still good. After my clash with Leo, however, I realized that others might not be as supportive of my mission as I had thought, and might even attempt to stop me. I had imagined this moment as a victory lap, or part of the celebratory procession of a parade, but I now understood that I would have to act in secrecy.

I busied myself with hiding the *Tengu* in an attempt to forget Leo, the way he looked at me as he faded away. Every strain I put on my shoulders, every muscle I pulled when hauling The Machine, helped take my mind off him. My hands, stripped raw by the *Tengu*'s thick ropes, were no longer the same ones I had used to Morse, to hit, to push my only friends away. Whether this pain was the burden or the freedom I'd accrued from disappearing Leo, I couldn't tell.

I stashed my ship temporarily in the back alley behind a row of restaurants. The nearby dumpsters were all empty, so I could assume that the week's garbage had already been collected. The hiding spot was more or less safe; covered up, the *Tengu* appeared to be just more trash. And anyway, should someone attempt to steal the *Tengu*, its weight meant they wouldn't be able to get very far.

Leo's final expression shot through my mind once more, and I closed my eyes tightly to drive the image out. I could still feel the soft gasp he'd let out reverberating in the hollow inside my chest. His last moments weren't of agony, but of peace. Then why did they trouble me so? It hurt to remember how he'd lifted up off the ground, staring down at me with that mixture of pity and forgiveness before disappearing to wherever the imaginary goes. I didn't want to see another person look at me that way ever again. If all went according to plan, I wouldn't have to.

During the morning rush, I went inside one of the diners to kill time, only to find myself having to leave every few minutes to check on the *Tengu*. I could tell everyone inside the restaurant was aware I possessed something valuable. It was in the fleeting glances they cast towards me, the hushed conversations I couldn't quite make out. I had to keep reminding myself that it wouldn't be long before I could launch.

Where should I launch from? I pondered this question and stirred my hundred-yen coffee, careful not to make eye contact with anyone. All of the preparations for the ship were completed, but the actual details for liftoff were still hazy. I scribbled a couple of possible launch sites on the back of a napkin, which I quickly hid when the waitress came to give me a refill, obviously trying to catch a glimpse of my secrets as she did so. I strongly disliked the coffee; in fact, it was the first time I had ever ordered it. All I wanted was the caffeine. Meanwhile, everyone in the diner continued their charade of mindless chatter, poorly hiding the fact that they were plotting against me.

I had read about this phenomenon, this feeling of being watched, some time ago. The legend of the *mokumokuren*: the phantom with a thousand eyes. There are stories of people being driven mad in their own homes, after waking up in the middle of the night to find eyes peering at them from behind sliding doors, up through tatami mats, down through holes in the ceiling—eyes watching with an unflinching gaze. A *mokumokuren* would never harm those who returned their stare, but their presence alone could drive you to insanity. Those who dared look away would be found later, still alive, but blinded, both of their eyes poached by the apparition. I could only assume Sakita as a whole had been haunted by one.

For an hour or so, I tried avoiding the eyes of the saboteurs around me as best as I could, until the pressure became unbearable, forcing me to escape through a side door. I sat down beside the *Tengu* in the alleyway, resolving to stay by its side until it was dark enough for it to be properly concealed. The stench of drip coffee and nearby dumpsters threw off my perception, and I began to see mirages when I peered out at the streets. The bodies of passersby stretched and deformed, fusing with one another, revealing the horrors normally hidden by their human forms.

When did the weather turn like this? The piles of snow along the sidewalks were now melting and stained with mud. At some point, the sun had risen high above, beating down as if it were the peak of summer. The clouds had cleared out, stripping us of shade, and I wondered if this cruel light was, perhaps, Amaterasu's judgement. I shed my coat in response, still sweating, as the world boiled beneath my feet.

Though I was exhausted, I was too afraid to close my eyes for fear of falling asleep. Those who walked by could be scouting out the *Tengu*, trying to find a way to take it from me. The tapping of their footsteps were hidden Morse code messages, provoking me, attempting to lure me out. There must have been hundreds of them, maybe thousands, and I was increasingly fearful that they'd attack me all at once. I could fight off one, maybe two at most, but an entire army was out of the question. My throat was sandpaper dry, and I longed for a drink. Rather than coffee, I should have had water. Through the walls, I could still feel the eyes of the people inside the diner watching me.

I felt one gaze in particular bearing down on me, from farther up the street. Whoever it was, they were still too far away for me to see clearly, although I could make out their general form. It was a man, judging by the width of his shoulders, the gait of his walk. He walked towards me calmly, making no attempt to chase me down, trusting that if I ran he would catch me. And I was still so thirsty! I wondered how thick my blood would be from dehydration, how dark my urine. I swallowed my saliva in a doomed attempt at fooling my body. It occurred to me that this powerful figure might be the only person I actually needed to fear. In fact, it wouldn't be so far-fetched to imagine that all of the eyes I feared were acting as agents for him. He knew exactly where I was hiding, and was getting closer.

The only people who had seen the *Tengu* were my grandpa and the late Leo, which meant that whoever was pursuing me didn't know what the ship looked like. In stubbornly sitting next to the

Tengu like a malnourished guard dog, I was placing my own creation at risk. I struggled to my feet, head swimming from low circulation, and fled the scene. Once I had decided on a location to launch from, I could return and retrieve the ship closer to nightfall. For now, it was crucial to lead this figure as far away from the *Tengu* as possible. I craved a drink desperately, but was too aware of the risks of slowing down. Behind me, the man continued his steady, deliberate pursuit.

My steps were uneven, faltering from thirst, pained from a migraine. If I turned downtown, I could lose my pursuer somewhere in Sakita's urban maze. For the first time in my life, I thanked my city's developers for their relentless lack of foresight. I backtracked slightly to take the turn I needed, shortening the distance between us, and avoided looking in his direction. He was getting closer. I could feel it.

I was too distracted by panic to realize that I'd made a monumental mistake. I had to concede a point to him: what he had done was a stroke of genius. By herding me into the city, he had brought me into an entire swarm of people who were secretly working for him. Everywhere I turned, a thousand gazes met mine, robbing me of any privacy I had left. *Mokumokuren! Mokumokuren* everywhere! They wanted to know where the *Tengu* was, were planning to strip me of everything I held dear.

I pushed my way through the crowds, ignoring their feigned looks of indignation. As if they didn't know what they were doing. It was all I could do not to scream, knowing that I was being toyed with. A young couple asked if I was okay, attempting to trap me with pity. The moment I accepted their offer for help I would be doomed, and they would take the *Tengu* away. When pity failed, the group attempted to break me down with taunts instead, some kid yelling out "Schizo!" from a pack of friends. I passed a teenager who reminded me of Leo, the same naive compassion registering on his face. Perhaps I'd deserved to lose him, after all. The heat was unbearable and I longed for air, water, and space, please gods, give me space—space away from these people, space away from anyone who would sabotage me. I had created Leo to be different from the others, but in the end he had been just like the rest of them. Saw himself as a saviour when all I wanted was a friend.

I found myself on a street I wasn't familiar with—a literal dead end in an alleyway blocked off by construction, no doubt that man's doing. He was closing in on me, and at that point all I could do was defend myself. I searched through my backpack and closed a fist around my house keys, metal sticking out from between each knuckle. Hopefully, this would be enough to break through skin. The man was approaching, I had barely any time to prepare. I could hear his footsteps echoing. Coming closer, closer . . .

When he turned into the alley, I rushed him, landing a solid punch into his side. I felt the keys sink in smoothly, and pulled back. The metal had ripped through his dark-green canvas shirt and was now sticking out of his flesh. He looked down with confusion at his wound, then pulled each key out one by one, making no show of pain. Almost as an afterthought he held out his hand, offering my keys back to me, now streaked with blood. I was out of options, unsure what to do after my first blow had failed. I took the keys back without a word, and for the first time met the eyes of my pursuer.

I knew this man. I had seen him hundreds of times before in archived newspapers, history books, and magazine clippings. He was short, but carried himself with authority. It was The General. Only now, he was thirty-four years old, the age he'd been when he fought his last stand. He straightened his uniform, then spoke.

SATELLITE

. . .

ANNA

"WHY DID YOU PUNCH me?"

The General's face was younger, fresher than the one I was used to. Despite still being twice my age, he seemed like a child now. He was wearing army fatigues, crisply ironed as if brand new, and had slung his iconic rifle across his back. I noticed with slight discomfort that a few of his fingernails were all but gone, worn away by battle. A pool of black blood, to which he paid no attention, was spreading along his side, darkened by his camouflage uniform. He didn't seem to be in physical pain, just confused.

"Why were you following me?" I responded.

"Answer my question first."

"I punched you because I thought you were following me. Now tell me, what are you doing here?"

"I was out for a walk and thought I recognized you from somewhere."

I looked at him suspiciously. It was a pathetic excuse, but the way he spoke struck me as truthful. That was another odd thing: on top of appearing as young as he'd been during the sixties, he was now speaking and listening perfectly, and from the way his eyes moved, I assumed he was able to see as well.

"You don't remember me?" I asked.

"So we do know each other!"

"My name is Anna Obata, and you're The General."

"The General? I'm Takuya Aoyama."

Aoyama. Blue mountain.

I made note of this. Out of concern for his privacy, public reports had censored his full identity, and The General as an old man had never told me his family name.

"Yes, but I call you The General. Out of respect."

He paused, pulling up memories from his future, before he realized who he was speaking to. "You're the delusional girl. The one who visits me on Mondays! I wouldn't recognize you except by touch. Come here."

He reached for my hand, which I was too stunned to pull away, and took it in his. "They're just as small as I thought they were. Where did these calluses come from? Your skin used to be so soft."

"I've been working with my hands a lot recently."

"A girl your age should find a man to do that kind of work for her. No use straining yourself."

"Why are you younger?"

He looked up from examining my fingers one by one, fascinated by every mole and crease.

"What do you mean, 'younger'?" he asked, an honest confusion apparent on his face.

"Last time we met you were seventy-four years old, deaf, and blind. People don't typically age backwards, right?"

"I suppose not, but does it really matter?" he asked. "The whole world is going to chaos these days. *Even Hell itself is a dwelling place.* What's forty years between friends?"

I took my hand from his. It felt unnatural for us to use anything other than Morse code to communicate.

"What does your boyfriend think of these calluses?" he asked.

"Boyfriend?" I pretended not to know who he was talking about, trying to fool myself into forgetting who Leo was.

"He visited me once, pretending to be you back when I was still blind. I was nearly fooled at first, but when I held his hand I knew. He thought he got away with it, too!" He laughed. "I'm old, not senile."

"You could touch him?"

"Of course. Why? Does he not like being touched?"

A fresh wave of nausea hit me. The General had been able to interact with Leo in the real world. Or maybe where they'd met wasn't reality at all. It was a violation for The General to encounter one of my delusions—the two were never supposed to meet. The lines between worlds were blurring, as though someone had run their sleeve over it, smudging the ink. Who belonged where?

"What did you and Leo talk about?" I asked.

"Is that his name? He mostly kept his disguise up, asked questions about what you were like when we first met. He wanted to know you better. Forgive me if I'm overstepping, but I believe he loves you."

"Loved. And you're not overstepping."

"Did something happen to you two?"

I stepped back. "Just a disagreement, it's fine. We're better off apart."

I could smell the faint aroma of roasted sweet potatoes from afar. Someone must have been attempting a barbeque, and I imagined washing down that smoky flavour with cold barley tea. My throat ached from thirst, and to make matters worse, I was getting hungry as well. The sweet potatoes made me feel a homesickness I hadn't experienced in a long time.

"In all honesty," The General admitted, "I failed to realize Leo wasn't actually you until after he left. In the moment, I was too worked up to think clearly. It was only after he escaped that I put two and two together."

"Escaped?"

He started to say something, then drifted off. "Is someone roasting potatoes in the middle of the city?" he asked, appearing grateful for the distraction.

"It seems that way . . ."

"How bizarre. It reminds me of the Philippines; the village I hid near used to cook those constantly. It nearly drove me insane with hunger, and to tears more than once."

"You never told me that."

"It never came up."

He saw me eying the rifle on his back and smiled, then offered to let me hold it. After I declined, he sat down on his knees formally, legs folded underneath him, and removed the rifle from his shoulders. Like The General, it showed no signs of wear, which became even more apparent as he began to dismantle it methodically, cleaning every part with a cloth pulled from his back pocket.

"I never told you exactly how I was captured, did I?" The General looked down at the pieces that were once his rifle and continued. "When I was fighting those police in the mountains, every six hours, without fail, a woman would sing the national anthem for them."

"To signal them to change shifts?" I asked.

"I believe so. It was the harshest pain of my life, hearing that voice taunt me twice a day. Her voice was so charming, the first warmth I had felt in years. But it also had this edge. You're too young to understand, but there was a harshness to it that made it all the more appealing. I decided that, even if it would be the death of me, I wanted to see the woman behind that voice."

"And did you?"

Whenever The General spoke about lives gone by, a wistful, melancholic expression would usually fall upon him. This time, he remained sharp, staring me straight in the eyes as he finished his story.

"When I heard their squadron coming for me, after I ran out of bullets, I had the option of running. It wasn't much, but I knew the jungle much better than they did. I could escape if necessary. And yet, when the time came, my desire to meet that voice overpowered me. I figured I could fight my way out later, but first I had to meet her. Can you guess what she looked like?"

"Beautiful?"

The General gave a pitying smile, as though I had been the one subjected to his pain.

"On the contrary. After I was detained, I told my captors I would speak only to that woman. It took a while for them to understand who I was talking about; they told me there were no women among them. But when I began humming that national anthem, when I described her piercingly clear singing, they started to laugh. They explained that the voice I had heard twice a day wasn't even live. That every six hours a recording would play over the radio, a voice singing through the machine."

The General turned his gaze to the gun and began putting it back together. He had laid each part on the ground carefully, and was rebuilding it faster than he had taken it apart. Once completed, he propped the rifle against his shoulder and pointed it at me.

"I forgive you, you know," he said, staring at me through the scope of his unloaded weapon. "Of course, it doesn't fire anymore."

"You forgive me?"

"For when you destroyed my home. You're young and confused. I did much worse at your age. I even enlisted in the army to get it all out."

"I thought you said you were fourteen when you enlisted."

"Those are just details, Anna. My forgiveness comes with a condition, however."

"What would that be?" Even knowing that his gun was barely more than a prop, being at the barrel end of it made me nervous.

"Come back to the real world. You've been playing make-believe for too long, and soon you won't be able to return. *The blind man does not fear the snake.*"

He pulled the trigger, my heartbeat quickening as I heard the click, despite having seen that the gun was empty moments earlier. And with that sound, the implications of what he was saying became clear. I had been called delusional by The General, by Takuya Aoyama, a soldier whose actual status as a soldier was shaky at best. Here was a man who didn't exist in any military records, who had been too young to actually fight in the war, who wasn't even Japanese. Up until that point, I believed that he and I existed in a state of mutual misunderstanding, trusting that neither would question the other too far. By asking me to "join the real world," he had broken this sacred trust.

"What squadron did you belong to?"

"Unit 24 based out of Okinawa; I was a captain under General Oogumi," he recited. "I was never a General—you're the one who began calling me that."

"What was your mission?"

"I was part of a classified guerrilla combat squad, tasked with maintaining choke points vital to Japan's defense of her peoples."

"A choke point in rural Philippines?"

"It offered a tactical advantage. You wouldn't understand on account of your inexperience, but—"

"There's no record of you anywhere. General Oogumi doesn't exist, neither did Unit 24."

"We were classified, so of course there's no record of us anywhere."

"Don't you ever call me delusional again. You screamed for Valhalla even though that was the first battle you fought, wasn't it?"

He stood up, leaving his rifle on the ground.

"I haven't thought about Valhalla in a very long time."

"That's because you don't deserve it. You were never a warrior."

The General glanced at the rifle by his feet, savouring the perfect words he had on the tip of his tongue.

"I envy you. I never made it to Valhalla, but you will," he said, his tone ceremonial and befitting a man of honour.

"I will?"

He nodded, and for the first time, I caught a glimpse of the force of nature he had once been. Standing before me, finally, was The General I had always imagined, capable of holding out in a standoff for days on end, too preoccupied with glory to fear dying in battle, eagerly anticipating his own death. Here was The General who believed in the purity of ideals, unafraid to sacrifice his own body for an abstract thought, whether it be duty, love, or obsession.

When he spoke, it was as though he had purified me, cleansed me of the blood spilled between us. The anger I had felt moments earlier had washed away, as smooth and clear as water, and was replaced with a profound sense of duty. I suppose if I were to attribute a single word to this sensation, it would have to be *epiphany*. The General was giving me my final mission; all that was left for me to do was obey.

"I can smell the death on you. Your time is coming. The next time we meet will be in the hall of Valhalla. Maybe your imaginary boyfriend will join us, too."

As he spoke these final words, he began to lift off the ground, gently, just as Leo had. He was beginning to fade, but rather than a look of pity, the final expression he shared with me was one of trust. It took less than a minute for The General to fully disappear, entering that hollow space inside me where Leo and The Prince now lived. Left behind in his place was a blue hitodama, slowly floating higher and higher until I could see it no more.

I found myself suddenly, painfully, alone. Leo, The General, and The Prince had all succeeded in abandoning this rotten world. Only I had failed to escape. My only hope was to be reunited with them up in space.

The *Tengu* was waiting for me, its lights pulsing with promise—an offer of safety, an offer of fate. As I walked back towards it, I could feel my face was wet with tears. I quietly said my goodbyes to this world, a psalm lost in a sea of noise.

SATELLITE

ANNA WAS GONE AND I was alone.

I didn't know how long I'd been missing from the world. I only knew that I had passed over a threshold into another reality, a holding room of sorts. I will never know death the way actual people—people such as Anna or Soki—will. All that I will know is this other place, a world held in radio static, where imaginary people such as myself wait. It reminded me of my time in space before Anna called me down to Earth. All that I could do was think.

I wondered what would have happened had I recited *Namu Amida Butsu* before Anna cast me off, as the Prince in my dream had done before his death. During my time in Anna's purgatory, all I could think about was The Prince, my sole stake in individuality. It was a mark of autonomy, something that separated me from her. As long as I could be sure The Prince was my creation and not Anna's, I could maintain my free will. If only I had thought to recite *Namu Amida Butsu* before death.

Then, as suddenly as I had entered this hazy realm, I was pulled out. I found myself in Anna's room, with not even The Prince to keep me company. The same quality of light I had seen that morning was filtering through the papered windows, this time not from sunrise, but sunset. I was at peace, but more than anything, I was grateful to be back in this imperfect world. I didn't know why Anna had brought me back, or if she was even aware she had, but none of that mattered now. I had returned.

This feeling of calm lasted only a few minutes before I realized that both Anna and the *Tengu* were gone. There was only an outline on the ground where dust had settled. I wasn't sure how much time I had before she launched, but my continued existence told me that Anna hadn't blown herself up—yet. With her actual passing would come mine. If I could find her before she detonated her ship, I could prevent her death, the deaths of anyone in her proximity, and, more selfishly, my own as well. And yet I could think of no suitable place to launch from, nowhere close enough for her to move the immense *Tengu* to, with enough open space to properly prepare for lift off. Why hadn't I thought to ask where she was bringing The Machine? I began rummaging through her room for any sort of clue to her whereabouts.

To create something of this scale, Anna would have needed a plan, a guideline to follow. A survey of the papers covering the windows yielded no results, nor did the unmarred books on rocket science. It wasn't until I thought to dig through her personal belongings that I managed to make progress. Shoved atop one of her dressers I found a stack of notebooks, water-stained pages warping the spines. While the outside covers had school subjects written on them—Arithmetic, History, and Science—a quick look between the covers revealed them to be something else. They were the workbooks in which she had tracked her progress on the *Tengu*. Anna may have been skipping school for the most part, but the few days she was compelled to attend, she would continue to work away at her designs, undetected by her peers.

While the log read straightforwardly at first, containing only technical notes for the structure of the ship, the further I went the more unpredictable, more frantic, her entries became. Details about her personal life began to seep through, musings about what she felt the rocket represented, what she was accomplishing. Her handwriting slowly warped into an illegible scrawl, spilling over the margins, as though every word was being chased off the page.

I had failed to realize, maybe even refused to realize, the full extent of Anna's deterioration. As if in penance, I began going through those notebooks, reading the cries for help she had written right under my nose. Eventually, it became clear that Anna had no idea where she was going to launch from either. How was I supposed to find out where she was headed if she didn't know herself? Still, I was convinced the answer was hidden in those workbooks, even if only in subconscious hints. I just had to look.

There was one entry in particular which struck me. It was from the day she'd sent me on my mission to visit the General, then waited for me at Lucky Ginseng, smelling strongly of gasoline. Until this morning, the only time Anna and I had been separated was on that day, when I can only assume that she had been gathering fuel for her machine. It was logical for her to have scouted a location at the same time.

The entry was long and rambling, starting with a string of dubious equations to calculate fuel use, before continuing as follows:

> Went to Fumie's home to steal gasoline today, and met Leo at Lucky Ginseng after. Surprised it was only ten minutes away. Now, the Tengu has all the fuel it needs. Fumie, that kitsune, was the last suitable target I had. You steal from, you get stolen from. It's

only fair, and judging by the home Fumie lives in, it doesn't look like she's ever lost anything in life. She's walking-distance to a pool, which must be how she keeps her tan.

6 degrees Celsius. Overcast Weather. Threats of snow.

I recognized Fumie as the name of the girl Soki had been with at Tonuki Café, and was suddenly faced with the question of how deeply I understood my own creator. Was Anna aware she had built a bomb, even if only vaguely? Was she aiming to kill herself? Even worse, was she planning on taking someone else's life as well? The Anna I knew would never commit such an act, yet after reading that passage, I couldn't help but worry that she was aiming her launch directly at Fumie. Imagine my horror when I turned the page and found Fumie's lipstick-stained napkin stapled to the back.

I quickly compiled a list of locations with possible significance for Anna, but only managed to come up with a few. Her orbit was much less predictable than those of other humans. The first place I wrote down was Tonuki Café; while it was far for her to move the *Tengu*, I imagined that with an entire day she might have managed it. If she was looking for a symbolic revenge against Fumie, the café would make the most sense.

The second location on my list was Fumie's home. I had no idea of its actual whereabouts—and without her full name I couldn't look up her address—but I knew from Anna's workbook that it was nearby. I checked the phone book that Anna had been using to prop up a desk to search for any pools in Sakita and found one that was close by. Wherever Fumie lived was ten minutes away from Anna's house and near a pool, so if I were to comb that area, finding a sixteen-year-old girl with a 2.2-metre-tall bomb should be manageable.

I had no idea how much time I had left, but all I could hope for was that Anna would wait until nightfall to launch. Tonuki Café or the pool: I only had enough time to check one of the two. I decided on the pool. As I ran out the door, a memory from days gone by passed through me. A conversation I once had with Anna.

"Did you know," Anna had asked, "that most ghosts are women?"

Where and when did this conversation happen? I couldn't remember. It came to me as fragments from a dream, two voices hovering somewhere inside my consciousness. I chose to remember it as taking place in outer space, to make it easier to picture. Anna and me, floating above the Earth, orbiting each other. They say that space smells like hot metal, but all I could smell was her strawberry shampoo.

"What do you mean?" I asked. "Do women die more than men or something?"

"No. At least, I don't think so," she said. "I guess you don't know how ghosts are made, then."

"Enlighten me."

"When people die, usually they just move on to the afterlife. Only those who have suffered or hold grudges turn into ghosts."

"And women suffer more than men?" It felt nice to be weightless again. I swam around Anna a few times for good measure. I wasn't wearing any metal plating, yet even in my human skin I felt safe. Somehow, space debris and solar flares couldn't hurt me here.

"I would say so. We don't forgive as easily either," she said.

"I'm surprised you know so much about what happens after death."

Anna moved her gaze from me to the Earth. "It's pretty obvious. The answers are all there, you just need to look hard enough."

"Do you think you'll become a ghost when you die?"

She looked back to me. "I've been unhappy enough, so it would make sense for me to become one. I won't, though."

"Why not?" I asked.

"I found pictures of these ghosts in my books. They usually have long black hair, high cheekbones, beckoning hands . . ."

"And?"

"They're gorgeous. I'm not pretty enough to be a ghost."

*   *   *

When I reached the public pool, it was already dark. No one was out at that hour, and there were no signs of Anna or her machine, either. I searched for her everywhere, shouting her name as I struggled to make sense of Sakita's streets. The pool was surrounded by thick tangles of suburbia in every direction, a much larger area than I had planned on searching. The hopelessness of my efforts dawned on me. It would be impossible to find Anna in this neighbourhood, and if she was at Tonuki Café, it was far too late.

I sat down by the edge of the road, determined to meet my end gracefully. I had no idea when my death would come. Up until that moment, I had only thought of my passing in abstract terms; now, I contemplated whether it meant returning to that unnerving empty realm. As I waited for my second passing, a Shiba, chubby from love, waddled up to me. I stroked her head and wondered how Anna was feeling. I would never get the chance to say goodbye to her, my flawed creator, to whom I owed everything.

The Shiba tried to jump up on me, perhaps wanting to play a game. Maybe in my next life I would be a dog and not a satellite. At least then I could interact with the real world; be more concerned with trips to the vet than micrometeoroids. The novelty of that image brought a smile to my face as the Shiba turned over onto her back, demanding belly rubs. Her fur was soft, unlike any sensation I had felt before. Perhaps I could spend my last hours on Earth counting every hair on her body. I understood now why so many people kept dogs as pets—unconditional love must be difficult to go without. She snorted lightly in response to my touch, just as I realized what that meant.

The dog was able to see me, and more than that, was able to interact with me physically. I kept stroking the Shiba's stomach, stunned, afraid that if I stopped I would break the spell. First The General had been able to communicate with me, and now this Shiba could as well. I was slowly entering the real world, independent of Anna. I was tempted to provoke the dog into biting me, to see if I could be hurt by the real world as well, but decided against it. I already knew I could.

I consulted Anna's notebook again, scouring it with renewed interest. The Shiba looked on disappointedly as I freed my hand from her belly to go through the pages, flipping desperately to find one of her final entries.

> Went to Fumie's home to steal gasoline today, and met Leo at Lucky Ginseng after. Surprised it was only ten minutes away.

I had misunderstood the passage. I had thought that Fumie's house was ten minutes away from where Anna lived, but reading the entry again, I realized that it was Lucky Ginseng that was ten minutes away from Fumie.

Lucky Ginseng was the ideal launch site: near enough to travel to by foot, with a parking lot that would be spacious enough to fly from. More than anything, it had a full view of the satellites she saw at night—a clear shot at her objective.

I left for Lucky Ginseng, sure that Anna would be there. The Shiba followed me, nipping at my ankles, before eventually howling and giving up in protest. Her plaintive cries echoed through the neighbourhood, a reminder of what it meant to live on this Earth.

ANNA

FROM WHERE I SAT, waiting to launch, the *Tengu*'s form was silhouetted delicately against the night sky. There was a rhythm to its grotesque form, a certain beauty in its deformities which, when projected against space, was breathtaking. I noticed that there were more satellites than usual flying above that night, making it the ideal time to join them.

I had decided to launch the *Tengu* at exactly midnight. There was no specific reason for this, it was just the romantic within telling me what to do. I checked my wristwatch. It was 11:33 p.m. I would leave this world in less than half an hour.

I went over the *Tengu* one last time, made obsessive by my impatience to launch. The string lights I had threaded across the outer shell, combined with the light from Lucky Ginseng's neon signs, provided a soft fluorescent glow for my inspection. After finding nothing out of place, I entered the cockpit, shutting the door tightly behind me. Inside, it was pitch-black and difficult to breathe, but the few holes I had cut into the vacuum sealing around the fridge door made it manageable. The slight claustrophobia only excited me more, reminding me of the greatness of what was to come. It took a few pushes to get the door to open back up, and I welcomed the clear air from outside.

It was now 11:42 p.m.

A goodbye cut short is much better than one dragged out, I firmly believe this. So what was I supposed to do with my remaining eighteen minutes on Earth? I had to fight off the sadness that could jeopardize the entire mission. There was nothing left for me on this planet; moving on to greater heights was the next logical step. For the final time, I regarded Sakita's skyline, the full moon silhouetting its jagged spires. The city was as ugly as ever. I was starting to cry again, and turned away to hide my tears—but from who? How pathetic it was to miss a city more than its people.

11:47 p.m.

I knew that if I were to walk a little farther from Lucky Ginseng I would end up in Fumie's neighbourhood. This was the most important part of the plan: I had agonized over whether the explosion from the *Tengu* could be seen and heard from her home. Her luring Soki from me was the last time I'd ever let the cruel and the mundane take what was rightfully mine. Would she eventually tell Soki of this, too? That she had seen the night sky light up, as though the sun had suddenly chosen to rise? And would Soki know to feel awe, rather than fear? Despite how things ended between us, I had confidence that he, of all people, would understand the significance of my act.

What a shame it was to go on this journey alone. Even with the stress of preparing to launch, I still felt a twinge of loneliness. I had built this ship for two, but Soki and Leo had chosen to stay behind. I hadn't planned for a solo escape. Of course, none of this would matter much, as I would soon be gone, far into space, away from this rotten world.

11:55 p.m.

I could hear someone running towards my location, feet bouncing off the pavement at a wild pace. I was worried that if they got too close, they might be injured by the explosion of takeoff. Their footsteps echoed sharply through the midnight air, sounding familiar, as though coming from a dream. Or was I the dream and those footsteps reality? I was curious about who they belonged to, but I was running out of time. Two minutes to launch. I began to prepare the *Tengu*.

SATELLITE

ANNA ONCE TOLD ME that when people go through periods of extreme crisis, time slows down. The world comes to a halt, as though everything revolves around that very instant. In the midst of an emergency, the brain stores all the details that would normally be forgotten, and in retrospect, the sheer amount of information retained throws the entire event into slow motion. A simple, yet potent, quirk of the human brain. A quirk painfully absent as I locked my sights on Anna, too far for me to reach.

The sight of Anna crawling into her ship, then, occurred in double-time, confirming that I was not yet human. Someone had set the metronome to a tempo I couldn't keep up with, my footsteps struggling to stay on beat. By the time I reached the *Tengu*, she was already locked inside, fighting for air in her refrigerator cockpit. I'd been 17.5 metres too far, 4.3 seconds too late. The air outside of her makeshift rocket was freezing, and I was surprised to see clouds of my breath come out in sudden, harsh bursts. I was becoming more and more a part of reality. The Christmas lights she had strung around the ship cast my shadow in blues and reds, a shadow that had not been there that morning.

Thankfully, in Anna's haste, she had entered her chamber prematurely and neglected to light the fuse, leaving the *Tengu* lifeless. I stood outside the refrigerator door, pressing my forehead against its cool stainless-steel shell and catching my misted breath. The feeling of the metal against my sticky human skin made me nostalgic somehow. Like I was going home. I could hear Anna muttering to herself inside.

"Can you breathe in there?" I asked.

"I can, don't worry." Her tone sounded uneasy, as though she were trying to discern any ulterior motives on my part.

"You're not cold, right?"

"I'm wearing a spacesuit. If anything, I'm a little hot."

"Too hot?"

"No, not really."

I tried opening the door and only succeeded in opening it an inch. Whatever was holding it in place was secure, though I still gave it a few more violent pulls. My hands began to pass through the handles, my body not quite able to decide whether it existed or not. In a couple of instances I was sent flying backwards, suddenly finding I had nothing to hold on to. I gave up only when I saw that I was shaking the entire machine. It might all topple over, Anna included.

"I locked it from the inside. I don't want the door to blast open when I take off." Her voice was muffled, and I could tell she was struggling for air. I held the fridge open as far as I could to let more air in, not sure if I was making any difference.

"Anna, come out. Let's talk this over."

"Talk what over? I've already decided. I'm leaving."

"Your ship isn't going to work. You're going to kill yourself."

She held on to her silence for a moment. "Please don't fight with me, Leo. Don't let that be the last thing we do. I'm not going to come out."

"Okay, what do you want to talk about? Just speak to me."

"You don't have to speak. I'm happy just knowing you're here."

So we didn't. We didn't talk. I wouldn't have known what else to say. At the very least, her soft breathing told me she was alive. When I look back on my time with Anna, I realize now that our relationship was one of silence. Our conversations were punctuated with it, both of us content with just being side by side.

I kept holding the door open until my hands passed through the handles once more. My body was flickering in and out of existence. Anna was trying to forget me, but couldn't do it. I could feel our collective memories seeping in and out of me, my creator wanting to hold on as much as she wanted to let go.

We were at an impasse. Anna could only activate the *Tengu* by getting me to light the gasoline reservoirs, which I would refuse to do. She could only launch if I left, and I would only leave if she wouldn't launch. We were locked into orbit, with neither gravity nor weightlessness strong enough to make a final decisive pull.

There was no way to remove her from The Machine, so I had to come up with a compromise. Anna was running low on air— the less time she spent inside her cockpit the better. I devised a plan stemming from my newfound ability to interact with the real world. Up until that day, I'd been completely ethereal, passing through whatever I touched. In the last hour, however, I had managed to pet a portly Shiba, see my own breath, and watch my shadow dance across the ground.

If I joined Anna in the cockpit, I could remove the lock and then, moments before the *Tengu* detonated, throw her out of the ship. The key was to act at the last possible moment, to ensure the *Tengu* would be destroyed without any chance of relaunch. Should I throw Anna out before she lit the fuse, she could simply make me disappear before trying again. The problem was that I had no way of knowing how tangible I had become, or if I was still transitioning between realities. My odds were fifty-fifty. I prayed that when the time came, I would be able to grab on to Anna and not phase through her instead.

"Anna, how many satellites are out tonight?"

"Thousands, millions. It's a shame you can't see them. You must be nearsighted."

"Tell me about them."

"They're calling for us, telling us to come and join them. Up there, everyone is kind, people are friends. Don't you remember any of this?" Her voice was growing softer.

"And how are you going to meet all of these satellites? Don't you want someone to introduce you to them?"

"That would be ideal, but I have no choice. You didn't want to come."

"If you open the cockpit, I'll join you."

"You promise?"

"Of course."

The door to Anna's ship opened soundlessly, and I thought how odd it was to enter my own casket. The Christmas lights, mixed with Lucky Ginseng's fluorescent glow, bathed Anna in an artificial lustre. She was wearing a makeshift spacesuit, its construction as dubious as the ship itself—a mismatch of reflective materials sewn into a poorly fitted costume. Light played off her, reflecting erratically, giving her a holy aura.

"Come in," she whispered.

The cockpit was surprisingly small, although I managed to fight off the claustrophobia by reminding myself it was Anna I was pushed up against. Our faces were touching, noses overlapping on each side. When she spoke, I could feel her lips brush mine, every breath sending heat down my neck, every blink tickling my eyelashes.

"Should I light the *Tengu*?" I asked.

"No, it's my responsibility. I'm going to open the door, light the gas reservoirs, then quickly shut us in, okay? If I time it right, we'll be able to secure ourselves before launch." She spoke firmly. I was amazed by how little fear her voice betrayed. Unlike her, I wasn't prepared.

"Just give me a moment. Please, just one more moment."

She waited as I ran through a list of things to say goodbye to: katsu curry, rickety trains, drive-in movie theatres. The smell of incense, of gasoline, of perfume. The feeling of asphalt under my feet, of snow on my face, of Anna's hand in mine. There wasn't enough time. Even with thousands of devotions, I would never run out of final goodbyes.

I wasn't sure what would happen if I failed, or even if I would fail. I needed to act with complete clarity of mind. My first mission was to save Anna; my nerves could kill us both. The faster I acted, the greater my chances of saving myself as well. Now wasn't the time to worry about the metaphysics of death, or where my soul might be heading. All I needed to do was stop being afraid.

"I'm ready," I said, trying to imitate her confidence.

Anna leaned out and reached for the lighter, unstrapping it from the side of a fuel tank. It was slightly more than an arm's length from the cockpit, and she had to stretch her whole body out the door to reach it. Almost as an afterthought, I recited *Namu Amida Butsu* to myself, as The Prince had. Anna heard this and turned back to me, delaying our launch just a moment more.

"What was that?"

"*Namu Amida Butsu*? It's a prayer."

"A prayer?"

"You say it to protect yourself."

"Huh." She looked at me quizzically, turning her head slightly to one side. "I've never heard that one before."

She'd never heard that prayer before? What did that mean? The implications were profound, but I had no time to consider them. Anna flicked on her lighter, pulling the fuse close with her other hand. She held the two together, as though offering a prayer to some obscure god. We had passed the point of no return; there was nothing I could say now to prevent the launch. The flame caught the end of the wick, moving upwards and into the tanks, erupting into blue rings atop the pools of fuel. She shut the door, but hadn't yet locked it. It was the exact moment I needed to act. If I threw her out now, the *Tengu* would be destroyed, and the two of us saved. I moved quickly to push her from the ship before she trapped us both.

My hands passed through her. I had lost my physical form, had ceased to exist. She never even noticed what I had failed to do as she closed the latch with an audible click. We were locked in, waiting for her machine to activate. My biggest regret is that I never thought to take one last look at the world.

On January 31, a half hour past midnight, the *Tengu* detonated.

GRANDFATHER

I HAVE AN AWFUL feeling about tonight. Something in the sky bodes badly for the future. Still, the air is refreshing, though I'm not sure where I am walking. I seem to be in a suburb of some sort.

I must have gotten confused. I have moments like this sometimes, episodes where everything seems unknown and I forget where I am, who my daughter is, who my granddaughter is. It takes a while, but eventually these memories come back to me. I suppose the only issue is that these periods of confusion have been lasting longer and longer lately. I'm concerned that lucid is no longer my usual state.

Oh well, I'll just have to wander around until I find my way home. It's almost midnight; a beautiful full moon is floating in the sky. There's a statue of Jizo by the side of the road. How lovely. Whoever stacked the stones here was really committed—it's more of a mountain than a pile. It goes all the way up to my waist! Surely the child spirit these stones belong to will have no trouble moving on to the next world. I bow my head briefly, happy for their luck.

The sky is so vast tonight, it feels as though it could swallow up this entire world. I miss the stars from my childhood, the time before light pollution washed out the heavens. I once heard that it takes so long for starlight to reach our insignificant planet from space that some of the stars we see now already perished millennia ago. What glitters above us instead are echoes of an older universe, a time when the humans craning their necks upwards regarded what they saw as gifts from the gods, and not as explainable scientific phenomena.

Looking up now, I can count only a handful of stars, maybe twenty at most. I wonder which among them still exist.

Ah, this night sky brings back memories of stargazing with Yoshiko. Or was it Anna? I can't recall now who I spent those nights with, whether it was my daughter or granddaughter who I had raised through a telescope lens. In either case, I always felt a profound sense of pity whenever I looked upon her young face, thinking of that casually cruel world about to open up to her. For her to live a full life with no regrets, that was all I desired. I was already a full-grown man by the time humans landed on the moon, and I wish my life had taken a path that would have let me make discoveries of my own. I suppose I didn't want that child to feel the same regret.

Anna must still be at home! I've gone wandering about late at night and left her alone at the house. How irresponsible of me. I should get back to her, it's half-past midnight.

Suddenly, I hear a great roar coming from the depths of the Earth. It's accompanied by a bright flash, illuminating the entire neighbourhood for a half second. The ground shakes. A gas pipe must have exploded, or maybe even a bomb. Whatever caused that eruption was big, and I don't want to be caught up in it. I need to get home as soon as possible.

Already I can hear sirens. I'm about to turn around when something unusual happens. I see a blue orb of light appear above where the disturbance was. It is floating in the air, as though suspended by a string hung from space. The ball is splendid, luminous, bathing everything in an azure calm. In all my years on Earth I have never seen such a thing. I feel a profound tranquility rush through me, grateful to have witnessed such beauty.

If only Anna was here to see this.

SOKI

THERE'S ONLY TWENTY-THREE PEOPLE in my class now. We started off the year with twenty-five. Then Anna got caught in that explosion, and Fumie moved to another school. So now we're twenty-three.

There are funeral flowers on Anna's desk, which strikes me as strange. She's not dead, just sleeping. When I mention this to Ms. Tanaka, though, she just gets upset. Tells me I'm being insensitive. But it's everyone else who's being insensitive. It's not like Anna is gone, she'll be back. You can't sleep without waking up, right? Even if it takes months more than it already has, she'll wake up.

Fumie is gone too. She said her mom was worried for their safety. Apparently, Anna detonated her machine near their neighbourhood. The explosion woke the entire family up, and for a couple seconds, the night sky went blue. Don't know if they moved homes, too, or just schools. Maybe they aren't even in Sakita anymore. Either way, I think they overreacted. Anna isn't dangerous. Still, if they're afraid then that means they have faith Anna will wake up. If she slept forever there'd be nothing to fear. That's not too bad, then. Knowing I'm not the only one who thinks she'll get better is reassuring.

Never knew Anna well. Talked to her a few times towards the end of last year. Felt like I understood her, somehow. Or really, that she understood me. She's the only person our age who took the kami seriously. Who didn't think it was weird for me to believe. We didn't speak much, since she barely came to school, but maybe we could have been friends.

They say Anna's lucky to be alive. That she should have died in the explosion. She survived because she locked herself in a fridge. The impact broke a couple of her bones, blasted the door off. Even still, the flames that came through the opening should have killed her. Whole thing's a mystery.

Police said it looked like there was somebody else in the fridge, shielding her. There were bruises on her arms shaped like hand prints. The thing is, they didn't find anyone else there. Some people say it was a ghost, but I don't think that's true. Still, I avoid the place where the accident occurred.

Everyone's acting surprised that Anna did something like that, as though she had been the outgoing star student before. Mina even pretends to be grieving, and gets lots of sympathy from the teachers whenever she says they were childhood friends. Makes me sick. Maybe if Anna had someone to talk to, this wouldn't have happened.

No one knows what she was trying to achieve, or what that bizarre machine was for. At one point, the police came to school and asked us a bunch of questions. None of us could give any answers. The only person who might know is Leo.

That's the biggest mystery. Who is Leo? When they found Anna, body smouldering, her brain was already bleeding, but she hadn't slipped into a full coma yet. She didn't realize how injured she was, just kept asking where Leo had gone. Kept saying she couldn't see him anymore. She was also mumbling about Valhalla and outer space, but mostly she was worried about Leo. They launched a manhunt for him, but nothing ever turned up. It was like he disappeared into thin air.

I visit Anna a lot. I'm the only one from our class who does. Used to be every weekend, but now it's every couple of days, for an hour or so after school. Maybe I feel bad for never really making the effort to get to know her. Nurses always give me pitying looks. Must think I'm Anna's boyfriend or something.

To be honest, visiting her is the highlight of my day. First I went out of guilt, but now I look forward to seeing her. I'm not sure if me being there will help her recover, but I go all the same. One day, she'll open her eyes again, and I want to make sure I'm there when she does. It'd be too cruel for her to wake up to an empty room.

The right side of her face was burned pretty severely. The doctors say it won't heal fully. Looks painful to touch. But even with those scars, she looks at peace. Makes me wonder how she felt when those flames caught up to her. Makes me wonder if she was ever afraid.

Mom once told me that there's different kinds of fire. There's unclean fire and purifying fire. Some Shintoists even burn paper dolls of themselves for spiritual cleansing. The paper doll absorbs all of a person's impurities, and is used as a sacrifice. Hope the fire that burned Anna was purifying. Hope it burned whatever hurt her right into ash.

The nurses say that me staying by Anna's side will help with her recovery. Don't know if that's true. Feels like they're just trying to comfort me. One even said that when someone's in a coma, it's a good thing to speak to them. You never know what they're able to hear. The problem is, I'm not good at talking. I thought I could just sit there in silence.

So, I asked my dad to teach me a prayer. That way when I visit Anna I can have something to say. He was reluctant at first, and told me I should go to a real priest for answers, but when I told him who it was for, he said he'd consider it. Then the next morning, as I was leaving for school, he handed me something. The words to a prayer. I recognized the rice paper he'd written it on. It was the same paper he hid deep inside his desk.

I was surprised he still remembered those devotions, and in a way I was relieved. Guess those prayers will always be a part of him. They don't just disappear. Even if you intentionally let them go, they never fully escape. Hard to let go of what you used to believe.

The prayer he taught me is called the *daijinju.* No one knows the exact meaning and origin of this prayer—not even the priests can accurately translate all the ancient words. But my dad told me that's not important. The words are just a device. If you recite them with a sincere heart and a pure mind, the prayer has power. It lets you create a connection to the kami. And if you repeat the prayer one million times, it gains extra power.

Now, whenever I visit Anna, I recite those words. I make sure to purify myself first, although usually just with tap water. Then, I sit by the foot of her bed, close my eyes, and recite the *daijinju.* It's tough, keeping the words straight, since they barely sound like Japanese. That shouldn't matter, though. If I say them with pure intentions it works the same, even if I don't understand them. Sometimes, I swear I can hear a whisper too. Where is it coming from? It's like a murmur from the heart.

One time, when I was in the middle of praying, Anna's mom came to visit. I stood up quickly and bowed my head, but she was too distraught to notice me. She was heartbroken, barely able to string together a sentence. Just kept apologizing. I couldn't help but notice how similar she looked to Anna. Same wide-open eyes, same pursed lips.

Seeing adults cry like that makes me uncomfortable. Being an adult seems tough. Never imagined Anna having parents, honestly. She never talked about them, and seemed so independent, I never gave it a thought. Makes sense, though. Everyone has a family, even one they don't talk about.

Anna's grandfather was there too. He seemed confused. Like he didn't know what was happening. But he had this content look on his face, not upset at all.

"And who might you be?" he asked.

"Soki. I'm one of Anna's classmates."

"Oh, is that this girl's name?" He reached out and put his hand over hers. "How pretty. I have a granddaughter who looks just like her."

I didn't say anything. Thought it would be rude to correct him.

"And what were you mumbling, just now?" he asked.

Felt my face go hot. Anna's mom was still talking to Anna, hoping her apologies would be heard.

"It's a prayer," I said. "So that the kami can help her get better. Called the *daijinju*."

"How lovely! It's rare for someone so young to know how to pay respects."

Even though I wasn't done reciting the prayer, I thought it'd be best to go. I shouldn't interrupt her family. The sun was going down, too, and I didn't want to be late for dinner. But as I moved to leave, Anna's grandfather addressed me.

"Would you mind teaching it to me?" he asked. "The prayer."

I stopped, not sure whether to stay. Anna's mom wasn't paying attention, so I could have slipped out. But the expression on her grandfather's face caught me. The same curiosity as Anna.

I sat back down. "It's a little confusing, but I'll show you," I said. "First, you have to close your eyes."

He closed his eyes.

"Then, you put your hands together. Like this."

I took his hands and brought them together, in that special way my dad taught me. It's a secret method, so I wasn't supposed to be showing it to others. But I figured that, just this once, it would be okay.

"Then, you start by saying *a-ji-ma-ri-ka-n*. You have to say it slowly. And really low, too. Listen to how I'm saying it: *a-ji-ma-ri-ka-n*."

Anna's grandfather started to repeat the words, although he ended up getting lost halfway, saying *ki* instead of *ri*.

"*A-ji-ma-ri-ka-n*," I repeated.

"*A-ji-ma-ri . . .*" He trailed off.

"*—ka-n*."

We went back and forth like this for a while. He had trouble getting the prayer to come out right. I was patient, though. Just sat there, re-teaching him the words. There's an entire other section after that, parts that even I have trouble remembering. Decided not to teach him those yet. Just the first step was enough.

"*A-ji-ma-ri-ka-n!*" he said, finally getting it right. He smiled. "*A-ji-ma-ri-ka-n*. What does it mean?"

"Not sure. But, it's not important."

He smiled. "How lovely. Thank you."

I got up to leave again. He was nice, and I wanted to talk to him a bit more, but I felt like I shouldn't linger. Anna's mom was done speaking to her, and was just sitting there, weeping. It was time for me to go home.

"Thank you, Soki," Anna's grandfather said. I was impressed he got my name right. "I hope we meet again."

And actually, we did. Doesn't happen a lot, but whenever Anna's mom visits, he comes too. The thing is, his memory isn't very good. So I have to reintroduce myself, and we have the same conversation every time. And I teach him the prayer every time, too.

"*A-ji-na-ri-ka-n,*" he'll say.

And I'll correct him: "*A-ji-ma-ri-ka-n.*"

"*A-ji-ma . . .*"

". . . *ri-ka-n.*"

At first, it was kind of frustrating. Wanted to move on to the rest of the prayer. Thought it would happen eventually, but so far it hasn't. But then I started to get used to his forgetting. Every time he pronounces the words right, I feel just as proud as the first time. I know it's useless, since next time he probably won't remember my name or the prayer, but I don't mind. Just repeating those words with him is enough. I wonder what Anna would think, seeing me with her grandpa like that.

Anna, a lot has happened on Earth since you went to sleep. The world has only gotten harder to understand. And when you come back, someone will have to help you re-learn it all. I think, maybe, I might be able to do this for you.

I'll wait forever, if I have to, but come back soon. I have so much I want to ask you. About where you went, about where you're going. You probably don't even remember me, but I'll be here, teaching your grandpa those words, even if he always forgets them.

Every so often, I see movement under your eyelids. Once your mouth even twitched. You looked happy. Anna, wake up soon. I want to ask what you're dreaming of.

. . .

IT COMES QUIETLY, SOMETIMES. Like the chirping of a cicada. Like a light layer of snow. Like a signal, still pulsing, so far above: *A-ji-ma-ri* . . .

ACKNOWLEDGEMENTS

THANK YOU, MOM, FOR your constant encouragement and for making sure I never had to run alone. Thank you, Dad, for instilling in me a love for literature, and for the countless late-night drives and chats over coffee. Thank you, Yuki, for being my closest friend.

Many thanks to my extended family in Japan—my cousins, aunts, uncles, and grandparents scattered throughout Kyushu—as well as to the dozens of Japanese exchange students I've taught over the years. The flavours and locales of this story wouldn't exist without the time I've spent with each and every one of you, all of whom have made an impact on the book in your own way.

While the act of writing is—usually—done alone, the process of publishing certainly isn't. Bringing *Satellite Love* to print wouldn't have been possible or even worthwhile without the wonderful and talented community I'm blessed to have around me.

And so, my thanks go out to Ruth Ozeki and Molly Zakoor for their immense wealth of kindness, and for being the first people to champion the manuscript in its earliest stages.

I'm thankful for my agent, Lucy Carson, a patient and powerful ally, whose enduring passion for the written word was truly encouraging throughout the entire process.

Many thanks to my editor, Anita Chong, for her keen editorial insights as well as her humour and compassion, so crucial in bringing the characters of *Satellite Love* to life. ありがとう!

Thank you to designer Emma Dolan for the stunning cover and illustrations, as well as the elegant design of the text itself.

Thank you also to my copyeditor, Melanie Little, and my proofreader, Rachel Taylor, both of whom made sure no contradiction or unintended quirk went undetected.

And of course, my eternal gratitude to everyone at McClelland & Stewart, a vibrant and vital cornerstone of Canadian fiction, which I feel so privileged to call my publishing home.

Outside of publishing, I'd like to give thanks to Caitlin Jesson and the rest of my family at Book Warehouse on Broadway for providing me a place to work while writing out my earliest drafts. If you, dear reader, are ever kicking around B.C., I strongly recommend you stop by one of their stores! And bonus points if you happen to have bought this book at one of those locations.

My thanks to Kelsea Gorzo, who I've known since I was two, for helping me figure out how the coma in the story would occur.

Thanks also to Carlo Ghioni for teaching me the responsibilities that come with telling stories.

And finally, thank you, Dasha. Without you, this story wouldn't have its soul.

- .... .- -. -.- / -.-- --- ..- / .- .-.. .-.. -.-.--

*　　　*　　　*

The "Lost Kitten" lyrics that Anna recalls on page 16 are the author's rendition of the traditional folk song.

The sutta that The General quotes on page 66 is taken from "Ekadhamma Suttas: A Single Thing" (AN 1.21-40), translated from the Pali by Thanissaro Bhikkhu. *Access to Insight (BCBS Edition)*, 30 November 2013, http://www.accesstoinsight.org/tipi-taka/an/an01/an01.021-040.than.html.

The translations of the Japanese Buddhist proverbs spoken by The General on pages 78, 98, 172, 173, 233, and 237 are from *In Ghostly Japan* by Lafcadio Hearn.

The poem that Anna quotes on page 136 is "The Herd Boy's Star," from *The Tales of Ise*, translation by Peter MacMillan (Penguin Classics, 2016).

The *ajimarikan* chant from the *Daijinju* prayer recited on pages 266–268 is from *The Essence of Shinto: Japan's Spiritual Heart* by Motohisa Yamakage (Kodansha International, 2012).